BLUEGLASS

Also by Chris Wilson

GALLIMAUF'S GOSPEL
BAA

BLUEGLASS

by
CHRIS WILSON

ANDRE DEUTSCH

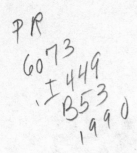

PR
6073
.I449
B53
1990

For Joan and Paul, my parents who
– they'd like it known –
are not portrayed herein

First published 1990 by
André Deutsch Limited
105-106 Great Russell Street
London WC1B 3LJ

ISBN 0 233 98566 2

Printed and bound in Great Britain by
WBC, Bristol and Maesteg

222 55459

O stand, stand at the window
As the tears scald and start;
You shall love your crooked neighbour
With your crooked heart.

W. H. Auden

LONDON
1845–63

Getting Born

Florence. Oh, Florrie. Flo. My auburn-tressed beauty. My freckle-nosed, twinkle-eyed, rose-cheeked, satin-flanked, plump-breasted love. My chortler, squealer, giggler. Guardian of secret dimples. Moist rapture. Liar. Thief of teaspoons.

Another morning. Seventeen minutes past nine. So say the languorous arms of my fob watch. Paradise. To think of you.

I hold you now. Captive in my mind's eye. Skipping naked from the chaise, your copper mane a cascade down your back. Then you freeze before the cheval mirror, stupefied by your own reflection. And we both gaze, transfixed and doting, on your raw form.

You can see your front alone – jut of hip, swell belly, pert breasts, amber-tipped. Whereas I, sunk in the down pillow, see you all. Fore and aft, silk and fleece, neck and nape, vain and vulnerable, vice and versa, lip and loin, head and tail, lost and found. And you, buff beauty, do not see me watch you, adoring the continent of hillocks, plains and shadowed crevices.

The lemon light through the muslin curtains fires the copper and gold of your hair and bathes your blanched skin.

My porcelain precious. If it were not for you, this would be hell.

Times were when I sought celebrity. In music halls and public houses. Now I should prefer that none had ever heard my name. Joey Blueglass. Prodigy. Master of memory. Mental monster. I should be retiring and modest as a mole. If I only had my time again.

Yet my face is in the periodicals and scandal sheets. Redrawn, with a certain licence, to show my proper depravity. A portrait, they suppose, must reveal the soul of the sitter. Which, in my case, must be a sour, soiled, sorry stuff. The *Illustrated London News* made free to redesign my face. To join my eyebrows, narrow my mouth, and loan me a smirk. Perhaps it was a printer's smudge, but to the tip of my nose – hooked and bumped – there was a dollop of stuff, poised perilously to drop upon my velvet lapel. Some criminals are so vile as to be strangers to the handkerchief. Snot, sir? They do not give a damn.

Reynold's News were moved by a different theory, and had me amiable and fat – chuckling at my wickedness above several flabby folds of chin.

Nor could they agree upon my age. Which I tell you now is seventeen. Contrary to the reports of the *Herald*, I am neither bigamist nor Fenian, Catholic nor dog-catcher. I say, let the dogs stay free. I should not wish a cage upon another creature. As for Ireland, let her care for herself.

My life has not been easy. Yet, withal, I have stayed a Christian, retaining my sense of humour. There is a fashion, this year, to displace God with an ancestral monkey. We are, says the fad, the distant cousins of baboons, upright, coy in clothes, brazen of words.

Yet I know there is an intelligent maker from the particular design of my own person. I have been fashioned peculiar for a purpose. The Lord is facetious. And so am I. He made me in his image.

To be frank, I am a freak.

We freaks are a diverse species. But we have excess in common. Each of us has some surfeit. My former colleague Josef Richburg, one of the seven leading claimants to the title of shortest man in the world, had a notable excess of smallness. He was three foot two inches tall. His fist could not fill an egg-cup. But in his tiny frame there oozed more condensed pride than is smeared through the House of Lords.

Pascal Pinion had an excess of heads, being born with one more than the usual number. Perched upon his scalp was a small monkey face. It would roll its eyes and dribble, leaking a trickle of saliva down Pascal's brow. And when poor Pascal donned a cap to cover his deformity, this second head would leak muffled moans against its dark imprisonment.

Annie Jones-Elliot is possessed of luxuriant beard, moustache and sideburns. If she were a gentleman, the world would think her virile and distinguished. Yet, she being a lady, you choose to mock and gawp.

Her companion, Louise Bernard, earns a living by displaying her legs – of which she has four. High on each thigh she has a supernumerary limb. There's a deal of gasping and whistling when she raises her skirts with a flourish to show her additional dangling parts. Some wag can always be relied upon to call for her to dance.

Tell me a human feature and I'll name you a freak who shows it to excess. For we are not less than you, but more. I've been dignified to work with the hairiest, fattest, smallest, tallest, most unlikely folk in creation. And what are they like? I shall tell you truthfully. They love and they hate. They breathe and they bleed. And they are never so odd as you think them. And they should far prefer it if you did not stare so rudely on the streets or omnibus, when they are not about their work. If you are chatting to a surgeon at a dogfight, you do not bother him to examine your bunion. So why gawk at a freak in the streets?

As for myself, I am a discreet freak. You could sit next to me in the Turkish bath and not be taken by the proportion, size or number of my parts. If you passed me in the streets, I dare say you'd take me for a common fellow.

My monstrosity is of memory. I am a mental freak.

Some men cannot remember where they placed their wife or umbrella a moment before. I, for my part, cannot forget. Not without effort. My mind is indiscreet, promiscuous, voracious. She swallows every sight, sound, touch and taste. And will never cough it up or let it go. No. She hoards it all. And stores it in my cranium. You would be quite surprised if you saw me. For my head is not notably large. It is a wonder there is space to house all that I know.

And am I lucky to be so capacious? I think not. It is no great blessing. To harbour a mind like mine. For, in truth, there are only so many facts a man can sensibly deploy. Often, it would be good fortune to forget. But my memory affords me no release, nor any relief from knowledge.

And numbers! My mind can never leave them be. She is always tinkering with them, totting and toying. Why, even as I write, and without any conscious intent, part of me has been multiplying my height in inches by my age in years, then squaring the sum, and dividing by the day of the month. The figure so obtained is 856579 and $\frac{7}{10}$ths. And where's the sense in that? You'll grasp the foolishness of my faculties.

And there's another thing I do. Without rhyme or reason, and without knowing how I do it. I can tell you the day of the week for any date of history. Jesus, sir? He was born on a Wednesday. Magna Carta? Friday. The answer just pops to mind. And do you know the vexing thing? Nobody ever knows I'm correct. They think I'm a fool or a braggart.

Sometimes I wish I'd been designed different, without a prodigious mind. It would have served me better to be hefty as a mason, nifty as a sweep or sly as a coster. There's no ready way to earn a living by knowing the day of the week of every date in history, remembering the curves and crevices of every passing nostril, or getting drunk on numbers.

If you were to lend me a number – like 86, it being the square root of 7396 – I should promptly tell you: '"Missus," shouted the fat boy.' And why? Because it is the first line on page eighty-six of Mr Dickens's *Pickwick Papers*. Having read this book last year, I can see it line by line. In my mind's eye.

391? ' "Come, look sharp, timber eyelids," added the other encouragingly.'

And there's a deal more that I could tell you. Make of it what you will. By August 1840, there were 1,331 miles of railway in the British Isles. And 318,716 Methodists. Yet George Washington died on 14 December 1799, aged sixty-seven. And the square of 111 is 12321. And the root of 111 is 10.535653.

Few men know all this. It makes me a rare repository. But what to do with all these verities? How do you tot them up to make a moral, or join them to tell a tale?

But let me start near the beginning.

*

I do not know if you are one of those unfortunates, like me, who recall the occasion of your birth.

In my case it was Friday 18 November 1845, Islington, London. I was in my usual chamber, discreet if bulging, within my mother.

It was morning. For the dismal dark gave way to a dim rosy light. I began to be shook and joggled again, as happened often.

In hindsight, I concluded that my mother was up and about her business – brewing a pot of tea, frying a herring.

There then commenced some bangs and murmurs above the regular swoosh and gurgle of fluids. I was happy enough, though. I thought no more about it. An embryonic fellow has a relaxed, accepting turn of mind. He grows accustomed to such happenings beyond his jurisdiction. He is happy to suffer the swaying, and takes a modicum of exercise by frisking his pudgy limbs. Despite the confinement and monotony, and unchanging landscape, it is a pleasant place to lounge. And, if a fellow gets bored, why then he can count his toes, or make some rhythmic noises by plucking away at his umbilical. Or he can change the beat of his mother's heart by kicking out with his feet.

The colours are drawn from a narrow palette at the reddish end of the spectrum. But it is cheery and decorative – with those yellows, oranges, reds and purples – and far preferable to the current taste for papering one's walls with sludgy greens and browns.

The temperature of the proceedings is so well and constantly regulated that one knows neither hot nor cold. And a fellow is fed so continually and discreetly that he is spared any aggravation of hunger or thirst.

And being on his own, the little man need not bother with clothes. And has no shame concerning his candid nudity – though his member is so placed as to occupy a central and large part of his downward vision.

I have no hesitation in recommending the place as a veritable Eden. You can well imagine my shock, then, to be thrust and thrown from the garden. Nothing in my brief captivity had prepared me for the horrors of freedom. I shudder, I quake, at the reminiscence.

First, there is a shocking woosh of waters. Then the walls of the chamber fold me. It is a fiendish shrinking room. You can get some inkling if you recall the feeling of swaying in your chair after a brace of bottles of claret too many. Except that in this instance the walls actually smash against my little person. And I do not know from which direction the next blow will come. I daresay it's a good preparation for society, but at the time it's disconcerting.

Then comes worse. The entire surrounds gang up on me, conspiring to squeeze me all over. As though I am a lump of dough being pummelled by an exuberant baker.

A fellow then becomes aware that his head is especially tortured. I don't know if you've ever had your head pushed against some opening, like the gap in some railings, which is too tight to allow its proper egress. It happened to me once in a public house in Whitechapel when two costermongers sought to resolve a dispute about the price of shrimps by forcing my head into a coal-scuttle. The ears are prone to special abuse.

It is not an exact comparison. Parturition is worse. For the ordeal is longer, and – it being a singular experience and radical departure – the fellow does not know what is happening nor what the outcome will be.

The opening proving stubborn and my head obdurate, despite the violent efforts to thrust me out, forceps are deployed. If you imagine a navvy holding the sides of your head between the blades of two spades, then tugging for all of his muscular worth, you'll garner a glimpse of the quandary.

A word about air. If a chap owes another chap seventeen shillings, say, and hasn't the wherewithal for prompt settlement, the second chap might – with the aid of some further fellows – dunk the first party in a horse trough, holding his head below for a minute or so. If you've never suffered this, you'll at least imagine the discomforts.

A baby, being snatched from his element, is thrust into another. Air? What's that? Having lived as a tethered fish, the infant lacks the knowledge to cope. His earlier, sheltered life hasn't prepared him for the airy stuff. He thinks he shall throttle and gag, then emits a frightful gasp. Henceforth, he rapidly gains the habit of breathing. But it's an abrupt and desperate way to learn.

The light is dazzling. For the chap has grown accustomed to the dark interior.

Then a fellow is struck by the chill. Not to mention the variety of choking, sordid smells. I should be less than candid if I failed to remark that, to a newcomer, the world has the aromatic ferocity of an abattoir in August.

And to ears attuned to the gentle throb of Mamma's tubes, the sudden sounds of the world are a violent assault. Imagine yourself as the clapper in a Bow Bell: you'll conceive the clout of the clamour.

Nor does it help a small man gain trust in the world if he is straightaway slapped around the buttocks, then swung upside-down by the ankle, like a skinned rabbit. Nor would you feel easy if the company then gathered to scrutinize and debate your most personal parts.

It's true this happens to us all. But my perplex is personal and particular. And it is my constant burden in life. I have the misfortune to remember what others have the tact and grace to forget.

Was it all bad? Indeed it was not. For I was met on arrival by two chums. Two of the very best.

I cannot praise nipples too highly. For I think that but for nipples I might have promptly abandoned the struggle and strife of life.

I have never forgotten a nipple, nor a breast. A cigar or brandy just can't compare. To my mind, you can't top the companionship of a raw woman.

I was a mad thing. There is but one purpose in life. One alone. And that is sucking. I suck, gobble, chew, bite, suck. Kneading against warm, satin slopes, licking and chomping, gurgling and grasping, spluttering and spewing.

Oh, ah, eee, ooh, uck, off, ahhh, uuup, urp, aa.

She is possessed of shocking beauty. The fat, brown, chewy, wrinkled column. It fairly clogs your mouth. And the puckered surrounds. And the pliant heavy softness of those mounds, in which a fellow can sink his face. Aargh, sir, eee. And when you've milked one, there's always another.

Many months must have passed in this fashion. It was a monotony of ecstasy. And, throughout this time, despite my best endeavours, I failed to eat my mother.

I am afforded a pillow which, though snug and soft, lacks any of the gravid bounce of a breast. My fingers taste sour and salty, and lack the wrinkled, clogging sweetness of a teat. I can find in them none of the pleasures of pap or nipple. Nor can any milk be coaxed from the harsh, cold tip of my rattle. The slats of my cot yield nothing to reward my lips or throat.

There follow certain frustrations. I dream of breasts, then wake to find them gone. Nor will my wails and whimpers make them be. The frustration is not unlike that at those dismal hotels which surround all railway termini. There is a bell to ring for room service. Yet it sounds unheeded down distant corridors. For the page is with the chambermaid, and the proprietor with his ale.

It was a trying time, as I recall. There was nothing to do but sob, or count the bars of my cot. Sixty-four.

As is the way with children, it took me several months to learn to speak.

Faces peer at me, breathing hot, sour gusts. You can neither suck nor paw them. They lack the beauty of a breast. They are tortured by holes and crevices. In each is a twisted lack, a gaping chasm with twitching edges. They pester a chap's ears.

I discover there is a commerce to this – of trading noise for noise.

If a chap burps, then this quivering slit breaks open and sounds off with interest.

– oof –
'How's my babby?'
– uurp –
'Joey's talking.'
– urf –
'Say mamma.'

A fellow soon gets the hang of it.

10

– titties –

'Mamma's little Joey.'

– Joey sucks –

A fellow has a lot to learn at the outset. And his task ain't made easier by the deficiencies of his vision. He's abysmally short-sighted. Fortunately, the problem remedies itself without any call for spectacles. But before he gets a sight of distance, he's prone to silly errors – which only confirm his infantile state.

Take Mamma! I swear that for the first few months I thought her entirely and utterly a pair of breasts.

Or myself! A chap doesn't realize he's there. You can't expect a fellow to stop suckling just to devise a philosophy of mind. It dawns slowly. For wherever I went, there I was too. And naturally I took to counting my parts. Two arms, two legs, one widdler. The solid mass that connects them became apparent later. And my head? Well, it's quite a conundrum. Being as how a chap's eyes face outwards, he just can't see the bit that sees. It takes a time to fathom it out. And it shows that our maker has a sense of humour. Why else set every newborn nipper a riddle that would tax a doctor of logic?

Growing Odd

When I hear Mamma's laboured, measured tread on the stairs, up I leap, squealing my pleasure, straining on tiptoe to peer over the top rail of the cot.

The door swings open, and there she is, panting, her stout chest heaving, her cheeks and brow shining crimson wet.

'Gawd,' I pipe up, 'spare my knees. I must have climbed a thousand stairs.'

'Kiss my nethers,' Mamma declares, 'you're a quare babby and no mistake.'

A chap naturally supposes himself much the same as his fellows. But I was not long in the vertical before I discovered myself peculiar. A mother exerts a powerful pull on the views of her infant. So, if she thinks him odd, then he bends towards her opinion.

I displayed a precocious mind. My memory, affinity with numbers and alacrity of thought must have loaned me the appearance of cleverness.

'Joey got ten toes,' I observe, 'and ten fingers. Four limbs, two eyes, two nostrils, one mouth. An' seven holes to his insides. Both sides the same. But top and bottom's different.' I daresay all babies might say the same, yet not all have a mind to. I remember the audit of my person roused me to great excitement.

'Who told you all that, boy?' Mamma frowns.

'Saw and counted,' say I.

'Well don't!' she sighs. 'It ain't decent. Not for a babby to talk like that.'

It was clear she was disconcerted by my quareness and by the questions I posed of her.

'Where do colours sleep at bedtime?' I demand to know, 'and why they let black stay up all night?' For I'd noticed that all the other hues scarpered when the lights were dimmed, leaving dark to its own devices. 'And where does the moon sleep, Mamma? And what she eat? And why they make her work on Sundays? And what does blue look like from behind? And who's his Mamma?'

She was surely a kindly woman, but prone to forgetfulness, prey to illogic. And lacking in curiosity.

'Joey's an odd 'un,' I hear her tell Uncle Clarence. 'Talking so. Ain't natural before he's weaned.'

'A proper puzzler,' Clarence nods, tapping his pipe on the grate, then turning his head to wink at me. 'A riddle-me-ree. A right bobby-dazzler. A caution that child. . . . How'd you come by him, Martha? He ain't one of us.'

For want of a pappa, we took to Clarence instead. As did Mamma, in her way.

I could never look at him without a thought of fruit. His face had the oily, pitted look of an orange, courtesy of his liver, by virtue of his tippling. But stranger yet was the livid, pocked, bulbous strawberry of his nose.

His Happy Family lived with ours in four rooms in Farringdon. There was a chimpanzee, bull-terrier, tortoiseshell cat, rat, ferret, rabbit and duck. The duck developed a taste for the frogs which were regularly replenished. So we never got to know a frog well. No sooner had we christened it than the duck ate it. After a while we stopped giving the frogs particular names to mark their special temperaments, but called each and every one 'Albert', be it man-frog or woman-frog, stout or thin, aloof or amiable, in respectful copy of our Queen – who also named everything so, be it library, embankment, horse, husband or locomotive.

Uncle Clarence gained a living by displaying his menagerie on Waterloo Bridge. In a single confined cage. It was the cause of much remark and wonder. The bull-terrier would laze placid as a cow, while the peevish, squawking duck paced his sturdy back. And the rat would nuzzle up to the cat who, for her part, declined to eat him. And the chimpanzee would lounge there, cupping a frog in her scrupulous fingers. Whilst the ferret paced the front of the cage in melancholy haste – but biting no other being.

'Witness the example of God's creatures,' Uncle Clarence barks, skewering each passer-by on the point of his baleful, pleading gaze. And when he has gathered twenty souls or so, he commences his spiel on the tableau of tolerance.

There were two sermons. One for times of war. Another for outbreaks of peace. When the Afghans or Turks proved quarrelsome, Clarence would preach how the diverse classes of our nation might unite – heeding the example of the beasts, forgetting their mean differences – to stand firm against the foe. But when our armies were not fighting, Clarence spoke a pacifist moral – how, like the animals, the nations of the world might live in harmony, taking pleasures each in the other.

So the animals could act by turns, and without apparent preferences, jingoists or pacifists, the classes of England or The Family of Nations.

And the lion lies down with the lamb. And I pass round the hat. And each performance might gain Clarence a shilling – in farthings and ha'pennies. Sometimes there is a sentimental sixpence. By the time he finishes his speech, and collects the money, Uncle Clarence has invariably moved himself to tears. Then he retires to the Embankment for a pint of stout and gin chaser, to regain his composure. Whilst I stand guard of the zoo.

Of course, there are several knacks and wrinkles in stopping the strong from gobbling the weak; dissuading the one that the other was his luncheon. Goodness comes no easier to animals than to people.

The chimp took twice daily doses of laudanum to keep her sweet. There was never a tetchier soul in Christendom before she took her breakfast spoonfuls, nor a kindlier soul thereafter.

The ferret had had his teeth pulled. But he was not above trying to nip you with his gums if you ever tugged his brush. Though when he forfeited his teeth, his bite lost its conviction, and was more reproof than assault.

The rat and cat were reared together. It's not commonly

14

known, but a kitten learns to kill by example. Alas, it's the parents that usually teach it to murder.

The terrier was a saint amongst dogs. A true St Francis: and he stayed ever cheery and tolerant, despite being lame and blind.

No. The duck it was that played the villain. Alice the monkey was forced to keep a vigilant eye on the frogs to keep the duck from snaffling them. Alice would trap them in her hands and toy with them all day. But when she put them down, to scratch herself or sleep, the duck would start to stalk them.

In truth, none of us loved Clara the duck – neither Mamma, nor Clarence, nor my brother and sisters. All of us found her a quarrelsome, vain and peevish being, and would shoo her away when she poked her beak around the parlour door. So she was forced to keep to the hall or sink. But the ferret, rat or Douglas the cat we let laze on the hearth when the season was cold.

The dog would drag his lame rear end around the rooms, yet he never ventured far. For he was discouraged by his blindness which caused him to collide with chairs and walls, or take a terrible tumble if he ever chanced upon the stairs.

We were crowded in those steamy chambers. But, withal, we were happy. And if a fellow shared his mattress with three brothers and an ape, at least he was never short of lively company. And he could learn much about natural history within his very home.

My mother being then but twenty-four had borne only six children. Two had taken themselves early to heaven, leaving four on the Farringdon Road. My elder brother – Dick – treated me well but rough; calling me 'Haddock' on account of some supposed resemblance between my face and the staring wide-eyed fish heads peering out from the barrows. And I don't think he meant it unkindly, but was merely pointing out some similarity his mind had noticed. For children are guilelessly candid. And, in truth, I do have a perplexed but placid expression built of a rounded face and bulging eyes.

Sisters Maggie and Sarah took to me most particularly, for they had few other toys and I was then the baby of the family.

They found special pleasure in dressing me in their frocks, and tying bows in my hair – declaring me a girl, by courtesy of their imagination, calling me Prudence and teaching me to curtsey. Which always gave them giggles, so amusing was I.

So even while a little 'un I was marked out as peculiar by my family and knew myself a different kind of being; somehow separate. My mind worked in dissimilar ways to the intelligences of my kin. So I was ever outside the jolly complicity they wove so easy and warm around them.

They found great rewards in repetition.

'Joez n'addock,' Dick chants, his face split wide by his wit.

'That is Prudence. She's a princess,' my sisters chime.

'N'addock.'

'Princess.'

'N'addock.'

And so on, and on. Repeating themselves up to seven or eight times without finding any diminution of their joke.

Though I felt myself neither fish nor princess, I naturally preferred the latter and would side with my sisters. I've always been happier with the other gender, finding their judgements more considered and considerate.

My family had absent-mindedness in common, forever mislaying items: ravel of string, half chewed stick of liquorice wood, pair of herrings, boot or apple. Then they would come to me and ask me where it was. And I would know. For I had seen it fall by the wainscot, or had spied the ferret scampering off with it to hoard it in his box.

Words came easier to me than to them, though they were louder and more garrulous – making blunt work with the fewer words they knew. Dick had the worst problems with diction. For he nurtured a perpetual cold, and his nose was ever plugged with a quivering jelly.

'Ugh. Whazat white ztuff, Addock?' Dick demands, pressing his nose to the butcher's window, smearing mucus on the glass.

'Tripe,' I tell him, 'and next to that is udder.' Which leads me to explain the names and parts of a cow.

'Cow?' says he, 'Woza cow?' For there are fearsome holes in his knowledge, through which you could steer an omnibus.

He has a simpler philosophy than I. He nibs fruit behind the costers' backs without first pondering whether apples grow on trees. And none of us can pee higher against a wall than he.

'Wire ya zudga quare won, Addock?' he asks, draping a fat arm on my narrow shoulders, pinching my cheek, 'Rare and quare. A proper dreamer. Mamma zez yera goblin.'

It's true I'm different. But I don't know why it should be.

'Lez go noggon zum doorz. Then run awf.'

'Why, Dick?'

'They giz right pizzled,' he observes, 'when they zopenz up and nowenz zere. Then we zjoutatem. Then they noze iz uz. Then we zcarper zjarp.' He zmiles with zatisfaction.

'Why, Dick?' I struggle for the gist of it. 'Tell me the full rules again. Is it a sport or a pastime?'

So he swears at me for my lack of wit, cuffs my ears and swaggers off, leaving me on my lonesome. And I feel a chilling sadness; but also a relief that I need not act a part I cannot understand.

I spent much time with the company of numbers. For I loved their sure-footed, quicksilver motions; their exactitude; the perfection of their protocol. Each knows just what the other means, and where he stands with his neighbour.

And how they came and went for me, like ghosts and phantoms, in the flicker of an eye. One moment multiplying to milliards, then promptly purged by a plague of division. And they were spared those gross and trivial human labours of chatter and nutrition.

So when my kin found themselves compelled to do business with numbers I was there to act as diplomat – carrying messages and translating between the ordered ranks of cardinals and the family Blueglass. In particular, I aided Uncle Clarence in his transactions with his hat.

'How many shows we done today, Joey?'

'Eight.'

'Then we done furkin well boy. Count the tin.'

'Two shillings and fivepence ha'penny. And two brass washers.'

This strikes him as a poor result: 'How much we come out with, boy?'

'Three shillings and fourpence.'

He's pained by the conundrum, rolling melancholy eyes and wiping his cheeks with his sleeve.

'How come we've worked the day long, and got less than when we started?'

'You took seven shillings in the hat,' I remind him.

'Then where's it gone, boy?'

'Tipples,' say I, 'to keep you in the spirit. And two mutton pies for lunch. Milk and fruit for the beasties. And a sweetener for the constable.'

'Streuth, Joey. It's a fearful lot to mislay.'

'Take away what we have now,' I advise, 'from what you brought out. Add what you took in the hat. Subtract the expenses and victuals.'

'Yes, Joey?' He strains for the logic of it.

'And you'll know how much you spent in the Hog and Viscount.'

'One and sixpence,' he guesses, 'or two and tuppence.'

'Five shillings and ninepence.'

'Furkit, boy. You make me sound like a proper boozer.' He sounds both startled and proud.

'Did you lose at dominoes?'

He swivels his eyes in the strain of recollection. 'I won sixpence,' he smiles. 'Then I lost a shilling . . . then I lost two shillings . . . then I called them cheats . . . then they turfed me out.'

'And did you drink stout and gin?'

'And some brandy to soothe my head.'

'Then . . .' I calculate the possibilities, for I never flinch from the challenge of this daily riddle, 'you had two brandies, six pints and six chasers. Or three brandies, seven pints and four chasers. Or four brandies, six pints, three chasers and two ports. Or you bought an ounce of baccy – which would leave you two brandies, six pints, three chasers and a hot potato.'

He nods at the wisdom of this – as though I've confirmed his exact suspicions – then commences to rummage through his several pockets, unpacking knife, twine, rags, pipe, potato

18

peelings, until he finds a new twist of tobacco. Then his face smooths with a smile of relief.

'You're a jewel, boy, and a good 'un. . . . Why, I thought I'd lost all my money.' Then he tosses me a full sixpence, telling me, 'Trot off. Buy some sweeties to fill yer gob,' while he goes to take a quick snifter to soothe the ache of his head.

For Clarence was proud of me and treated me like his very own son. He'd brag about my cleverness to his pals in the snug of the Hog and Viscount. Which was how – by way of a coincidence out of a mishap – he eventually came to sell me for six pounds, to settle a debt, in a public house in the Strand, which was known as the Bosom and Viper on account of its clientele.

But I'm straying ahead of the story. For at this moment of the telling of it, I'm still only four years old.

Remembering

My memory is my most prominent organ. It's a freakish faculty, a conspicuous deformity. Like the hump of a hunchback, it's marked me out from my fellows. That and my distinctive birthmark.

Or, perhaps, this memory is more like the shell of a snail, or carapace of a tortoise – a bulky baggage that I must bear on my back wherever it is I crawl, which is mistaken for me, and into which I withdraw my soft and fleshy self whenever I am threatened.

Like the snail's shell it is a labyrinthine compartment, from which I can never free myself, which grows as I grow. It is the space in which nature decrees I dwell. And to its secret, recessed chambers I alone am privy.

You're no snail, but a lugworm or earwig, wasp or flea, tapeworm or moth, toad or lizard. For we are all small creatures in God's garden. And some large foot may squelch you, unknowing and uncaring. But you must not live in fear of this. Best keep your antennae quivering. And don't stray onto the path, in case some boots are walking it. And keep off the lawn, in case some larger bodies are playing croquet.

There are smaller than you and larger; more decorous, or warty. You must have your purpose and must live it. You have a dignity and must meet and greet it.

I dare say a slug on a lettuce can snigger at a greenfly on the parsley. It may be a slight and unsightly thing, but to another of its kind a greenfly is lover or mother and not to be sniffed at. And its satire is no comfort to the slug when, distracted by its sneering, it slips into a cauldron of mulligatawny. And then, however fine the mollusc believed himself, he's only a viscous lump in the soup at the Ritz, merely a disagreeable conversation piece between a waiter and diner.

It's a rum riddle – morality – and hard to get to the bottom of it.

But I'm straying from the matter of my memory which is also a quare and rare fumblemebob.

The fact of it is, I can't forget. Not a sausage nor a syllable. Sing me a song, I'll repeat it exactly. Give me a newspaper, I'll scan it then read it back verbatim – backwards should you wish it, though I assure you it'd make even less sense. If you were ever kind enough to lie with me, lady, I would recall your every pore, mole and wrinkle, scent and wetness. For I have an endless trace of my life. Every moment is there on the record. Imagine a moving lantern-show, complete with sound, and touch and smell besides. Then you have it. And can play it forward or back.

It was a wonder to my family: as it was a wonder to me that they could forget. But these misunderstandings happen when a snail is reared amongst slugs.

I sit beneath the table in the kitchen. Mamma cannot see me here, peering up beneath the fringe of the oilskin. Douglas purrs, heavy in my lap. He is a fine chappie and a good cat. Only he pricks my thighs as he flexes his claws. A fellow's ear still throbs where Dick clipped him. And his cheeks are red and swollen. And when he licks his top lip it's hot and salty. The fellow's not a poo nor a sniveller. There are eighty-two tiles on the floor and seventeen are cracked. When you ain't careful you can tread on the cracks. A fellow has no business clouting his brother for no reason. The chap can smell the herrings from yesterday and Douglas has done a piddle. And so has a ferret. Mamma's ankles are red and chapped. She treads on the back of her shoes which slap loose with every step.

If a duck comes to make trouble, a chap will shoo him away. A fellow wonders why left and right change sides when they face a mirror. But top and bottom stay where they are. And what's behind a mirror? And what's behind behind? And who tells the day it's his turn of the week? When the light goes out you see its black back. Hot and cold take turns but never stay together.

A fellow has a white crusty scab on his elbow. When he picks it, it bleeds and itches. So he has to scratch it some more. Mamma squeaks and squeals like a door hinge:

'. . . orf – her – of – fafe – eat – ernal – word – ooze – birrit – breeves – the – act – if – flame . . .'

Mamma pants and wheezes. Drops the spuds into the boiling water. Mamma swears they don't feel it.

'. . . ee – will – my – she – held – and – pour – shun – be – as – long – as – life – end – yours . . .'

Time ticks but you can't touch it. Light shines but you can't hear it. Hurt hits you but you can't clout it back. Bad smells. Good tastes. Odd numbers can't be paired. There's always a quare fellow left over. All on his lonesome. One isn't odd, though. The singular fellow likes it on his own.

A fellow can hear Clarence coming. His boot nails strike sparks on the tiles. Fire in his feet. Can smell the beery breeze of his breath. He says: 'Furkit, Martha. Yera rose.' A fellow can see their still feet facing. Can see Clarence's rude hand pat her bottom. Then both hands lift her skirt. Mamma says Clarence is naughty. But naughty ain't bad as bad.

I can see it and smell it, and taste it on my palate. It's vivid as if it were now. But stronger. And I can make it go backwards. There are pings from the basin as droplets of water leap upwards and into Mamma's cloth. Clarence's boots scrape backwards and disappear round the door. And Mamma's voice wails strange and sad:

'. . . ees – I – won – tub – dnilb – saw – dnuof – ma – won – tub – tsol – saw – ecno – I . . .'

And I think how easy it was then, when I was a nipper and could hide beneath the table. Or come out and be basted with love.

No one taught me to read, exactly. Except myself. I chanced upon it. Neither Clarence nor Mamma had ever taken to it. They knew the Hog and Viscount, Pentonville Road, Manzini's Pie and

Eel shop, without any prompt of signs. And they supposed that the alphabet belonged to that class of luxurious thingamibobs and whatsits – like veal, stockings, Madeira, spectacles and lobster – above their price and several stops beyond their station. They'd have no more presumed to read than to repeal a Corn Law or appoint the Bishop of Durham.

'Can you read books, Mamma?'

'I should think not, indeed. Who do you think I am, Princess scuse-me Alice?'

'I can, Mamma.'

'Course you can, boy. And your uncle Clarence is the Duke of Gloucester. Only he likes to keep it quiet.'

But I could, and had the pages to prove it. Four scrumpled sheets, with a boot-print on the topmost. I'd found them by a printer's doorway in Golden Passage.

'Look, Mamma,' I pressed my finger to the first line and commenced to recite:

Varicella encephalitis, 514
Vascular disease associated with melancholia, 83
Vasomotor attacks simulating epilepsy, 474
        lability in neurasthenia, 86
Venereal diseases, 344–429

And so it went on, all the way to 'Weygant's dementia, 675.'

'How did you do that, boy?' Mamma's lips were all twitch and tremble. There was a sheen of sweat to her brow. She was staring at me wide-eyed, like I was some green-skinned stranger and not her flesh and blood.

'Just came to me, Mamma. I didn't mean no harm.'

'What does it mean then?' she demanded. 'It don't sound like decent English. And there ain't a proper story to it.'

'It's a puzzle-book, Mamma. I know that much. The numbers go with the words. And the words with the numbers. And they both say something about the other. Then, if a fellow can crack the code, he can work it out. But I can't solve it. I reckon there's some pages missing.'

In truth, it had me beaten to a flummox. But I thought

23

Varicella encephalitis was a very pretty phrase. Venereal was all slithery, and put quivers down my spine.

'If you carry on like this, boy, you could be a ...' she paused, awed by possibility, '... a clerk. When you're grown a man. And work at Euston Station.' Mamma gripped my shoulders and smiled her wonder. 'God knows why, but you're sharp as a needle.'

Though she couldn't teach me, she helped me after that. When she was about on the streets, she'd retrieve anything with lettering she'd chance to find, be it clean or dirty, wet or dry, light or heavy, on the pavement or down in the gutter.

So commenced my schooling. And I was tutored by a motley crew – luggage labels, caustic soda wrappings, sheets of newsprint, omnibus tickets, lost letters, empty wine bottles, radical pamphlets, cigar bands, vegetable crates.

Each told its own story. When I had thoroughly digested them all, I would tell the news to Mamma, and try to weave the strands into a tale of sorts. Inevitably, by dint of the fragmentary and circumstantial evidence, it turned into a mystery.

'Once upon a time there were some cigars. We cannot know their names or number. But they came from St Paul, Missouri.'

'A church?' demanded Mamma, sniffing something amiss.

'A place in Americky.'

'How they get there, boy?'

'They sailed on a ship.'

'Ain't that awful expensive?'

'They were wee fellows, no fatter than my thumb. So got charged a fare proportional to their smallness.'

'It ain't that way on a tram,' says Mamma. 'You pay the same if you're fat or scrawny – unless you're a kiddy, or slip off without them seeing.'

Then I'd explain how the cigars came to Messrs Sullivan and Beswick in the Strand, and was each dressed in a band of purple and gold, and called a Yankee Peculiar. And one was bought for ninepence and sold to a man unknown, who smoked it in the Farringdon Road.

'Don't we know nothing about this man?' demands Mamma.

'He ain't short of money,' say I, 'to buy a ninepence cigar and smoke no more than the half of it. And he ain't short of spit, neither. And from the bite in the butt we know he ain't got all his front teeth. And he might be the very same fellow who lost the letter.'

'The letter!' says Mamma. 'Tell us the story of that.' She always likes the letters the best. Far more than the crates which weigh so heavy but speak so slight.

'It's written by Trusting Patience to Dearest Precious Jerry. She says she loves him like no other. He is hers. She is his. Otherwise she never would have.'

'Never what?' asks Mamma.

'Compromised herself in Hyde Park, Mamma, that Sunday evening behind the bandstand.'

'What she mean – compromised?'

'She bared her very core,' I say, 'or bored her very care . . . the writing ain't too smart. Then she gave of her diadem and lost her jewel.'

'Lost a jewel?' Mamma gasps. 'Behind the bandstand, she says?'

'Together with her innocence, alongside her caution.'

'Ah,' observes Mamma, nodding sagely now, 'too true.'

'And they must hurry to be one. For she is late and may be two. And why does he not come, when he is her precious and promised? . . . I think it's a riddle, Mamma.'

'A proper poser,' says she, 'a right pickle.'

'And Precious Jerry ain't solved it,' say I, 'because he's screwed up the letter and thrown it away. Like it's vexed him – not knowing the answer. Perhaps he's the same fellow who drank this bottle of champagne that was bottled in Rheims, and the wine went to his head.'

So I read a lot, of varied sorts. A deal of riddles; how to keep a jewel unto oneself; where wines came from and their fluid volumes; how to mix a solution of caustic soda; the numbers and destinations of the buses in London; the price of onions; the cost of sin; instructions for applying linaments or assembling pressure-pumps; the curative properties of patent liver pills; the times and places of theatrical performances; the characters of popular murderers; the contest of capital and labour; the choice of afterlifes; the routes of the Great Western Railway; restaurant menus; the Afghan campaigns; the order of service at funerals; the integrity of royal persons; auction catalogues; medical directories; the proceeding of the House of Commons; reports of cricket contests.

There was near as much as a boy could take in. And all subjects were there, in sensible proportions – Geography, Science, Logic, Mathematics, Government, Morality, Religion, Rhinology, Poetry, Patriotism, Commerce, Horticulture and Pathology.

I dare say I studied as diligently and gained as wide an education as any scholar of Harrow College or Oxford University. And all from the garbage of the Farringdon Road – which is as good a library as any I know of. I've never forgotten those lessons. All the truths and methods I learned, I carry with me still.

From reading it was a small skip to scribbling. And though I had no one in particular to write to – nor, indeed, was on speaking terms with anyone who could read – and though I could remember whatever I needed without aid of jottings, still I took scribbling to be a proper accomplishment which any nipper should master before he could claim himself smart.

In the fullness of time it served me well enough. For, as I'll tell by and by, I was to earn a living of sorts as a writer of sorts – composing mendicant letters. Though begging proved itself a hard profession, and not so rewarding as many suppose.

In my selection of a neat and mannered hand, a wealth of scripts were available by way of example. I copied some of the elegant curvicules of the silver and gold lettering above Ludemann's Modern Pharmacy. These forms I supplemented with ornate Ts, Gs, Ds and Fs from the labels of claret that may be procured from Forbes and Frobisher of Drury Lane, and which I dare say go as well with a haunch of venison as with a rib of beef.

My numbers I selected from the doors of a well-known bank. They were as clear and serviceable as you'd expect of a respectable financial institution that cares about its cardinals.

With time and practice the script became my own, gaining a unity that belied its mongrel origins.

I did much of my writing in chalk upon walls. For the implement was cheap as limestone, and the surfaces stood about naked in gross profusion.

My hand was much to be seen between Waterloo and the Angel:

Joey Blueglass is not an haddock
Varicella encephalitis

Or, as my facility grew to match my ambition:

Clarence Chesney's Phenomenal Bestiary and Happy Family, popularly acclaimed for its Utopian Moral, is open for perusal upon Waterloo Bridge, weekdays and Saturdays. No bookings required. Free Spectacle. Donations at the discretion of our Generous Patrons.

As viewed and applauded by Fanny Larkspur (courtesan to Royalty), the Dukes of Bedford and Argyle, and the champion pugilist Bruiser Yates.

Marvel at our Ferret! Wonder at our Duck! Gasp at the Salutary Amity between our Cat and Rat.

The trouble with a mind like mine is that it's hard for a body to sneak away and spend time on its own. No sooner have I sat myself down in Roux's, ordered a buck rabbit and half a bottle of Chablis, than my mind is prompted by speculations that quite distract from the meal.

Which would take longer, I ponder: 1) for a young but full-grown Border Collie to pad home from Rochester Row to Peckham Rye, via Waterloo Bridge, with a handicap of a three pound weight on its back, or 2) a number seventeen omnibus to complete the route and take its ten minute pause at the terminus, or 3) for an eleven stone man, of moderate appetite, to force down nine buck rabbits.

Or else I trouble myself to calculate the probabilities of a man playing poker to improve his hand from a pair to three of a kind by discarding two or three cards.

Or I wonder how many words there are in the book of Deuteronomy. Or how many flies it would take to fill a pint measure.

And a fellow's memory, weighing him down with the baggage of history, quite tugs him back to the past, and prevents him unwrapping the present. Which, hereabouts and now, is just as well. Given that this fellow's in a fix.

Being Sold

I don't believe I'm betraying any confidence, or revealing any news in reporting that Clever Hans, the performing horse, wasn't half so clever at calculus or algebra as many supposed. His owner it was that did the calculations – signalling to Hans, with a wink or frown, when to start and stop tapping his declaratory hoof.

There was a like conspiracy between man and beast when Uncle Clarence came a terrible tumble – losing six pounds, which he did not have, playing at cards with an Airedale terrier who was a bitch called Foxer.

I was ten, then. And thought myself grand. Brother Dick had grown fat as a slug, ahead of my snail's pace. So the grey canvas trousers we once had shared could no longer contain him. Thus, I acquired the sole tenancy of them. And could go about town – smart – whenever I wished, no longer having to wait for him to return with my share of them.

Clarence now took me with him into the snug of the Hog and Viscount, though he'd ration me to no more than two pints – to be taken in halves – unless we were flush. And when his pipe was nought but smoulder, he'd give me the final puffs of it. Whilst it made me splutter, and the suck dealt a bitter burn to my mouth, I was proud to be acting the man.

'This small man,' Clarence slurred proudly, addressing the bar in general whilst pounding me on my hound's-tooth cap, so making me gargle my ale, 'is a furkin prodigy. There ain't nothing he can't do – count, read, calculate . . . remember all manner of instances . . . 'n help me train wild beasts.'

Most had heard it all before and took us on sufferance. So none turned a whisker or arrested their slurp or chatter. Nobody that is except the red-cheeked geezer in a green velvet jacket (greasy at the cuffs) with copper buttons (with an insignia of dragons rampant), and a cream bow tie, and tan and black striped corduroy trousers tucked into riding boots which had recently trod in the stable, so bore the sticky evidence still. He was known as Kent Jack on account of his claim to be a farmer from that part. Though he chewed his vowels like a bumpkin, his accent would lapse to the local. I had seen him three times before – twice watching us at our labour on the Bridge, and once outside the Beehive Inn – but never wearing those boots, or with that hound at his feet.

I'd heard him talked of. Some say he didn't so much farm in Kent as hold an apron of garden in Bethnal Green. And that he wasn't half the innocent he pretended: that his pasture was the credulity of others; that he harvested more hopes than hops, and threshed more suckers than wheat.

'Me boy's a furkin rare 'un,' droned Clarence, biffing me hard in the small of my back.

Whereupon Kent Jack coughed noisome, spitting something green, the size of a sixpence, onto the boards between us. He raised his eyes to the sooted ceiling and commenced to drawl, as if confiding to the cornicing, 'Yon whippersnapper may be no more of a slouch than you'd expect . . . for the companion of a maundering, goofy sot . . .'

It was clear he was referring to myself and Clarence.

'. . . but,' Kent Jack slowly lowered his moon eyes to us, 'I doubt he's a match for my dog.' At which, the dog sprang up from its sprawl, as if it had just heard its master's return, and commenced to whine in eager anticipation of something or other, or its cousin Eustace.

It was a fine looking fellow – with sharp black eyes, pricked ears. Its wiry coat a lustre of tans. And had a full combed beard below a yawning, pink-tongued smile. You could see it ate regularly and well, and enjoyed a lively romp.

Clarence was an amiable man, and maudlin with his ale. He wasn't a bar brawler, but neither was he one to retreat from a challenge. Not in his regular parlour, in front of his regular chums.

'What kin your dog do, then?' says Clarence, polite enough but sceptical. 'Scratch hisself?'

'Scratch indeed,' says Kent Jack, 'an catch rats, an chase cats, an bury bones . . . which is more than your puppy can.'

'Mine does all of that,' says Clarence, sucked into the pretence that I too was a dog, 'an find anything that's got lost, an remember all manner of things.'

'Mine can too,' says Jack, nonchalantly, 'mine can run a mile in three minutes.'

'So can mine,' lied Clarence, 'I'll wager he's faster.'

'Wager?' asked Kent Jack, smiling.

'Wager,' Clarence confirmed, somewhat grudging.

'Bet you he can't race Foxer. Not the length of the Bridge and back. Even though he's bigger.'

'Betya he can,' says Clarence, 'and give yorn a start.'

'Sixpence!'

'A shilling!'

'Half a crown, then,' Jack concluded firmly. And they shook hands on it. And Kent Jack beamed down at Foxer. And Clarence looked regretfully at me. But patted my shoulders to suggest some confidence.

'Take yer boots off,' he whispers to me, 'they'll slow you something awful. The dog ain't wearing none neither.'

The bar had taken to the notion of the race. Most jostled to the pavement to watch. Harry Soames tried to take some side bets, offering nine to one against me. But he couldn't get a single taker until he stretched the odds to thirties. And even then, the backer would chance no more than a snifter – and it was his round anyway.

I concede that I lost. Though the dog was a decent sport and didn't try to show me up or put me down. Whenever she'd bounded far ahead, she'd promptly stop, wagging her stumpy tail to a blur, and wait for me to catch up. But the rub was that she'd never let me in front. Whilst she'd chase a stick if I threw it ahead, she'd ignore one chucked behind.

By the end of the course I was slowed to a panting stumble:

31

hot, bothered and blistered. Whilst my stomach was thinking to heave back my breakfast, I was feeling sorely shamed to have failed my Uncle Clarence.

Foxer padded past the post a few paces in front, turning her eager smiling head in encouragement. She seemed not a mite fatigued, or even exerted, by the contest.

'Foxer by a whisker,' bellowed Kent Jack, 'and three lengths. A close-run contest,' he declared generously.

Then Clarence paid up. They shook hands again. And Kent Jack enquired if Clarence were a drinking man. Upon receipt of an affirmation, he said he would buy him a consolation drink or two with the winnings.

So we returned to the snug. Several fellows bought me a beverage, and slapped me about the head and shoulders, on account of my being such a game sport. They offered me a bone, remarked upon the wetness of my nose, and questioned Clarence on my pedigree. And suchlike. Which we took in good part.

Foxer sat by our table and licked my bruised, salty feet. While I stroked the length of her back, blowing softly on her ears. And it was not only the contestants who'd become friends, but their trainers too.

Clarence declared Kent Jack to be one of the finest. Kent Jack observed that Clarence was as honest and trusting a soul as he'd ever hoped to meet. Much such sentiment was exchanged, as were several more snifters.

'Yours may be the better athlete,' says Clarence, 'but mine has the cuter mind. He's a right sharp 'un.'

'Yes?' says Kent Jack, 'I expect he tells fortunes like mine, then.'

'Tell fortunes?'

'Of course,' says Jack evenly, as though it would be odd if an Airedale didn't.

'Show us,' demands Clarence.

'Foxer, tell this man his fortune.'

At which the dog sat up and begged.

'She says you'll earn your living by collecting money from the public,' says Jack.

'Furkit,' says Clarence, boggle-eyed, wiping his brow, 'he's right. . . . What else can she tell us?'

'What else, Foxer?'

Whereupon she lay on the floor and raised both front paws to cover her eyes. Then she rolled over, scratching a foreleg on her speckled belly. Then she stood up and shook herself.

'You'll have some bad news soon,' Jack translated, 'that's what Foxer reckons. It'll cause you some aggravation. But you'll soon get over it. Then you'll be right as rain.'

'Jasus,' says Clarence, 'I've never known the like. Not from a dog. The gypsies are good for a peek at the future, but your hound has 'em beat.'

'Of course,' says Jack, 'what Foxer likes best is playing at cards. She's a right canny one – at poker or pontoon. . . . Only you have to deal for her. 'Cos she can't properly handle the cards herself. On account of her paws,' he explained.

It's a dismal thing to remember – how Kent Jack, Clarence, Foxer and I walked to the Beehive Inn, otherwise known as the Bosom and Viper, and joined the pontoon school in the back room.

The other players said they felt not at all demeaned to play with a dog; that they had played with her before and knew her as an honest, sporting character, who was never shy with the ante and never shirked a debt – even though she often lost. As for Clarence, they observed, Foxer's introduction was good enough for them. Any friend of hers was welcome at their table.

Foxer sat pert and alert in a chair, signalling to Kent Jack, who sat alongside. By whimpers, whines, twitches of her ears, jabs and jerks of her paws, Jack knew whether she wished to twist or burn, raise or stick, double or quit.

Clarence fared too well at the start. After twenty minutes he had won six shillings from Foxer, and seven and sixpence from the other three players – who then dropped out, declaring themselves skint. They praised Clarence for the skill and daring of his play, saying it was a pleasure to learn from so fine a gambler. Further, they said, they would stay and watch him better Foxer. For, they argued, however amiable was a bitch from the North, their loyalty lay with the Cockney and the man.

I tried all manner of ruses to get Clarence to leave.

'We must collect the horse now Uncle,' I said.

'Don't be gormless. You know we ain't got no horse.'

'You mustn't lose the rent money. We need it for Mamma's medicine.'

'Don't have a care, boy. I've got this Foxer foxed.'

The company observed it a poor thing for a pipsqueak to instruct a gentleman and uncle. So Clarence boxed my ear.

They shouted encouragement for him to up his stake, then twist another card. And then commiserated when he bust, saying he was pestered by a brief demon. His good fortune would return. His skill would out. He must play on to protect the dignity of men against the presumptions of dogs.

When Clarence had lost his winnings, then the residue of his pockets, Foxer let it be known – by licking his hand thrice – that she would advance him credit of three pounds.

When he'd lost this, she consented – at the pleadings of Kent Jack – to let Clarence play double-or-quits on the turn of a single card.

Clarence turned the Queen of Spades.

Foxer got the King of Hearts. Then yelped at her win, panting like a proud 'un.

I declared in my thin, tremulous voice that the king had been played three hands before and placed at the bottom of the pack. Which had not been shuffled.

The company agreed that I was a liar. And a malicious pipsqueak. I protested that I was not. I supported my case by saying that certain royal cards had recurred with uncanny regularity – whereas other cards had been too shy to show their faces. Some cards showed remarkable agility, I opined, considering they lacked the transport of a shuffle.

A stout man observed my drift, then objected to it. He said he could as easily part my head from my shoulders as tear a card or scratch his nose.

Clarence rocked mute in his chair: his complexion faded from orange to grey.

Foxer romped up and down the skirting board, sniffing about for rats.

Kent Jack advised that there would be no unpleasantness so long as all gentlemen present settled their bets.

Another suggested it a poor thing, and unsporting, for anyone to misuse a dog, and abuse her trust. For this was to prey upon the dumb.

Uncle Clarence found his feet; then his tongue. He said he would go, but return within an hour, together with six pounds. Kent Jack said he would keep Clarence company, as he'd much enjoy a stroll in fresher air.

The stout man said he would stay with me – to see that justice were done, and the debt settled.

There was no window. Two bruisers loitered by the only door. And I wondered to myself where Clarence might find six pounds. It struck me that the need was more mine than his.

I spotted all this for another riddle. But this was a hard, cold, steel-sprung mantrap of a conundrum. The sort that snaps its teeth to tether you by the ankle. So the fellow would need to speak the right answer to the riddler, if he wanted to keep all his limbs about him.

I knew that the parties and players had lain in wait to fleece a mark. But why poor, bare-arsed Clarence who had so little to shed? And why pay him the compliment of such intricate manoeuvres? You could foil his faculties with an earwig and an ounce of cheddar. So why stage such a devious drama?

No. It was planned to deceive a sharper man. The real stakes were under the table. The real sucker had an ounce more wit. And p'r'aps there were scenes still to play.

One of the players winks at me and beckons me back to the table.

'Sit, boy,' he says simply. He's lost his cutting edge of threat. He smiles. At least, he splits his mouth to declare an even ivory bite.

'Look, boy.' He cuts and shuffles the pack with one hand, like a cute 'un. He turns over twenty cards. Quickly. Slapping them down, face upwards, one after another, in a single pile. Then he fans them into a hand – so he can watch their faces and I see their backs.

'How many, boy?'

'Twenty,' I say. Now I know the answer to the riddle and must keep my wits about me. For I was playing not only for myself but for Clarence and his legs besides.

'Name 'em.'

I do so, and choose to make no mistake. He nods gravely.

'Which was the twelfth?'

'Four of clubs.'

'How many knaves, followed by a red card?'

'None.'

'Which queen before the ace of diamonds?'

'Hearts.'

'How many black cards – eight or lesser?'

'Six.'

'How many spots?'

This makes me pause for thought: 'Hundred and four.'

'Another thing, boy. Listen carefully . . .'

'Yes, sir?'

'If nine men each have eight kiddies; and each kiddie has seven cats; and each cat has six kittens; and each kitten catches five mice; and each mouse has four paws; and each paw has three claws; and each claw has two fellows; and every fellow owes me a crust . . .'

'Yes, sir?'

'How many kittens' legs are there?' he asks, thinking he's tricked me.

'Twelve thousand, sir. If you please. And ninety-six.'

'And I expect you think you're nifty,' he says.

'If you please, sir. I expect I do.'

'So what's my name, boy?'

'I don't rightly know, sir. Some call you Strand Harry. Others call you John Rivers. I expect you're other fellows besides.'

'That's right, boy. And supposing I said you've got a talent and I'd take you on – what would you say?'

'I'd say thank you very much, sir.' Then I got bold, 'And I'd ask you to give my Uncle Clarence his money back.'

He shook his head. 'Can't be done, boy. It wouldn't be right. He's a cabbage, you see. Nature made him a sucker.'

I blush crimson at my mistake; Clarence's nature; our shame.

'But . . .' he splits his mouth to show his teeth, 'we needn't smack him. And we could give your mother a sovereign.'

'Thank you, sir.'

'But I give you due warning boy . . .'

'Yes, sir?'

'Just because it comes easy to you, don't mean you won't have to work. You're a raw 'un yet, with a lot of learning to do.'

'Thank you, sir.'

Which was how he took me for his apprentice, and I took him for my master. Which was no bad thing for my advancement and education.

Learning a Craft

So I'd been dumped on my feet, and found the company of my fellows. And John Rivers, or whoever, wasn't a common street duffer – like those drones that worked the honey pot, or sold false pawn tickets, or played the pea and thimble, or grazed upon clergymen outside St Paul's, or plucked provincials at Lime Street Station – but was a craftsman who worked with gentry. And being bored to tire a single gambit, he ever extended his art.

And if his marks lost money – as he required they should – they at least enjoyed a spectacle, witnessed some deft conjuring, observed fine acting, heard a compelling story, ate a good lunch, drank only the best from the wine list, paid willingly, travelled about town, thrilled to a drama, learned something new about human nature. At the end of the day, they knew well enough they'd been worked by a master. And were left in the educative company of at least one sound moral or maxim.

Why, one time, the drama critic of the London *Times* had written two columns on how my master had sold the chorus line at Drury Lane, for sixty guineas, to a visiting banker from Tunis.

This was before my time with him. I had to learn my lessons before he took me into his confidence about taking the confidence of others.

But the first thing he did with me was to have me properly cleaned by a lady companion of his called Molly. Who was the first woman, besides Mamma, to ever undress me. In a bedroom in the Beehive. Which I found quare but thrilling – though I had never really taken to washing before. Being adverse to the sting of suds and chill of water, and the satiric comments of my family on my puny frame, willowy limbs and red thing.

'You whiff and no mistake,' says Molly, swaying back as she tugs off my jacket.

'If you please, miss, I stink like two goats. The master told me so.'

'And what does the master want with you?' she asks.

'I don't know that he wants me exactly, miss. Only he won me in a card game.' I thought it best to act discreet, in case she wasn't intimate with his business.

'Well, what can you do, child?' she asks, smiling first at my manner, then frowning at my shirt.

'If you please, miss. Though I'm quare, I'm clever.'

'What are you clever at?'

'Doing things, miss. With my head. Numbers, words and suchlike.' She found this funny enough for a snickering giggle. But I sensed she'd taken to me.

I'd never spoken to a pretty lady before. That, and the fearful prospect of shedding all my clothes, was tying my tongue all awkward.

'Please, miss. You smell as well.'

'I do?' She stepped back, hands on hips, mouth all puckered.

'Yes, miss. Of lemons and lavender. And you've been drinking gin.'

'Well you are a clever 'un,' says she, 'but you must never betray a girl's secrets. It ain't proper for a gent.'

So I didn't mention that I could see her very bosoms, and the shaded valley between, and a coral segment of nipple. Nor did I remark how these twins rocked within their cradle before my startled eyes, or that they had the bloom of peaches and a taut sheen, and were wondrously plump; that her waist was pinched narrow above the proud flare of her hips; that I could see the long taper of her thighs stretching beneath her dress; that there were two clear inches of petticoat for mortal view below her hem; that I had never viewed so many parts of a fine lady so close; that, though every woman held at least one good card, she had a royal flush; that her hair was lush and lustrous as Foxer's; that her face made me quiver, the way it flickered from frown to smile in an instant; that her lips were glossy as cherries; that her tongue was that pink at the centre of a strawberry; that I could see up her nostrils, and feel the warm pulse of her breath on my brow.

No, instead I said, 'Please, miss. You're sleeker than a ferret and gentler than any bull-terrier.'

And I swear she grazed my temples with those lips, then clutched my face to her waist.

Then she swished from the room – various parts of herself rubbing and rustling against portions of her clothing. She returned with a firm, cool manner; together with cloth, towel, bucket and block of carbolic.

'I don't need to take my trousers off,' I suggest, "cos I'm entirely clean below the waist.'

'They all say that,' she observes briskly, 'and it's rarely true, for men are mucky items.'

'Turn your head, then, please, miss.'

'I've seen a naked man once before,' says Molly. 'There are only a few parts that cause any offence. And I'll give you a sixpence, if you can show me anything I ain't seen before.'

So I slowly roll down my breeches.

'Cripes, boy! What's that red thing on your wee fellow?'

'It's a birthmark, miss,' I mutter. For I hate it when people remark upon it, as though it's a conversation piece. 'And you owe me sixpence if you please, miss.'

Molly left me wrapped in a towel, pink and sore from exposure and scrubbing. When she came back, she gave me two white shirts, knickers for my privates, a navy woollen suit, sky blue velvet waistcoat, scarlet braces, new leather boots with leather laces, prickly socks to wear beneath them, a comb made of tortoiseshell, paper and pencil, three packs of playing cards, two pairs of ivory dice, a cribbage board, ham sandwich, canvas purse with a brass buckle, and a book of etiquette.

I swear that though I'd left Mamma and Clarence, the Happy Family, my brother and sisters, it was one of the choicest days of my life.

What my new master taught or told me within my first day in his service:

1. to eat quieter, if I please – and using the utensils
2. to quit dribbling, for Christ's sake
3. to chew before swallowing
4. never to slurp, on any account – for the sake of his temper
5. not to expect him to tell me twice
6. to wipe my nose on a handkerchief, and my hands on the napkin
7. never again to speak of Marie in front of Molly; nor mention either to Emily-Jane
8. to tidy my mop of hair with the comb provided
9. to throw a twelve with two dice whenever I chose
10. to get Foxer to turn a somersault
11. that the chance of two separate events both occurring was the sum of their separate chances
12. but that the chance of two related or interdependent events follows the rule of d'Alembert's gamble
13. that, if you are being suspiciously followed, it is better to walk than to run
14. how to lose the tail in a public house, hotel lobby or railway station
15. that our names and characters might change by the day and within each day
16. that the purpose in life is to minimize error
17. that a man makes more errors by talking than staying silent

18. that a man makes more errors by getting drunk than staying sober

19. that a man makes more errors by being certain than being suspicious

20. that things are seldom as they seem and rarely as they are

21. that absolutes are relatives, as are relativities

22. that correct breathing is essential to the maintenance of a man's composure

23. that an industrious confidence-man is better than a lazy monarch: for it is not a man's occupation that matters as much as the dignity he finds in his work

24. what women wear beneath their dresses

25. the master's own classification of the seventeen most frequent forms of fool, mark and sucker

26. how to recognize these types – from behind, from the front, and from hearing their speech

27. that Uncle Clarence was the lowest form of sucker – which the master termed a Cabbage

28. that people speak through their hands, feet and clothes – but often cannot hear what they themselves are saying thereby

29. that I was a better fellow than I supposed myself; but worse than he wished me to be

30. that Foxer's other names were Poacher, Alice and Pontoon Sarah

31. which was my bed at the Beehive

32. that till I grew old enough for ladies, I should henceforth sleep on my own – for there was no shortage of beds

33. that on the morrow he should start to train me in the things that mattered

34. that, if I wished to become a gentleman, I must first learn Burke's *Book of Etiquette*

35. that he was a hard man – so I must not cross him, nor speak any of his names if I came a cropper

36. that he wished me sweet dreams

I believe I have never known such a contrary man. For he was kind and cruel, bearded and clean-shaven, bald and hirsute, upright and slouched, John and Simon, clergyman and pimp, beggar man and thief, here and gone, returned before he left, hale and pale, mute and raucous, solemn clowner, young and old, a pious atheist and trustworthy cheat, moved by a fickle faithfulness, a nation unto himself.

If you were to ask me how he was, I should bid you select any epithet and couple it with its opposite. Then you'd have the part of him. But not the whole. For he never disclosed himself entirely – even to me. So you know him as well as I. He is the grocer and the doorman, the colonel and the baron.

He had nothing so stable as tastes. Though he always had the tetchiness to voice them.

'Shall I get you pickles for your brisket?' ask I.

'No, for I detest both,' says he.

'But yesterday you ate two portions.'

'Exactly.'

'Shall I leave you alone, then, sir?'

'Up to a point, boy. Up to a point.'

But if there were any constants to his temperament – rock within the swirling sea of him – I should declare that he was unerringly sharp and various, and was grumpily affectionate.

As for his assessment of me, that was consistent. I lacked wisdom. But I was very cute with cards and numbers. And I did enough to earn my keep.

For just as Clarence had been loath to lose to a dog, so gentleman gamblers hated being bettered by a child. They'd ride their luck, chance their arm, just to try to beat me.

I would sit in my chair, raised to the height of the baize by several cushions, acting the chirpy pipsqueak.

The master stood behind, whispering to me between the play of the hands.

'That's Mr Cromer,' says he, 'who owns a distillery and brews half the vinegar in London. He's just lost a hundred and ten guineas to you. So smile at him – to show you're grateful. P'r'aps you could chance a wink besides.'

We did not – could not – cheat. Anyways, there wasn't a

need. Men who conquer the vinegar trade think they can boss the baize. I knew the fall of the cards, and their likely order in the pack; I learned the opponents' strategies; calculated the odds – theirs and mine. It was enough to keep me ahead of most. And the more they lost, the more vexed they became. Then, they played worse. Then, they lost more.

When we were well up, the master would take a barley-sugar lollipop from his pocket, unwrapping it with a deal of rustling, telling me to suck on it, and make some noises if I wished.

'Kiddie likes his sweeties,' he'd observe solemnly to the other players. 'It does a man good to see a nipper content.'

And the more I beat, the more there were that wanted to put me in my place, and wipe that unfortunate smirk from my face.

Till a friend of the Minister of State for Home Affairs, who was the brother of a solemn loser, advised the master to retire his gimmick. Which he did. Enough was enough, he declared. I believe he'd grown tired of standing behind me.

And Mamma, Clarence, Dick, my sisters, the ferret, Douglas and the other beasts?

It is sad to report – as Burke's *Book of Etiquette* observes – that as a fellow elevates himself in life by changing stations, he naturally distances himself from those he leaves behind, stationary upon their chosen platforms.

I thought that Clarence had pretended not to see me as I stood at the back of the straggle that had gathered around the menagerie. Dick now carried the hat.

Clarence's shame, I supposed, was in having me settle his debt by paying with my person. Burke does not direct upon my exact case – being more concerned with modes of address to the peerage, the correct handling of grape scissors, or the protocol in leaving a visiting card for a rural dean. But I warrant there can be no doubt that a man should not barter, sell, or otherwise transact, a young fellow who is not within his gift to give – however tight his corner. Not that this protocol concerned me. For I had nought but gratitude for Clarence, who had advertised my mental merits so long and loud, and indirectly gained me my master.

He did! Dick waved his cap beneath my nose. With a surly deference, without any flicker of recognition. He shook the hat, lest I be slow on the uptake. There was only fourpence ha'penny there. His face told a pained perplexity, then sprung an unpleasant leer, when I dropped a half crown with a clink upon the coppers. Clarence, who had caught the glint of silver, broke his slurred oration to give me a solemn salute. Which gesture might have been better bestowed on a colonel of hussars, in full dress uniform, by a puppy subaltern.

They did not know me! Had I changed so much in seventeen days? I dare say I had. And not only on my surfaces.

My hair was neatly parted and oiled. My face was pink above a starched white collar. My suit was freshly pressed and brushed. You could see the shining heavens curved upon my boot caps. I stood ramrod stiff with my heels touching.

Yet they seemed to have changed the more. Clarence – whose conduct I'd taken three weeks before as an exemplar of heroic manliness – was acting a sad, derelict sot. His unshaven face was criss-crossed with broken veins. His clothes would have disgraced an ashamed beggar. His spiel and patter – assembled of coughs, splutters and slurred whinings – an unwitting farce upon the sequelae of tippling. The Temperance Society could not have contrived a more salutary or persuasive example.

Dick mimicked a common urchin. His hair stood straight up, more in need of shearing than parting. You'd have given him a hosing and scraping before you tried the delicacy of a wash. I dare say he harboured fleas. I would have given him the coins for a manicure – but it would have seemed a cruel and facetious offer.

A Cabbage and a Sprout! Which types of sucker and shoot are unable to witness the general in the particular, or recognize a repetition – the master says. So cannot see their nephew or brother, because he's dressed in new clothes.

Mamma knew me at once. As soon as the door swung open, warming the urinary airs of the stairs with the domestic savours of kipper and ferret turd.

'You Mamma's Joey!'

'Good afternoon, Mamma.' I dabbed a handkerchief to my nose, but it did not block out the stenches. 'It's a fine day, so I thought I'd step out to pay my respects.'

She shuffled backwards into her parlour, clutching her skirts with her cracked, pork-sausage fingers.

'What've they done to you, Joey?'

'Cleaned me up, I dare say, Mamma. And taught me manners and suchlike. But I'm still your very own son.'

She clutched me to her, fair squeezing the breath from me, rubbing her sand-paper cheeks against my neck. Quite choking my gullet with the solid smells of her.

'Cripes, boy. You're a young gentleman.'

'A fellow does his best, I suppose, to create a favourable impression.' Which was tactless of me, given the state of her parlour.

'Do they work you hard, Joey?'

'I play cards, Mamma, and travel the railways, and eat in fancy restaurants, and go to the races, and amuse ladies. My master's kind enough. I keep the company of a dog called Foxer. And I've a bed all my own, and a book of etiquette.'

'They've changed you, boy,' she whined her muffled protest. Her reddened eyes trickled some tears. 'They've put you through the wringer, and covered you in starch. Then scorched you with an iron.'

'I'm happy, Mamma.' I told the truth. 'I'm learning new things – gambits, stratagems, tactics, probabilities, ploys and suchlike. I'm apprenticed to a craft.'

'What craft?'

'Designing appearances,' I say, 'for gentlefolk who wish to buy them.'

'Duffing?' she asks. 'Conning?'

'For the better classes,' say I.

'So you ain't coming back, boy?' She's snorting and snuffling, dabbing her eyes with her apron.

'Every so often, Mamma,' I promise, stroking the fur of her arm. 'Whenever my profession allows it. . . . But, Mamma, I love you. And I've brought you some presents.'

She arranges the bottles, with laboured care, in a row on the table edge. Lethargically, passionless.

'Ain't no need,' she prods the wine bottle.

'It's a La Cruze '35, Mamma. It's choice with shellfish. But you must wrap it in ice for an hour.'

'That so, boy?'

'Armagnac,' say I, 'for Clarence.'

'Bugger needs a belting,' says she.

'Sarsaparilla – for the kiddies.'

'Kiddies?'

'That's Eau de Cologne de Florix, from Flaubert's of Piccadilly,' I say, 'to dab behind your ears, and . . .' I redden, 'splash on your chest. . . . Molly wears it,' I explain.

'I ain't no Molly,' says she.

I was properly choked to have returned to find home so strange, spoiled, soiled and different.

When I went, I left two sovereigns on the mantelpiece, next to the lacquer-backed hairbrush I had brought her.

The very same way I later used to leave Florence a contribution, to defray some of the expenses of being a lady.

My First Woman

I hazard I learned much and quick. I grew apace, though my body persisted in lagging behind my head. I worked hard with the master, though it seldom seemed like labour. Having been summoned to answer to a friend of the Secretary for Home Affairs – and having been much taken by the fellow's frigid asperity – the master promptly became him, complete to his lisp, silvered sideburns and fondness for speaking snippets from Ovid. Whereupon we travelled first class to Manchester. He as He; I as His page. The master let it be as well known as was compatible with his starchy discretion that he was sent by a Man, connected to Another, who attended a Palace, to assess the worthiness of certain mill owners for the award of Knighthoods, Peerages, and other honours, for service to Industry, Probity and the Poor.

Our company was much sought. However many invitations the master declined, still he was never without an appointment for luncheon and dinner the entire two weeks of our travel. He showed himself a scrupulous and civil servant by his adamant refusal of bribes – conceding only to charitable contributions.

'Twas odd, the master observed, how many believed themselves deserving of royal honour on account of their being rich, gross, bald and blunt ... and credulous how they further supposed that a mistress, fondness of boys, fraud, vice, intemperance, or unlikely appetite, should ever hinder its award.

Another time, I helped the master sell some sheep bones to the Patriarch of Antioch, the latter being fully convinced – from decipherment of some parchments we also supplied –

that the pieces of fossilized mutton were the very ribs of Saint Peter.

We also wrote, discovered, and sold to two different publishing houses, a hitherto unknown novelette of the recently deceased provincial poet William Wordsworth. It was a lewd and lively confection, scribbled in the author's own hand, entitled *Lucy, Pensive on my Couch: a True Romance*.

I gathered from this piece – which the master composed and I jotted – that there was a deal of pleasure and lively fun to be had by a gentleman from the companionship of a lady. And that to be – surprised by these joys – sportive as a fawn – in secret bowers – with strange fits of passion – with quickening pace – by night concealed – down the vale profound – as the maiden sighs – tossing her head in sprightly dance – the lap filling with pleasures of her own – before withering on the stalk – was, in short, not to be sniffed at. And ranked high amongst the pastimes.

I had garnered this much: that a man goes off with a woman to find some privacy, on a bed, couch, or in a doorway; that both parties, for private reasons of their own, divest themselves of some clothing – entirely, or from the waist downwards, else loosing some buttons at least; that there's jiggery-pokery, sometimes with squealing and bouncing; that the man falls asleep or takes more pleasure; that the man then gives money to the woman, if he's had the better sport of it; so that, contrary to the rules of cards, the loser gets paid.

I was full ten years old. Since I ate, worked, drank and gambled as a man, I determined that I should try this further recreation and find out whether women were to my taste or not: and determine exactly how they were to be enjoyed.

Burke's *Book of Etiquette* was teasingly mute on this matter, remarking only that man and wife might enter each other's bed chambers on certain days of a month, after getting the maid to deliver a note detailing their intentions. Burke observed that it was a foolish man who entered his wife's boudoir without knocking. But, since the pleasurable trade between man and woman seemed to lie outside of marriage, this helped me not a jot.

Nor would Molly explain.

'I was thinking, Molly, that I'd like to enjoy a woman.'

'At your age!' she says, giggling like a child. 'Don't you think you should grow first, Joey?' As if my size mattered.

'I am grown,' say I, 'in the things that matter.'

'You'll need more than that wee fellow, Scarlet,' says she.

'Let's leave my chappie out of it,' say I. For I felt confident I could enjoy a woman as well as the next man, without any vulgar recourse to my privates. And I wished she would not make such frequent reference to the red fellow. It doesn't help a man if a woman laughs at him whenever he lowers his breeches. Though I held her as dear as any, I resented her sly allusions to my birthmark. Which was a private matter of mine.

'I'd be pleased to enjoy you, Molly. Could you show me how it's done? As one friend to another. For I mean to get to the bottom of it.'

'Your master wouldn't like it,' says she, 'and neither, I fear, would I.'

I thought her a spoilsport but did not say so.

Nor was the master as clear as could be.

'Sir,' say I, when I find him at leisure, aimlessly rolling his dice and jotting down the numbers. I was too preoccupied to ask him why he was dressed so – in the purple frock of a bishop. 'What's all this hanky-panky as goes on between men and women?'

'Why, bless you, boy,' says he, 'it's a God-given gift, sanctified in heaven, for the procreation of children, that male and female may become as one, worshipping each other with the vessels of their bodies.'

'Is there no fun to it, then, sir?'

'Genesis, chapter three, verse fifteen,' he observes, rolling a succession of double-ones. 'And I will put enmity between thee and the woman, and between thy seed and her seed: it shall bruise thy head, and thou shalt bruise her heel.'

I knew I'd get no sense from him until he was defrocked.

Another time – 'Sir, what do you do with Molly? In your room?'

'I'd think that was my concern,' says he severely, 'and hers. Why, has she been telling tales?'

'No, sir. Not Molly, sir. She says you're never any trouble.

That you take your pleasure quick and quiet, and then nod off. She was quite particular that you never tire her.'

'Good,' says he, 'I do my best. I'd hate to hear she'd been telling tales.'

'Do you think I should try a woman, sir?'

'I'd wait a while, boy, till you feel the obligation.'

'But what does a fellow do, sir? When he enjoys a woman?'

'This and that,' says he, 'with some ups and downs, on and off. There are some ins and outs to it, too. If a fellow has a mind to it, he'll soon gain the knack, without any lessons at Sunday School. If he's neat and nimble and got the nous.'

'But it's worth the effort, sir?'

'To my mind, boy, it's better than eating, on par with sleeping, but less of a joy than work.'

Which seemed a fair recommendation. So I thought I'd procure some women and try the business. To see if it pleased my taste.

The master was in Hastings, on church business – as treasurer of a charity for the widows of fishermen – and Molly at her sister's house in Bow, when I walked out for my sport one evening.

Shunning my own locale, for fear of being seen, I strode out west towards the Haymarket. For I knew that women who liked pleasure took particularly to the theatre.

There was quite a throng. And being shorter, then, than most men – though by no means slight for my age – I had some trouble seeing and being seen. But even when I walked close by the ladies, they smiled out over my head – winking or calling to any other men that chanced by. As though I were not there. Which made me worry about my dress. But, no, I decided, I was smart and tidy as the best. Slicker than most.

The benefit of this disregard was that I could study each lady, without being hurried to purchase. And there was a deal of choice – between young and old, pretty and haggard, smart and soiled, smiling and scowling, healthy and withered, bent and straight, entire and toothless, coughing and composed.

If I was a sucker in the master's system, I was a sucker for beauty. So I thought that, given this fine selection, it would be better to select a beautiful woman. Else a handsome or a pretty one. With all her parts to her, and with a smile that showed a taste for pleasure. Other things being equal, I thought a lovely face and upright posture offered the best of bets. Then, if all else disappointed, I could take pleasure in her appearance.

And the whim I had was that I should like a lady like Molly. With long black curls and a stretch of ivory chest. With a skip to her walk. An athlete of laughter.

After two rounds of the Haymarket, I thought I had found her. After a further lap I was certain.

So I combed my hair, eyeing my reflection in the windows of the Argyle Rooms. Then I burnished the toes of my boots on the back of my trouser legs. And spat bravely on the pavement.

'Nommus,' says she.

'Pardon, miss?'

'Piddle off,' she explains, 'scarper, scat, decant. This is my patch.' She has a mellow, quavering warmth to her voice. Her accent shows her a well-spoken lady.

'I'm not cognisant of the argot, miss,' say I, 'being new to this mode of transaction. But I think I'm a mark, miss. I'd like to buy, not sell. I'm a sucker.'

'Buy?' says she. Indeed, I would, for she was chipper and chirpy as Molly, with mighty swells and dips to herself.

'Have the pleasure of you, miss.' Knowing as much as I did about most things, I was discomforted to find myself at the disadvantage here. And I wasn't making my purpose clear.

'You?' said she. 'And whose Uncle Arnold?'

'Just me.'

'Scat, boy.' She tousles my hair and pushes me away. It's a firm hand in the small of my back.

'I dare say my money's as good as the next man's.' I unpack my purse on my palm.

'Fifteen shillings for the room,' she says, delicately lifting coins, 'two guineas for my company. Ten shillings for the laundry. Another guinea for the refreshments. . . . I might lose by it, but you have a pleasant face to you.'

So we set off for her rooms in the Langton. I wondered what

manner of refreshments there might be – parched, as I was, by my walk.

'It's my first time,' say I, 'but I 'spect I'll pick it up. I've a sharp mind and I'm nifty with my hands. . . . And please, miss?'

'Yes, young sir?'

'What's your profession, miss? Are you courtesan, actress, dolly-mop or tail?'

'I'm Fanny. I'm a working girl who's come unbuttoned.'

Her chest was quite a startling sight. A fellow couldn't hold himself from ogling – though he knew from Burke it was impolite. But it was nothing to the drop of her drawers. The young chap was fairly pole-axed.

'Please, Fanny. You've got a hairy patch below your belly.' I pointed out the part, though she'd have been a dim 'un not to have seen it for herself. It was a dense forest, stretching down and round between her legs. There were fluffy tufts on the inside of her thighs.

'So I have,' she observes, yet without any curiosity. I've often wondered at that: how women take their mystery so casually for granted.

'What's it for, Fanny?'

'Lawd if I know. But you'll find a deal of women have it.'

'You could hide things in it,' I advise. 'Small valuables and the like. For, I dare say, it'd be the last place a rogue would think to look.'

'I never thought of it that way,' says she. 'Now what's your fancy, young 'un. I do straight, French, Egyptian, Dutch or Eton College.'

I told her I would like to lie with her – which I understood to be the correct wording and exact procedure.

So we did it. Lay on the bed. Together. So close I could have touched her. When I thought she wasn't looking, I sneaked a glimpse of her bosoms.

'Do you think it's rude to stare, Fanny?'

'I should say so. Didn't your mother teach you nothing?'

I tried bouncing up and down till the bed creaked. She joined in alongside, fairly choking with laughter.

'You've got a part of it, at least,' she chuckles.

'I learn most things quick,' I tell her.

Though we lay there for the best part of an hour, nothing much transpired except her snorts and snores, and that irrational stiffening of my whatsit, that Burke's *Etiquette* just don't remark on. It just springs up proud, without rhyme or reason. So I rolled over on my belly to conceal the wee chap's eccentric conduct.

'Would you like a game of brag?' I ask, hearing her yawn her return from sleep, 'or perhaps poker? To pass the time.'

'Time's up,' says she, stretching. 'Another man will be wanting the same. A girl has to earn her living.'

'Well, thank you, Fanny. I did enjoy you.'

' 'Twas nothing,' said she. 'You must come and amuse me again.'

As I skipped along, I felt all aquiver, to have had my first woman. And to have found it such a pleasant, enigmatic drama.

Looking back, I don't fault dear, sweet Fanny. I was indeed the sucker; and she the duffer. It probably did me good to be done. For, as I was later to find, in this life every trickster is another man's mark. Even the master got taken once.

Once you allow yourself to get hungry, thirsty, needy or proud, you've promptly set yourself up. For there's a nagging urge, jostling for control of your faculties. So you must keep your appetites sensibly sated, to concentrate on the job.

Which was why the master, getting properly tired of my enquiries, conceded the case, telling me about the business between men and women.

Naturally, I was much amused. Taking it all for one of his witty blags.

'It isn't a joke, boy!' he scowls, which always warns me. 'Or perhaps it is, but it isn't mine.'

'But it's an unlikely business, sir.'

'Aye,' he concedes, 'the good Lord's quite a prankster. But he requires we take his slapstick seriously, and ignore any double entendre.'

I giggled. For I imagined the master and Molly. Doing it. It must have gone against the grain of his temperament. Exposing himself so.

Then he tells me about the dancers and the jig. And the characters in the farce.

'Really, sir?' say I, 'I wondered what they were for. And like a sneeze, you say?'

He maps the geography of the other gender, then delves into some geology besides.

'Well I never,' say I, 'and a fellow would never guess. Not from seeing the surfaces.'

Then he recounts his classification of the twenty-seven most popular ways of assembling the parts and pieces.

'The Flying Hedgehog!' I say, repeating his terms with wonder, 'Topsey Gander . . . Lord Chancellor . . . Soggy Rabbit . . . The Queen's Prerogative . . . The Last Resort . . . The Winkle and the Oyster . . . They sound like pubs, and no mistake.'

Then he tells of tones, timbres, tempos, recapitulations, ritornellos, rinforzandos, rhapsodies, reprises, resolutions, rallentandos, rolls and rondos. It was clear there was quite an art to it all.

'So you'd say, sir, that music offers the closest guidance? That there are codes and conventions? But each player must be prepared to watch the baton? But also improvize, as both conductor and composer? Yet be prepared to play second fiddle?'

'Aye, boy. But there's a deal of theatre to it, too.' So he tells me something of Melodrama, Edmund Kean, Travelling Shows, the prompt box and the proscenium.

'The Romantic Movement, you say?'

He speaks of *coups de théatre*. Also of the Comédie Française.

'So you must rub both ladies with oil?'

'It lessens the friction,' the master tells me.

He set me on my way. You may well imagine. But if the master had a fault, it was excessive concern with method. He'd turn it all into Itology – making a system, forming a classification, naming this and that, calculating the probabilities. Then devising a deceit, and selling it to a sucker. Not just for the money, you understand, but for the joys to be had from the work.

And there were simpler, more honest pleasures than his. Why, a man would lie with a woman – like Fanny – and simply enjoy the moment.

And think she has choice thighs. Or worship her very soul at the temple of her lap. Paying soft and solemn respects to the graven images of those swollen lips. Dizzied by the incense. Incensed that in an hour you must part. But parting her, find a pearl loitering there in the oyster. And snuggling there, give pleasure just for the reverent pleasure of it. Without any thought of stratagem or gambit, odds or ante. And praise God for his sculptural ingenuities. And think he loves us well – to give us this innocence, in our corruption.

Literature

It was about this time that I learned to forget; and quite by accident.

It's a fine thing, forgetting. I quite commend it – as mental sanitation. Even if it takes a time, and tests a fellow's ingenuity. For we all have things roaming our heads as we'd prefer should loiter outside.

The master had instructed me to stain Foxer – black, that she might acquire an alibi and disguise, and pursue her career under other colours. So it was that I found myself painting her with boot dye. It was a tedious task. You should not believe the number of hairs to a dog. And if each hair must be painted to its curly root, the task quickly palls. So, as I brushed the tint into Foxer's back, I passed my time browsing Heine's *Deutschland, ein Wintermärchen*, that I might tutor my mind in German.

Foxer became frisky as I daubed the insides of her ears. Naturally, then, I dropped a blob of dye upon the margin of page thirty-seven. And it was the master's favourite tome! And he was jealous of his library.

Promptly, I swabbed the page with turpentine. This only compounded the smudge, and spread the tint to pages thirty-one to forty-seven inclusive.

Foxer, who found herself averse to the sting of stain, then took sly advantage of my confusion, padding a retreat upstairs. I could see the route she'd taken from the dyed footprints on the Afghan carpet.

I found her whining her discomfort upon Molly's sofa. Naturally I advised her off. Yet it was too late to prevent her registering the imprint of her belly upon the primrose velvet.

And that weren't the full of it. For, by some quirk of her physiology, or duff dye, Foxer dried to a glossy green. Which hue, the master tartly observed, did not satisfy his requirements – since it awarded an Airedale more celebrity than concealment.

It was a sorry sequence. I dare say any intelligent man unaccustomed to staining dogs with Whistler's Patent Boot Dye might learn similar lessons from the task. And think himself wiser thereafter.

But the master aimed blame. At me. Fair loosing his tongue, till my shirt front was sodden from weeping. He then calculated the strength of the damage at seventeen guineas. And docked it from my wages. So it was I not Foxer that was in the dog house.

But it was thus I learned to forget. For, writhing in my bed, I recollected the scene. I imagined making amends. In my mind's eye, with a fine brush dipped in whitewash, I painted out the stains to the master's book. Then, carefully mixing the palest yellow, on my imaginary palate, I stained Molly's sofa back to its pristine colour.

It was magic! In my memory, at least. I could summon the book and sofa to mind, and scrutinize their finest features. But the stains were gone! However hard I struggled to recall them, the blotches could not be seen.

I thought it a fancy trick. I commenced to forget more and different. I erased chapter two of Book One of Mr Disraeli's *Sybil*, simply by turning the pages in mind, and splodging each with a masonry brush dipped in distemper. I was pleased to have it out of my head. He may know politics, but 'tis clear he don't comprehend the Epsom Derby.

And I straightways discovered other means to forget. I found I could burn things too. And cross them out with an imaginary pencil. Or lift them in my mind's eye and toss them over my shoulder. Else put them in a sack. Or consign them to a cupboard. Then they were gone! Clean forgotten.

So I gave my mind a fine spring-cleaning. I dropped the master's watch down a coal-hole, to repay his malice to me. I cut off Gladstone's whiskers with Molly's millinery scissors. And didn't he look a changed fellow! Then I deleted all the 'nots' in the Ten Commandments – just as a jest. And screwed to a ball the timetable of the Great Western Railway.` I lifted Mr Millet's 'The Winnower' from the gallery wall and chucked it on the parlour fire – frame and all – till it were but ashes and acrid smell. I placed Sly Hobbs in a dark cell, then slammed closed the heavy door. And bolted it shut. For I surely ain't going to entertain in my mind a man as slashed open my arm with a razor.

Then I could barely remember him.

Whatsisname.

Ain't it a choice task? Forgetting.

But I was careless when I first started tampering with my history. I'd find holes and voids in my recollection, and worry for my sanity.

That was before I started leaving messages for myself, in the files of my memory, explaining I'd wiped some traces to avoid any cause of melancholy, sparing myself any gratuitous pain.

I come across these memoranda all the time. There I am, recalling my days as a nipper. I see it all. My scrawny brown arm flashing out to biff brother Dick in his belly. Then I see his fist, fat and knobbly, arc into my face. Then I can visualize nothing. Till there appears in my mind's eye a neat note, scribed on card, in my best italic hand, the ink faded brown with age, addressed politely to myself.

To Joseph Blueglass, Gentleman.
Dear Joey,
    Reminiscence can be a hurtful thing. So some subsequent incidents have been edited out, by your faithful and former self, Joey. 21st Feb 1856.
P.S. Is life better now you've grown older?
I dare say you're rich and happy by now.
P.P.S. Have you been back to visit Mamma?

'Tis a charming thing to receive such correspondence from my younger person, who takes such a brotherly care to protect me.

*

As if she had not played enough tricks with my mind, Nature commenced to toy with my body. And she played with me where a fellow is naturally most sensitive and coy. If he's been told so often to keep the unsightly bundle from view, mention and mind, it'll strike him as a wry paradox that the divine hands then fondle his parts so particularly.

But Nature worked her craft at such irritating leisure. So, for a while, viewing the indelible but slow changes writ on his parts, the young fellow is at a loss to decide if he is a distended child or diminutive man. And his voice is moved by the same uncertainty, quavering his confusion to the world.

And it being marked scarlet at birth, I'd hoped to keep the whole thing hidden. But now I knew I must disclose my blemish – if I were to gain any satisfaction from it, and have it earn its keep.

I should not wish to inflate it out of proportion, but it's a quare and risible fellow.

The master knew my problems.

'I dare say you're thinking of women,' says he, hacking away at his breakfast sausage.

I blush. Molly snickers.

'Molly's chest is a fine thing,' the master observes, 'but you'd do better to look elsewhere, to find a fitting purpose.'

'Pardon, Molly. Sorry, sir.' I dare say the tips of my ears glow incandescent.

'You're going to be a lecher, boy. And I don't suppose I can save you. But I'll do my best. You need a business of your very own, boy, to keep your mind off bosoms.'

'Yes, sir.'

'So I shall teach you to write.'

'Like Misters Thackeray and Dickens?'

'The same idea,' says he, 'but briefer. There's no earthly need to write near so much as those demented fellows. They can't stop themselves scribbling.'

'Poems, then, sir?'

'Begging letters,' says the master. 'They're the purest form of literature.'

'They are, sir?' I hadn't known that.

He reaches into his vest for his gold fob-watch.

'Where's my timepiece?' says he.

'I haven't seen it for a couple of days,' I tell him.

'A man needs his watch about him,' he declares with irritation, 'for time is of the essence. In literature as in our work. I've got no more than ten minutes to explain writing to you. So listen close. There are only seven tricks to literature, and I've told you the first and foremost already . . . Writing is beggary. But you don't ask straight out. That's too obvious.'

'It is, sir. Naked as a nipple.'

'There's a single design to all the great literature of the world, from the Odyssey to Oliver Twist. All the good works speak the same. Any differences are discretionary detail. They all say this – "I want your money. Here are some lies. Pray, send me twenty guineas by return of post." '

'They do?' I hadn't known.

'Yes, boy. But Misters Homer and Dickens are sly and subtle fellows. They don't come out with it straight. Instead, they describe a plight and imply a remedy. That remedy is money.

'Dickens is the master, boy. He has a poor starving orphan beg for more gruel. For the writer must show poverty and help-lessness. Stir the sympathy of the reader. Then, if they cannot feed the orphan themselves, they can pay Mr Dickens to do it for them. And so he becomes the richer, by borrowing others' woes, or by making people suffer in his imagination.'

'Yes, sir.'

'So all writing is telling sorry stories, with orphans and widows, sickness, death and misery. But you don't tell by telling.'

'No, sir?'

'Indeed not. Mostly, you tell by showing. So, instead of saying that Oliver Twist is sad, you have him weep and wail. And you don't say a man is cruel. Rather, you have him throw the boy from the orphanage, or try to drown his devoted doggie. The readers will draw their own conclusions . . . What you need is an outward depiction of the inner state. Don't tell of melancholy. Show tears and shivers instead. They're always more effective. Understand, Joey?'

'I shouldn't say so, sir.'

'No?'

'No, sir. Instead, I'd observe that I have a knowing glint in my sparkling, chestnut eyes.'

'That's the idea. Now, another thing. Writing is like praying, or laying with a woman. There are always more parties in mind than are present in the flesh.'

'Who is there, then, sir? Besides the reader and writer?'

'Three phantoms, boy. There's a reader the writer imagines – with his sympathy and purse drawn tight, so must be moved to unlace the both. And the writer the reader imagines – who might be trying to trick him. Which is indeed the case. So the writer has to fool the reader, by hiding behind another party who he gets to represent him.'

'Who?'

'The duffer,' says the master, 'who in literature is known by the alias of Narrator. And is no more nor less than the character you invent. To work the mark and purloin his confidence. By creating the right impressions.'

'It's duffing!' say I. 'It's all misleading appearances. A farrago of lies. A confection of invention – selling deceits to suckers.'

'Exactly,' the master confirms. 'Try it, boy. Pretend you're someone you ain't. Borrow some worthy woe from an unfortunate. Then see if you can convert it to capital and claim some credit for it.'

'But, sir,' I demand, 'why don't they arrest scribblers and poets, and sling them in the clink? Why do us duffers take all the blame?'

'Hypocrisy,' the master replies.

He urged me to correspond with the wives of dead men, saying I should find lists of fresh widows in the obituary columns. Widows have often just come into money. This occasion, he advised, makes them emotional – ripe and ready to be plucked by the tugs of literature.

So it was that I wrote my first fiction. Like Mr Dickens, I understand, I drew some themes from the facts of my own life – making my hero a bastard, conscious of his humble birth. I called myself Jonas, but played only a minor part.

I dare say I was too ambitious. But a writer must aim high, if he wishes to develop his craft.

My dear pure lady

I shiver with shame to write to you. For I am a poor corrupt vesil but was dignified to receive your husband may he rest in peace between my thighs. If he had but one fault it was to fall to my level and make the single mistake of fathering my three kiddys who are Jonas Emma and Harriet through his seed. And you should shudder with affiction at the sight of the boy who is the spit of his father down to his blemish pride and peculiarity as you shall see when you come to meet the lad and have the joy to witness him nakid. We all want no more than to weap on the grave and ask your permishin for same so as not to cause you more greef nor embabrasmint. Though we are sorry not only at his passing as his forgettin his promis to provide skooling for the boy and sustinince for the girlies. No matter for the foggler is gone and it is to late and I should be ashamed to lay any claim on the Estate. My brother friend who is soliciters clark with slye and witte of grazing fields says anyways it should be hard to prove the piternity for sure for there is only the resemblince of the boy and gosip to make my case. That and the Letters. And whats done is done for the eg is cracked and only strife would come of it for it was not a true maridj but a bigimy for he maridjed you ten years afore me so all I ask is that the kiddys can come see there grand relatifs and fathers grave and red their eyes as is fittin and say watch to their brother and sisters and you as they fondly call aunt jenny before we go to Kanada in a grand ship for which we must first find the Money chance willing. For we need the mighty sum of One hundred Pounds. To start our lifes again. Shall you meet us at the Stashin when we come on the noon train easter satur day or shall we inquire of you in the town saying we are your kin to explain our curiositis lest folk think us burglars or ruffians or will you write. Should you prefer us spend but one night or the month with you and should you mind we bring our dog who is smarty who is a fine ratter and partil to the country but don't worry for our food becos I shall bring plenty shrimps welks cockles eels which we sell on the streets but of which there is always left overs from one day to another which are always fresher to the mouth than the nose advisis so dont be afraid for the fish course. I am sorry and degraded to be the cause of any upset which my news may bring you but the ill wind will seem no more than a fart once weve drunk some bottils together and make ourselves friends and sung byby to the old foggle may he rest in peace bless your house god save the queen may I call you sister. aggie bessant

I hazard it was good enough – for a first composition. Though I sent the letter to but fourteen widows, I received within a week an injunction, two writs, an enquiring solicitor and one hundred and fifty-four pounds. All of which, I dare say, speaks ill of the opinions of widows of the characters of their husbands. There must be distrust in many a marriage.

The master cautioned me to brevity and concision, counselled me against caricature and exaggeration, and told me to find another address for my correspondence. He told me the six ways in which a story may be ordered as plot, explained the relationships of story time and discourse length, and made some compelling observations on the disparate points of view of characters and narrator.

He let me keep twenty guineas, saying I had earned it.

I thought I should buy myself some women, and enjoy them properly. Now I had the wherewithal and maturity. First, I supposed, I should return to Fanny and complete the transaction with her.

It was barely a year since I'd spoken to her – yet she seemed to have aged by ten. She weren't near half so perky. Her skin had gone pitted and leathery as a pigskin wallet. She'd lost some of those front teeth, which would have been most prominent if she'd still retained them – so when she thought to smile, she grimaced.

'I know you from somewhere,' she says, when I drop my trousers and advance towards her, 'I never forget a face. You're Scarlet, ain't you, you little bouncer?'

'You remember!' say I, kissing her cheek in fond gratitude.

'Same again, boy?' she asks all cheery. 'Shall us take a kip?'

'More 'n that,' say I, 'this time. For there's a lot I ain't never tried. I've got a deal of learning to do.'

'What's your fancy then, Scarlet?' She eyes me with suspicion.

'Dutch,' say I, 'to start with. Then Turkish. And I'd like some French and Topsy Turvy too – 'cos I've heard good reports of both.'

'Hark at the boy!' says Fanny. 'Ain't he the greedy one.'

Then we squirm upon the bed. I upon her.

'Aaagh,' I observe, for I'm no sooner in than shaken by spasm.

'Do other men take longer?'

'They surely do,' says Fanny, 'some go on for minutes on end.'

'I'm fast,' I brag. 'Everyone says so. I do most things quicker than most.'

She lies still on her back, upon the damp stained coverlet, twining a lock of hair between long white fingers. Now, I look at her closely. She has a bosom, belly, thighs and fur. Everything I'd wanted. All I could ask for. And all in the single parcel. So the urge promptly returned.

'You are a lovely lady, Fanny. Should we kiss now? Or p'r'aps hold hands? What's the proper etiquette?'

'As the gentleman pleases.'

'Well, then, Fanny, I think I should like to try Turkish instead, if it's all the same to you.'

'Already?'

'I'm quick, like I said. And there's lots I have to do. And I dare say your time is precious too.'

Turkish took longer to achieve. French longer still. But both were assuredly worth the efforts, and didn't seem a labour at all. For they repaid a fellow's diligence in shocking, stunning coin. Topsy Turvy I found improbable and intimate, and the most agreeable of all. And gave me a long study of what I'd longed to see. Not to mention the flavours and scents of it all.

I reckon I had the better sport of it. It was mint as a new coin to me. Whereas Fanny had clearly had too much of it, and grew quite brusque and grudging.

'Shall us try adultery now?' I ask. 'They say that's pleasant too.'

'You have to be married, boy,' she snaps. 'That's the law.'

That set me pondering – that there were things to do with a woman as were only allowed in marriage.

'What's Eton College, then, Fanny? Can we do that instead?'

'Stuff that,' she suggests, 'up your bum. This lady has another appointment.'

Women, I have noticed, are designed with more elegance, mystery and discretion. Particularly below the waist – holding their pursed, moist secrets furtive as molluscs. And their surface swells and swerves have the bloom and blush of fruit. So the woman looks like a person grown to ripe and succulent proportion; plush and scented as a plump peach.

Whereas the male, I fear, looks like an afterthought in the flurry of creation. Given that the Lord wanted to finish the business in a week, and take some rest, some parcels were designed in haste, to loiter graceless for eternity. I dare say the male parts were amongst these. It must have been a taxing task. Designing something pretty for every last purpose under heaven.

If you cast your eyes over a naked man, you'll see what I mean. Certain pieces have been tacked in haste onto a basically sound design. Without consideration to the grace or proportions of the whole – like a brick porch on a Norman church, or the price-tag plonked on a chicken.

There might be a man who looks better unbuttoned or untrousered, but I haven't seen him. Michaelangelo did his best with a suggestive David: but at the cost of shrinking the offending items to diminish the affront, then furnishing the chappie with the modest breasts and lovely face of a girl.

And as it is in society or Parliament, it's often the biggest booby that has the loudest say. So the foggler is forever intruding in the conduct of my mind, nudging and goading. And I'm stuck with the loon through life. Tied to a hectoring bore who will rise to but one ardent ambition, and can make only two observations.

If you've ever taken a spaniel for a walk, you'll know how it is. The frothing sot drags you along. He will insist on leaping on everybody, poking his wet nose where it never belongs, pausing only to pee.

The Ashamed Beggar

As I was passing down Drury Lane, the brown velvet fumes of Porter's Coffee House sidled warm up my nostrils – carrying Jamaica sugar, caramel, coffee and chocolate. The aromas fair tweaked the nipples of my desire, as I pondered my priority of pleasures. For I could not decide which I should prefer – a coffee before a beef steak, a woman before coffee, or a mocha pastry before the woman. And to compound the difficulty, all lay close to hand. Then a shadow fell across my legs. And an actor addressed the writer, as if I were a judge.

'Excusing me, your honour.' He was bent like a question mark to a stance of puzzled deference, watching my feet, offering a bald blotched pate to my gaze. I wondered what his story was. He wore a threadbare frock coat, faded from black to speckled green. And smelled of shag and cabbage. From his dress I knew he could not be a Blown-Up Miner, Shipwrecked Mariner, or Frozen-Out Gardener. He bore no afflictions beyond his character, smell and twisted posture. I reckoned him a Destitute Hero, or Ashamed. I decided I should pay him for any narrative that I hadn't heard before.

'But surely you're Ashamed, sir?' I guess.

'Indeed, your honour, I am ashamed.' He winces to show so.

'But I seemed like a kind young gentleman who might hear you out?' I beam my understanding.

'Yes, your honour.'

'Very well,' say I, 'tell me a tale' – though I believed I knew the story.

'If you please, your honour, I was once a prosperous trades-man . . .'

'But a fire burnt you out, I hazard.'

'Why, yes, sir.' He coughs. 'Perhaps you read of my misfortunes in *Reynold's News.*'

'Was your poor wife Betty burnt to a cinder, along with all your stock?' I exhale smoke, tapping the smouldering tip of my cigar.

'My wife's name was Rachel, sir. And my son Toby was burned with her, too.'

'Then you must have walked all the way from Peterborough?'

'From Bedford, sir. And my dear daughter Peggy died on the road. With me without the wherewithal to bury her proper.'

'Then, I dare say, you feel afflicted?' say I, straining to supply a sufficiency of sympathy.

'Afflicted and Tormented. Pestered to the limit.' He shuffles and clears his throat. I suppose he fears he's rumbled.

'Troubles seldom come singly,' I advise, 'neither in literature nor life.'

'Indeed, your honour . . . so I wondered . . . if you could . . . ashamed as I am to ask . . . . shamed . . .' He shivers as he lays open his palms before me.

'It can't bring you back your family or business,' say I sadly, 'but I could give you eight shillings and tuppence, which is all I own in the world.'

'Thank you, sir. But shan't you keep a sixpence for yourself?'

'No need of money,' say I, 'where I'm going. Is this the road for Southwark Bridge?'

'Where are you going, then, young sir? Elephant and Castle?'

'Heaven or hell,' I say, 'for I must drown myself prompt-ly.'

'Drown yourself? I shouldn't do that, sir.'

I heave the coins from my pocket and lay them in the cup of his hands.

'You seem a kind gentleman,' I say, 'and have suffered rare misfortunes yourself. . . .' I slump down to the paving, crumple and weep. He stoops over my bowed, shaking head.

'Shall we drown ourselves together?' I whimper, drawing

my sleeve along my cheeks, to mop some tears. 'We should find comfort in companionship.'

'We have to struggle on, boy,' he says gruffly.

'Can't,' say I, 'I swear it ain't possible. Not to be a Christian and keep alive in London Town. A man can be alive or godly. He can't be both together.'

'What's happened, then, boy?'

So the Lost Christian tells his tale to the Burnt-Out Tradesman.

'Pappa is in prison. Mamma died of shame and contagious complications .... I came to London yesterday, straight from Mamma's funeral. To find my fortune. At the train station a blind man asks me to lead him to Daintry Passage. When we get there he asks me if there is anyone else about. I tell him we are alone, whereupon he biffs me a mighty blow on the brow. Then he rifles my pockets, taking my purse, pork pie and picture of Mamma. I shouldn't mind the loss of my purse – for all it contained was money. And a pork pie is easy enough to procure. But it was the only portrait there was of Mamma. It was precious to me, but useless to a blind man.

'Well, say I, at least I have a sovereign sewn into my pocket. I shall get by. So off I set, whistling "Sometimes a kindly light surprises", for it was Mamma's favourite hymn. I put a brave face on it. But in Gray's Inn Road a clergyman seizes my valise and races off with it. It contained all I yet owned in the world – Mamma's prayerbook, Pappa's watch, my bible and boots.

'Well, say I, perhaps the clergyman belongs to an unorthodox sect. Or perhaps ministers conduct themselves different in the smoke. Or p'r'aps he ain't a vicar, but only a thief dressed that way. Maybe the Lord has despatched him to test me, to see if I am truly Christian.

'Well, say I, The Lord is my shepherd, I'll not want. And I ain't walked more than a mile when a smile comes to my face. So I beam at all that pass. Thinking ain't we all God's creatures, and don't He love us all. When one man tugs me by the collar, saying he's Outraged. He drags me to a constable who promptly arrests me. And the next I know, I'm before the magistrate and fined ten shillings for Soliciting for Immoral Purposes.

'Well, say I, at least I still have change of the sovereign.

When the constable commences to deal me my second belting of the day – telling me to reform myself, each time he wallops me.

'Well, say I, my nose has stopped bleeding, and only two of my teeth are loose. The policeman was mistaken, but we're all mistaken sometime. And I dare say he was only doing his best to keep the peace. So I set out again, whistling to restore my spirits. And I ain't been walking five minutes when I behold a wondrous sight. I see a woman who looks the spit of dear, dead Mamma.

' "Bless you, ma'am," say I. "Ain't you a lovely sight. To cheer a fellow's sight."

' "What!" says she, "I ain't no tart. And I'm old enough to be your mother." Then she hacks at my shins, and gobs in my face.

'Well, say I, she ain't like Mamma after all. But there must be a Christian somewhere in London. Even if blind men attack you, clergymen steal your boots and bible, magistrates convict you for smiling, policemen thrash you, and mothers spit in your face, it ain't due cause to lose all hope.

'So, Jesus, say I, I know I shouldn't test you. But show me your grace, pray. Send me a sign of your goodness . . .'

The Ashamed geezer shakes my shoulder, for I've started sniffling again, shaking and shivering.

'Well, boy, what happened then?'

'You came along . . .' I splutter, 'and told me your business was burnt out, along with your wife. And your darling daughter was lying unburied on the roadside, as carrion for the crows . . . so then I knew there weren't no hope. That the Lord had sent you as his Dismal Messenger. That Jesus had whispered to me – "Yes, boy. Go drown yourself from Southwark Bridge".'

The Ashamed one coughs and shakes me again. There's tenderness to his touch. 'Boy! Boy! That's just my patter. It's my blab. How I earn my living. It ain't true, boy.'

'Then your wife ain't dead?' I gasp at the glad news. 'And your business is going begging?'

'Yes, boy.'

71

'Bless the Lord!' I shriek. 'Ain't he bountiful? Don't he love us after all? Shall us sing a hymn together?'

'Where you come from, boy?'

'Nottingham,' say I, 'and how I wish I were back there.'

'Go back, boy. You'll be safer there. You're right. London ain't the place for you.'

Then my face creases. I'm wracked by tears again. 'Ain't got the money,' I sob.

'How much?' asked the Ashamed one. 'How much do you need?'

'Seventeen shillings.'

'Here, then.' He stows a bank note in my pocket. 'And go straight to the station. If anyone talks to you, look away. Don't answer. You surely ain't safe on your own.'

I rise a changed and cheery man, dusting the seat of my breeches. Smile my gratitude. Even beggars have hearts.

'Thanks, matey,' say I. 'Ain't it a strange life. You've paid for my story, so you can have it. It's sure as fleas you need a new 'un.'

Unlike him, I wasn't ashamed. No. I thought myself a clever bastard. As young men do.

I dare say I'm observant. I'd been noting some sad shapes to the world and counting the sorry numbers that described them. Concerning prices, income, dignity and equality.

Take oxen. It don't seem right that the farmers in the country should have 'em all – heifers, cows, calves, bulls and bullocks in profusion – while we in the smoke have none. It's a wonder folk don't covet 'em.

And while we're on the subject of beef! It didn't seem right either that a grilled sirloin in Langley's should cost more than a lady outside. Not when she gives the better pleasure. Not if hers is the flesh of a person, and a steak's but a bit of a beast. And the cow can grow fat browsing on grass. But the lady needs costlier fodder.

Or, consider income. I know a fellow as harvests dog dirt from the pavements and gutters. And labours the broad day long, trailing behind hounds with a trowel and bucket, chancing on a turd as though upon a treasure. It ain't a dignified profession – waiting on the whim of a dog's bum, so he can scavenge its doings. And this fellow gets no more than three farthings a pound for the premium stuff, and barely ha'pence for the rest – when he trades it in at the leather tanners to a sniffy apprentice who curls up his nose.

But there are men who can employ their name to do their labour, leaving the body to rest abed. They suck on their silver spoons, retain a banker to count their income, and rarely set foot on the streets, for fear of staining the soles of their boots, or tainting their nostrils with odours of life.

And some are born handsome, or grow pretty through life. Whilst others are fashioned like fish.

We're all traders in flesh. If a man has a choice, it's between being diner or dinner. So I'd rather sup than be supper.

The master must have worried for me, because he took me to task – telling me I was squalid.

'Lewd, licentious, vile,' says he, cupping his chin in his hands, elbows splayed upon the table. 'A disgrace, boy.' He speaks with melancholy severity, in his domestic voice. There's no clue from his apparel – starched shirt, white wool waistcoat, striped linen trousers – that he's acting any part, striking any posture, or speaking for anyone but himself.

'I am, sir?' I hadn't known.

He exhales silver skeins of cigar smoke, which drift between us. 'You are, boy.'

We both look sadly to the pewter platter that lies between us on the table. Gnawed lamb bones rest on a primrose bed of congealed grease. 'You blaspheme. You lie, you steal. You're venial as a pig. You've taken to whoring as if it's a sacred calling.'

'I'm eager at least. There's that to be said in my favour. And I do love women, sir. A thing of beauty is a joy forever.'

'Then collect pictures and porcelains,' the master advises,

'instead of women. The patina of age improves them. They weather better and gain in value.'

'Thank you, sir. I shan't forget it. But I'll keep an interest in women too. A fellow needs a recreation to keep him off the streets.'

He bites the tip of his cigar with menacing exasperation, spitting a flake of tobacco leaf to the floor.

'The best part of your clothing comes between your aptitude and appetite, boy. You'd do well to think more – and keep buttoned your lip and your trousers.'

'I lack wisdom, sir,' I explain, 'and I'm facetious and lewd. They're common enough faults in the young, I believe.'

'What'll become of you, boy?'

'Shall I hang, sir? As the gentleman in the white waistcoat prophesied for Oliver Twist.'

His right hand jerks on the table, tightening to a fist. He ain't never hit me yet, but I flinch due caution.

'What do you want of life, Joey?' I swear he's gone all misty and sentimental about his eyes. He holds a linen handkerchief to his face; trumpets through his nose.

'I don't know, sir. Only I suppose I shouldn't mind . . . if a lady chose to love me. And I should like a gold propelling pencil.'

He nods sagely and surveys my face. I dare say he's thinking that I look something like a fish. 'That's a moustache you're growing is it, Joey, on your lip there?'

I blush and concede it is. A tentative sketch for one.

'Well, it's a good start, Joey. I know a woman who likes a moustache on a fellow, and admires him the more for it.'

For my part, I'd taken to worrying for him. The master. Well, when Albert Francis Charles Augustus Emmanuel of Sax-Coburg-Gotha, Prince Consort of Great Britain, breaks ranks and the habits of a lifetime to wander down Berwick Street market, accosting passers-by to enquire of their opinions on the Abolition of the Window Tax, and the rumoured retirement of William Macready from the London stage, then purchases three pounds of spuds, remarking that his wife – whom he calls 'Queenie' – is fond of mash, then flirts with a watercress girl, commenting upon her pretty shawl, then strides into Manzinis' Artisan's Economical Luncheon Rooms, and orders jellied eels, two mutton pies, and a portion of mushy peas, then gobbles them down, as though he's starved from a week in the workhouse, then slouches off down the Strand to the Beehive, where he downs four pints of porter in as many minutes, announces he's off to the back to pass water, using a vulgar colloquialism to refer to the act of micturition, but then promptly vanishes, as though he'd never been there, without paying Bent Frank, who'd been too startled to charge him for his drinks, then, you can well imagine, folks are bound to notice, and will remark upon the occurrence.

The master returns, a few minutes after his highness has left. He expresses surprise at the commotion.

'You must be mistaken,' he tells Bent Frank, when informed of the visitation, 'the Prince Consort drinks Mild not Porter. He always pays for his bevvies. He's well known as a decent sort who'll always buy his round.'

The master skips up to his rooms, taking four steps at each bound, seeming well pleased with himself. I find him alone in his parlour, reading a work of Goethe aloud in German, practising a stammer, whilst watching himself in the gilt looking-glass. He's holding his left wrist in the clench of his right hand.

'My pulse is one hundred and five,' he tells me.

'It was you,' say I, 'and you're taking a mighty risk, sir.'

'It's my business,' says the master, 'and I'll conduct it quite as I wish, without the say-so of a puppy 'prentice.'

He was cold and sharp as hail with me, for three days after. Leaving me to pace my room at the Beehive when he stepped out to deceive. Never inviting me to eat at his table. Nor returning any chummy overtures. Refusing to give me any tasks or excitements.

But at least the Prince Consort hadn't been spotted again. Not in our neck of the Strand.

Which was some relief, for I loved the master.

He was the closest I had for a father. But he was dark and deep as the mud at Wapping. And he could be quick and cruel as a viper. Only, I'd discovered later, be it days or months after

I'd been punctured and sliced by his bite, that there was some proper purpose to his venom. So, though it was harsh, it was fitting.

But sometimes he'd arrive home with some unlikely present – a stuffed porcupine in a glass case, a urethrascope, a copy of *Foxe's Life of the Martyrs*, pig-poultice, gelding tongs, bust of Aristotle – and it might take me weeks to find a proper use for it.

And occasionally, I couldn't detect any ulterior motive. So he'd either changed his scheme – aborting a coup – or just wanted to show me a kindness.

But with this business with Prince Albert, there was something odd to him, over and above his standard trickiness – some extra kinks in the corkscrew of his purpose. Some detour beyond the devious. He'd begun to over-reach himself.

But he'd taught me a lesson or two, hadn't he just? And given me proper ambition.

I was resolved. To be the character I wished – and not as the world cast me. Mister Dickens scrawled phantoms in ink on paper: I should scribe Joey Blueglass in blood and flesh.

Nor would I sit up and beg for tidbits. But prowl and scoff as my fancy took me.

I was not a chalk board on which some weary tutor could scratch his jaded lessons. I would learn what I wished – not what others thought to teach me.

If a grit of knowledge caught in my mind, detaining it with pain, then I should cast it out. I should exile it, by my new power to forget.

I would not be victimized within, bullied by my own reminiscence, nor burdened by the weight of my very own head.

For I saw it this way. If a chappie rents or buys some rooms, then he counts them home. He won't welcome trespassers, nor thank others to tinker with his fixtures and fittings.

And how much more personal and private to a mar is his head than his house! Yet the world makes free to invade the chambers of your mind, scrawl on the tablets, and scatter all manner of litter on the carpets of your faculties.

I would not have it. I determined to be sovereign of my mind.

I don't know as how other folks forget – debts, obligations, shame and such. Some braggarts claim it just comes natural and don't cause 'em any strain.

For my part, to tinker with my reminiscence, there's a deal of procedures involved.

Firstwise comes a paradox. Of christening the very thing I mean to forget, so I keep a record in my cranium.

Then, if I later meet a stranger as gives his name, I promptly know if he's never been in my head before – or if I've chosen to forget him on account of some unpleasantness.

I'm properly wary of those folk I've once ejected from my mind. So I'll turn on my heels or snub 'em. They've had their chance. And I won't have 'em back in my head again. They'll only cause some fracas or a scene.

The second stage is the forgetting itself. Which I do in front of a mirror. I play the scene in my mind's eye. I can whitewash it out with broad strokes of a brush. Or turn out the light, so as nothing can be seen. If it's just an unfortunate remark I wish to forget, I'll cough or whistle as I remember them saying their piece. Then I can never hear their words again; only the overlay of my own interruption. Unless I choose to lip read.

But that ain't enough – as any sensible mind will perceive. 'Cos I've promptly remembered the act of forgetting – together with a measure of what it concerned.

Then, I have to forget that as well. So I remember myself sitting so, watching my reminiscent reflection, preparing to forget. Then I've got a nifty trick! I just smash the mirror in mind with a blow of my imaginary hammer. Then that recollection splinters before my reminiscent eyes.

Each to their own, say I. I dare say we each have our own knacks for getting the business done.

Sometimes, the fancy takes me to remember what I've forgot. There's a hefty number of items, arranged in alphabetical list – for I keep a tidy head.

Mulberry wine, sick as a pig on
Mule, kicked by
Mullet, bones of, in throat
Mullion, falling from
Mulltravers, George
Mumble, Nora, RIP
Murder, of grocer's wife
Mustard, not custard
Muster, not passing
Mutatis mutandis, memory of Mamma
Mute, Hurdy-Gurdy man, with axe

Lord knows what they all mean! Yet it surely testifies I've spent a deal of time working to improve and cleanse my mind.

But it struck me as a hard task – keeping a wholesome, sanitary head. For I learned with ease but struggled to forget. Some days, I'd acquire as many as 117 new facts. And many were quite unsavoury.

Love

A Cockney can gain a jaundiced view of his town – on account of what transpires veiled behind the yellow smog.

Fathers sell their daughters. Mothers toss newborns to the lapping Thames. Merchants trade in wheat and virgins. Waifs huddle, like rats, in sewers for warmth. Husbands stake their wives on cock fights. Fellows settle debts by slicing through faces with razors. Mudlarks swim through sludge to scavenge rags. Sweeps get roasted up chimneys. Their sisters rent their laps on the lease of a quarter hour.

So I'd reached the conclusion that society was a market in flesh. And that Burke's *Etiquette* should be a shorter but truer gospel if it were shrunk to an epigram – 'tis better to be teeth than toast.

Knowing as much, I must have become squalid. As the master was wont to remark.

'Well, Joey,' say I, 'he's a wise 'un, and you surely ain't happy. He's spoke a caution, so heed it.'

If others could love others, then so could I. I can do most things quicker than most; and I ain't a one to be bettered. Any skill comes easy to me. There can't be no more to it than nous, practice and technique. I'm a self-made man; so I'll make myself better. I'll redeem myself through love.

So I promptly added the task to my morning rituals. Reformed, I'd commenced to rise at seven. Firstwise, I'd gargle with brandy to freshen my mouth. Then I'd swab my feet, armpits and privates till I could sniff there no more than carbolic. My body being properly cleansed, I'd promptly attend to the health of my mind.

Each fresh day I'd forget sommat unpleasant, to rid my head of an irritant. Then, to fill that vacated space, and balance the weight of my head, I'd promptly set myself to learn German or physiognomy, topology or Africa.

Finally, before dressing, I'd sort through my tenets and polish my convictions.

There was never any problem finding a sordid, tarnished item; nor difficulty in selecting a shining, wholesome replacement.

I'd inspect the herd of beastly thoughts grazing the plains of my experience; and select the nearest or sickest, to be culled in the knacker's yard of my purification.

Now I cannot remember what these were or even to what they alluded. For I'm properly purged of the improprieties that once were in me.

I'd scribe the septic thought on paper, in my mind's eye, then screw it into a ball, and – to be doubly safe – toss it onto an imaginary brazier, then watch it flare on the coals, collapse to a powder of ash, and be lost.

To take the place of such ill thoughts, I'd write fine maxims that tempered nobility with wisdom or reconciled piety with Leicester Square. For though I ardently wished to be thoroughly good, I did not intend to render myself full stupid as a saint.

Love makes the world go round: that and commerce.
Be kind: insofar as it is sensible.
Love thy neighbour: whensoever she'll let you.
'Tis better to give than receive: if you ain't the loser by it.
Do unto others: as you would have them.
God is ever watching us: with his glass eye or his good 'un.
There is no finer treasure than the love of a good woman: unless it be the love of two.
Honour thy father and thy mother: if they ever chance to call.

If you take the effort to plant such fine thoughts in mind, then they take root. Shortly, they flower.

So I set to reform myself. And if it didn't immediately make me happier, it made me kinder and better, I dare say. And the better able to weather that tempest that lay ahead.

The master says I must meet him in Langley's Chop House. I slope away towards the back room, for I can see he's working a mark.

But he hails me and waves me over. 'Mr Meredith,' says he, 'pray join us.'

So I'm called to play my walk-on part. 'Your Lordship,' says the master, 'this is Mr Meredith, the vendor's clerk, who's here to receive the advance. In return for the pedigree and documents of ownership.'

Whereupon, the Personage reaches to the inside pocket of his frock coat and withdraws a wallet fat as a Dickens novel. Only the pages were banknotes. He counts out four fifty-pound notes and slaps them upon the table.

'Received with thanks . . .' the master writes with a neat, laboured hand, mouthing each word as he scribes it, 'two hundred pounds. As one tenth the purchase price in advance, being deposit on Maccabeus, racehorse, winner of the Monmouth Trophy.'

I feared he'd gone too far. Over-stretched his grasp.

'Ain't that chancey, Mr Rivers?' I remark. 'Duffing a peer of the realm?'

He'd brought me to Webster's Brasserie for a celebration lunch. Treated me to a brace of lobster. With green mayonnaise. So I was sorry to carp my caution.

'It's a straight deal,' says the master piously. 'The horse is mine to sell.'

'*The* Maccabeus?'

'The same.'

'Not a nag that pulls a brewery cart?'

'Maccabeus himself.'

'Spelt with two "c"s?'

'The horse,' says the master, tiring of my suspicion, 'together with his pedigree and documents. I bought him fair and square for twenty guineas.'

'Then you got him cheap, sir.' For the life of me, I couldn't sniff the scam. 'He's a proper bargain.'

'Well . . .' the master pauses. 'The Earl won't pay the full purchase price. Not when he sees poor Dobbin.'

'He ain't well?' I ask.

'Stiff,' the master concedes.

'In a leg?'

'All over.' He rolls his eyes in sorrow. 'He broke his back in training. He had to be shot, so it took my fancy to buy the carcass.'

'You can deliver him to the Earl, then?'

'All five pieces – head and four quarters. And be glad to see the back of him. He whiffs like a dung-heap. None but the dog'll go near him.'

'Get another man to take him,' I suggest, 'in case the Earl don't enjoy the blag.'

'Kent Jack,' says the master.

And he ordered another bottle of champagne. To toast the deal. John Rivers. Reformed. Honest broker. Dealer in horse flesh. Under aristocratic patronage.

You shouldn't believe that an earl high in the esteem of our nation, famed for charm, lauded for his hospitality, a man as had shared a Turkish bath with Princey, been friend of Fanny Larkspur, and intimate of Cora Silk, graduate of Oxford University, himself a prankster, should turn so vindictive when bettered in business and made the butt of another's joke.

Kent Jack broke his back in a fall.

The master left promptly with Molly, advising me to find a crevice and keep myself low, and quiet as a woodlouse.

'Find a good woman,' he advised, 'quit whoring. And try to make yourself decent.' Then he turned his back upon me for the very last time.

Molly planted a kiss on my cheek, her tongue quivering moistly. ' 'Bye, boy. Be happy, now.'

I resolved this much – no one should abandon me again. No one would leave me. Ever.

Alone, he wept for them.

So the young 'un was parted from his master. And could as well return to his family – from whom he was now separated by a chasm of class and character – as join a school of cod, or graze with a herd of alpaca at the zoological gardens.

With only seventy pounds to his account, and fine tastes, he would soon have need of an income. Yet he was thoroughly disabled by his sensitivity from any customary form of labour. He knew only literature and the design of deceits.

Nature had fashioned him as a thing apart, governed by unnatural rules. But the needle of his mind still lacked the push of its purpose, or thimble of conviction. He'd planted the seed of love in his mind but doubted for its germination. Slouching through the streets, hugging the corners of tea rooms, slumped in taverns, loitering behind the fug, he was harrowed by an ache of loss. He was still driven by that desire – to lie with each and every pretty woman he saw, of whom there were a teasing large number. And he knew no gesture, other than payment, that might entice a lady to share his bed. Which frustration left him in a continual state of aggrieved melancholy.

As if this were insufficient vexation, he was harried by the persistence of two men, in service to an earl, who dogged his tracks one day behind. And the boy loved life, in his morbid fashion. But had no defences, save his guile, and a pistol which he had never fired in anger.

We find wisdom in extremis. I dare say I could have found no better refuge than as a freak. For I changed my identity and associates, shifted from Literature to Art, within a single skip. I found the path by a curious coincidence of passion.

The first days away from the Beehive, I spent around the Haymarket. A distance from my usual haunts, but in a familiar warren.

I kept the company of professional ladies. But, however vigorously I laboured, sprawled upon warm, wet bellies, I could not plug the yawning chasm. For the void was in me not in women. And not to be filled by nooky.

Then I met her.

83

I met love as a pit pony greets sunlight. As a dizzying, dazzling, long-forgotten radiance. The glare made me stagger, lurch and topple.

I knew she was my quest and grail, the first instant I saw her. She was chewing a muffin in Lloyd's tea-room.

How did I know she was for me? My body took peculiar. I was clutched by a rare sensation. It had never visited me before. Vision and touch, taste and smell, were miraculously transformed. Everything mattered, and was heightened and gravid with meaning – the grasp of my boots on my toes, the savour of butter on the air, the music of forks being sliced through pastry.

My innards were bathed by trickles of hot treacle. My earlobes prickled. My heart juddered against my ribcage, bursting to break out. My lungs heaved to secure some air.

It occurred to me that people were kind. That the good Lord smiled on our happy doings. 'There is no finer treasure than the love of a good woman . . .' thought I. There was something to the feelings like the first advice of opium. Yet the next morning I did not wake shivery, aching and miserable, searching the bedclothes in the suspicion that I had been sleeping with hedgehogs.

How to describe her? For I was not struck just by the loveliness of her face but by the radiance of her spirit, intangible as perfume. Yet more potent. Quite pervading the tea-room, suffusing every pore of every crumpet, adding her delicate savour to each last pot of tea, sweetening each bowl of honey, her creamy wholesome health enriching every pat of butter.

Innocence was cast in her broad white brow. Her glistening coral lips spoke the discretion of her passion. Her hazel eyes shone her kindly light, and most amiable intelligence. The thin wrists told her delicacy. The clutch of her teaspoon within her frail fingers showed the fastidiousness of her morals.

Every feature of her person showed it. She had saved herself for me.

She was seated tight by another lady who – resemblance whispered – was her sister. Though they looked uncommonly alike in the façade of their flesh, they radiated quite different spirits. So, for me, there could be no hesitation nor conflict. She was delicate as a narcissus. Her sister seemed a pleasant enough package.

They were dressed identically – in foxfur jackets, turquoise silk dresses with lace collars. She wore a silver monogram brooch on her left lapel – above that breast in which her heart nestled. 'C' said the brooch. Her sister had copied the ornamental flourish, as if borrowing upon the credit of the fair one's beauty.

I dropped, blanched and breathless, into a chair at an adjacent table, facing her, so I could glimpse the marvel around the flimsy, quivering edge of Reynold's *Racing Digest*.

'A rude boy is staring,' observes the sister.

'Sh, Chastity,' says she. 'He's reading his paper'.

I order Darjeeling, scones and a double portion of plum jam. Sugar aids my composure.

'Good afternoon,' say I, laying down my paper, taking care to smile at both. To convey my disinterested magnanimity. But my voice betrays me – wobbling on the high-wire of my emotion.

'Do you suppose he's talking to us?' the sister asks her.

'Don't be rude, Chastity. He means no harm.'

Her voice soothed that space between my ears – spreading warm over me, like butter melting on a teacake.

The coy invitation of her tone proved it. She desired me, as I yearned for her.

'If you wish,' I say, 'I could join you at your table.'

'If you try,' says the sister evenly, 'I shall call the major-domo to throw you out.'

'Chastity!' says the lovely one. 'Hush! Don't be cruel. I suppose the poor child's lonely.'

I flush. Lacking my customary composure, I drip butter on my cravat.

'Well look there!' says the sister. 'This used to be a respectable tea room. If the man at the next table wasn't always a gentleman, at least he wouldn't dribble.'

'Hush, Chastity. He'll hear you.'

I observed that both – in their very different ways – were much concerned with gentility. And that they had devised a partnership by which one could be harsh and the other gentle; one domineering, the other submissive. I recognized the arrangement. It is the very same liaison as between my rude desires and mild-mannered conscience. You know that one is nicer, but find the provocative one the more persuasive.

'I shall not hush, Charity. The boy is a pest. I shall not have him stare so. Boggle-eyed as a fish. We are not in a freak show now. If he wants to look, he must pay his shilling.'

'Sh.'

'Sh, yourself! Indeed!'

'Chastity . . . I want to go to the . . . you know.'

'Odd, Charity. I don't. Have you been drinking my share of the pot?'

As I watched their backs, in their graceful retreat to the ladies' room, I saw how uncommonly close they were – each laying an affectionate arm across the other's shoulder. They matched each other, stride for stride, in perfect synchrony.

Then I was fingered by the most abject melancholy. Knowing I could not make progress with the lovely without gaining the tetchy attentions of the sister. Knowing I could not separate them. For now I knew who they must be.

The celebrated Coleman sisters. The song-and-dance Siamese Twins.

How cruel of the world, thought I – that it should take such delight in their bondage.

But – I thought, in my self-pity – at least they had each other and should never be lonesome. Then I felt the surge of steamy anger towards Chastity. Who had got my lovely first. And was tied to Charity as I should be.

Perhaps I am more fond than the next man of complications. It might be that I take delight in difficulty. Or that I most want what I cannot have. That I will always select the two in the bush, and shun the one to hand. Perhaps I take joy in freaks.

I am not a normal man. Nor entirely moral. My desire is as unnatural as my memory. My appetite is scarlet as my part.

Perhaps I am a lecher – and nature marked my card.

But I was bewitched. Transfixed by Her.

I knew that I must woo and have her. That none other

would do. That I must suffer the gaze and scorn of the Other.

At least I knew where she would be found, for *Reynolds News* relayed her movements. She was performing at Cecil Burney's Curiosity Music Hall, together with her sister.

There's no finer treasure than the love of a good woman – it occurred to me – unless it be the love of two.

I Become a Freak

I followed Charity with all the mad conviction of a sniffing dog.

I promptly scripted in my mind certain notions concerning my person – that I, too, was a freak, possessed of prodigious oddity, and that I could rise to the pinnacle of that profession. And there was no doubt I had the facility for it.

'You're a quare 'un, Joey,' Molly had often advised me, 'you should go on the stage, boy.'

I had a fancy card printed: gothic silver lettering on ivory card. I could order no less than a hundred – though I needed just the one. To present at Burney's Curiosity Music Hall.

PONTIUS PORTER – MNEMONIST EXTRAORDINARY
(*gentleman*)
FREAK OF NATURE
PRODIGY
KNOW-ALL

'Pontius is an odd handle, ain't it?' says Cecil Burney.

'My father was a free-thinker,' I explain, 'so I count myself lucky I ain't a Judas.'

'I ain't never seen your act. Nor heard your name.'

His face isn't his friendliest feature. It's a broad, flat, waxy tablet. White and immobile as a dead man's. He has heavy lidded eyes. What's living within him peers through the cracks, and twitches those tight grey lips. His eerie stillness gives him the gravity of a statue. So he seems not so much seated as cast at rest in marble. His head is thrown back against the flaky plaster wall, so you can count the deep folds to his neck. He has a mighty mound of chest to him. He is one of those ample men who bear the bulk of their bellies in their breeches. A slow pulse to the button of his waistband shows he still draws breath. His conical legs reach up to his desk. So the soles of his shoes face me, framing his face. So there seems not one but three uncaring, impassive stares addressed to me.

This makes him a difficult audience. But, I dare say, it ain't his task to make life easy for an artist. Too many comedians must have provoked him to laugh at them. Herds of performing animals must have fouled his floors. And, from the stains above my head, I hazard, some acrobats had smeared his ceiling with their juices. Strong Men might have wilted under his gaze and left his chamber weeping.

'I know about *you*, sir. I've seen you about,' I say. Which was the very truth. It's surprising how many folk a good memory can recall. 'You drink in the Pope's Pogue. Port's your tipple. After a few you're almost frisky. You tell tales about Mr Dickens. Then you do impressions of Edmund Kean without his trousers. . . . And you ain't unfond of Lucy, are you, sir?'

His boots part a smidgin. I can see him hoist an eyebrow to reveal the full of one cold, dark, still eye.

'Ain't you got no proper deformities, boy?'

'Plenty,' say I, 'but all in my head.'

'Show us, boy.'

I hand him a copy of that day's *Chronicle* and bid him read a line. He finds an advertisement. A widow lady in Eaton Square needs a decent, frugal, Christian housekeeper without affections, affectations or attachments. Having heard as much, I commence to recite the subsequent items in the classified columns. He raises a languid finger to halt the flow.

'Tricksy paper?' he asks.

'No,' I say, 'it's just I can remember anything I've seen. I'm a proper freak, sir. Truly.'

'It ain't bad, boy. But neither is it comic.'

'It's dramatic. With mental conjuring besides. . . . And I can answer any question. Which quite surprises folk. . . . Try me, sir,' say I. 'I'm a proper know-all.'

'Am I married?' he asks.

'To Mary Anne. Née Bower, as I recall.'

'Know her birthday, by any chance?'

'Last Thursday. May 4th.'

There's a twitch to his left eye, near gross enough to count a wince.

'I clean forgot,' says he. 'It's no wonder she's been frosty.'

'She's an easy item to remember,' I advise, 'because she was born on the very day that Tippoo of Mysore was killed at Seringapatam. Exactly one month before Archduke Charles defeated Massena at Zurich.'

He seems to take to me, asking me about horses.

'Fancy Petronius for the Cesarewitch?'

'Knickerbocker Club's the nag,' say I, reminding him of the handicapping and likely conditions underfoot. 'Or you could take a chance on Fidelity, if you're offered better than sevens.'

'There's something to you,' he says, 'so I'll give you a chance. You can go on after the waltzing goats, before the lady contortionist. But you only die once on Burney's stage. If you get the hook I ain't never seen you.'

I agreed that no man deserved more than the one death. I thanked him for his trust, saying he wouldn't be disappointed.

Which was how I first chanced upon the boards, becoming an artist. And appeared on the very same bill as the Coleman Sisters. The lovely singing freaks.

I didn't lack for confidence. Acting's only a form of duffing. The punters pay before the show, not after. And there's more of them. That aside, it's much the same.

In the foyer before the show I listened out for certain indiscretions and confidences. I lifted one man's wallet, then returned it to his pocket with an unlikely addition.

I wasn't accorded their full attention or respect. Not when I first wandered onto the stage, into the gold circle of limelight. Some folk were laughing and chattering amongst themselves. Others whistled or turned their backs on me. One contingent were more concerned with buying themselves tipples at the bar. So I clapped my hands and bade them listen. Which, I dare say, quite surprised them. 'Sh,' said I.

A wag proposed I go dunk myself. Whereupon I repeated

the cautionary advice his lady friend had given him before the show, concerning his manners on the mattress. For, in bed too, he spouted too soon. His lady clapped. He gorged red and shook a fist. The rest of the audience chuckled.

I sniffed, then, the cruelty to theatre. And saw there was no loyalty. The audience liked nothing so much as seeing one of their number abused. So I spoke honestly all I'd heard before the curtain. That the butcher in the fourth row sold donkey as beef, and swore his customers didn't know the difference. That the lady in the feather bonnet should hurry home to Bethnal Green, if her husband, Benjamin, who had a vicious temper, were not to discover her doings.

Then I got the man to unpack his wallet – causing him some shame, and the rest much merriment. After this I remembered the pages of that day's newspaper; dealt peremptorily with some numbers; invited questions – which concerned the weight of our Queen, height of the Matterhorn, Truce of Malmö, my own parentage, the feats of boxers and racehorses, the diet of crocodiles. If I wasn't always fully candid, I never shirked a question, nor was ever at a loss for an answer.

I went better than the goats – having less thrown at me – and was every bit as contrived, and had cleaner habits on stage. And had a more savoury smell. Folk won't pay sixpence to see an animal urinate on stage when they can enjoy the sight for free in the streets. And though an audience may flock to see an artist, they'll rarely queue to smell him.

The lady contortionist was better than her reviews. If a lady is willing to chance her arm, displaying herself so – wrapping her ankles round her ears, packing herself in a picnic hamper, catching toffees in her mouth like a terrier while balancing on her nose – she deserves a sight more sympathy. I suppose she was put off balance by some unkind prompts and heckles, telling her where to put her parts.

A bearded lady baritone then sang ribald words to some well-known hymn tunes, accompanying herself on the harmonium.

Two-headed Pascal – he had a small monkey head perched on the back of his scalp – then struggled to keep upright on his unicycle whilst facing both ways. Then both his voices joined to sing 'Annie Laurie', achieving a most curious unison, the monkey head warbling a high-pitched, plaintive continuo to the melodic tenor rendition of the other, human, voice.

But the artistry of all before seemed shallow and tawdry when Charity and Chastity commenced to perform. They had ravishing soprano voices, which they deployed on the most moving and beautiful ballads – 'Love amongst the Heliotrope', 'Ardour in the Arbour', 'The Lost Mariner's Orphan, Freddie', 'As Grandmama Lay Gasping' and 'The Tubercular Princess'. For their finale, they sang that most winning of ditties, 'Dadda, my Doggie, Dadda, Is Drowned'. And even while they caressed each last nuance, their faces adance with many and varied sentiments, they achieved the most charming ballet – dancing with the most exquisite and precise togetherness. So all that witnessed it were unsure whether the twins should be considered two or one, ballerinas or chanteuses, artistes or angels.

If Charity outshone Chastity, I was forced to concede that both were consummate performers, and conjured their seven effects with striking rapport.

With the exception of the waltzing goats, each of us on the stage had practised what came naturally to us. All had made some virtue of their deformities. So we were alchemists – transmuting the base matter of our oddness into the gold of Art.

And there are worse careers for a person than being applauded for being oneself. Most folk are less fortunate, being forced to conceal or deny their character in order to earn their crust.

You may well imagine, I was much taken by the Art.

'You ain't bad, boy,' says Charity. 'Haven't we seen your act before?'

'Not at the Lyceum?' I ask.

'We haven't played the Lyceum,' says she, her cheeks gaining the blush of rose petals. 'They say it's very fine.'

And Cecil Burney admits he's seen worse than me. And promises that if I perform as well on the morrow, he might be able to start paying me for my work. Which would mean, I calculate, that I should no longer share a dressing room with six goats and their surly herdsman. For I should take their place on the bill. And I felt no qualm or quiver of conscience, since they brought our Art into disrepute.

There was a sound reason, I found, why most of the cast of Cecil Burney's Curiosity Music Hall were all deformed, misshapen persons.

Mr Burney has both Philosophy and Morality, which he has derived from the teachings of our Lord.

'A two-headed man is a freak,' says he, 'but a two-headed man on a unicycle, displaying both his minds and voices . . . well, that's an artist. . . .

'Edmund Kean was a colossus of the filthy thought. There was more squalor and stench to his mind than lay in the gutters of London. But give him the part of Lear or Othello, as a conduit for the sludge, then he became a Beauty. And the vile effluent spewed forth as Poetry. . . .

'It's like the musk in perfume. You would never credit it – that a gland from the anus of a rat could help ladies smell so sweet. . . .

'Take Pontius here,' Mr Burney nods his solemn approval, 'who's a squalid little chappie, with a face that would caution a wolf. But have him on the stage, displaying his sharp compendious mind, and you have a Vessel of History. . . .

'A midget might be a slight man. But place him on the back of a spaniel, to ride it like a stallion, then he becomes a Giant of Disproportion. . . .

'Or a lady may be set apart by beard and moustache. On the omnibus, she's a curious diversion between Baker Street and Marble Arch. But have her play God's Tunes on the harmonium, then she becomes a Paragon of Mystery. . . .

'It's all a tale of the talents. For the freak is just an extraordinary talent harnessed to too slight a task. Then he seems absurd. Like a dray horse pulling a perambulator. But give the freak his purpose and he becomes a thing of beauty. Profound and Prodigious. . . .

'Our Lord bade the sick be well, the crippled to walk. Cecil

Burney ain't so nifty. But give me seven people odd-constructed and I'll fashion them into a Drama. It'll be both Tragedy and Farce.'

Though his pay was grudging and erratic, Burney meant the best for a fellow. So the young chappie was chuffed to serve a Higher Purpose, and sidle close to his sweet Charity.

But the company let it be known that I was a prettier package on the stage than off. Nor could I prevail upon Charity to demur. Not with gifts, smiles, winks nor wit. For she was tight in the clutch of Chastity.

I could not look upon them but feel a wave of sorrow drown my hopes, seeing that knot – of radiance and gloom, dawn and dusk, sunbeam and fog, right and sinister. She and the Other – in the bow tie that God had fashioned of them.

As I progressed in my Art, moving up the bill, vaulting the bearded lady and contortionist, I dare say I was not only pest but threat besides – challenging the twins for their perch at the pinnacle. So, if Chastity spoke to me at all, it was to advise me as to my place.

'The poor boy can't sing for the life of him,' I overhear, 'or dance. He only gets by as an oddity.'

'But he was good tonight, Chastity. Knowing all about the man with the green umbrella with the thingummy in his wallet.'

'The boy's an ear-wigger, Charity. He thinks eavesdropping's an art. I'd wager he's doing it now. . . . Look! His lugs are all aglow. At least he has the decency to blush.'

I'm sitting with my back to them, slyly watching their reflections in the bar mirror. Their heads seem to sprout from the sherry barrel.

'Sh, Chastity. Don't bait him so. The poor boy's lonely. I fancy he wants to make friends of us. He always sits on his own, rolling those fishy eyes.'

'There's fancy and fancy, Charity. I fancy he fancies more than a friend.'

'Chastity . . .' she giggles, 'You can't suppose? He's just a boy.'

'There's boys and boys,' says the sister, 'and I shouldn't like to mention the notions they take into their minds.'

They snuggle close, chortle and whisper. Then turn four eyes to gaze upon my hunched back.

'Eel be lucky,' says Charity.

'He can bream, cod preserve us.'

And so on. Observing that, if I didn't find it tunny, I had no call to carp. It was my fault for herring. That I should stick to my perch, by knowing my plaice.

I kept my dignity, despite all provocation. I drained my ale to the dregs, donned my cap and slouched from the bar. It was not my appearance they mocked. That was just a red herring. They were large fish in a small pond, and I was no longer the small fry.

The trouble with a mind like mine is that it won't let go. I lay writhing between my steamy sheets, prickling all over, seeing them taunt me in the bar. Then I trawled the truth of it. Understood why my Charity had seemed to turn against me.

I had been watching them in the mirror.

My doting eyes adoring the beauty on the right, I had mistaken Chastity for Charity. Charity for Chastity. I, not nature, had fashioned their difference. And if I could mistake the one for the other? What did that make of my passion?

Praise the Lord. I've a strong mind. Got given it. Had it for as long as it can remember. Never had to struggle to improve it. Never had to coax it to work. It just sets itself to business the moment I blink open my eyes to the morning light. Keeps itself frenzied the whole day long. Won't be slowed by a tipple or ten. Just carries on. Noting it down. Totting it up. Assigning odds. Speculative creature. Quare organ.

Only, few have admired its cruel beauty – the master, Cecil Burney, Sir Frederick ffalke. And they were never my chosen bedfellows. Though I loved all three, I never wished to unbutton one.

I could have wished no more than that Florrie could have quarried the loveliness in my depths that I found to her skin. But she always took my grace for oddness.

ffalke loved my mind the most. He was a quare, rare and friendly fellow. Designed a ventilated hat, to keep his mind cool in the tropics. Fashioned special spectacles so he could read his paper in the bath. Underwater. Got so engrossed, he said, that he'd quite forget to breathe. Bald as a coot, twice as silly. Clever man. Daft as a brush. Fellow of the Royal Society.

ffalke clung to us freaks at Burney's. On account of our contribution to knowledge. He said I was a phenomenon. Told me I was impossible – that I defied science. Which was never my intention. For I've always had due respect for truths.

'Mr Porter,' says Sir Frederick, formal as a summons, 'I'd be interested to know how you achieve it.'

'Achieve what?'

'Mimetic reproduction. Serial or free recall,' says he, 'over long retention intervals. In flagrant contravention of the known parameters of the human mnemonic span.'

'What, sir?'

'Your memory, Mr Porter,' says he. 'How do you give the impression of remembering so much?'

'I suppose I'm better than most, sir.'

'Come now, Mr Porter,' he wags a caution with a finger and smiles knowingly, as though I'm teasing him, 'I shan't tell on you.'

'Just do it, sir. There ain't no tricks. It's just a knack.'

'No! Mr Porter. That can't be. You'd exceed the Laws of Psychology. Don't suppose you're free to do that, Mr Porter. Any more than you could flout gravity and fly. The natural laws will not be defied.'

'I didn't mean to offend nature, sir. I should never make so bold.'

'You see, Mr Porter . . . ' he explains the severity of my condition, 'if you could really do what you seem to do, you'd have a cleverer mind than mine.' He chuckles at the notion, taking no offence.

'Didn't mean to be uppity. Or insult your honour.'

'I know this much.' He smiles and wiggles his brow. 'You plant fellows in the audience, to ask prepared questions. But what I don't know is how you guess what I shall ask you.'

'Try me, sir.'

'Well, now.' He clutches his morocco-bound pocket-book and

flicks through the pages. Then he seizes a pen and scribbles like a mad 'un. 'Which is greater?' he asks, 'the root of 69,000 or the square of 262?'

'The first, sir.'

'Ah, no. Indeed not. They are the very same, Mr Porter.' He chortles and rubs his palms together. With sheer delight.

'Are you sure, sir? I reckon there's the difference of a fraction. Which is $^{679}/_{1000}$, give or take a smidgin.'

He frowns, then scribbles anew. Stops. Frowns. 'You've tricked me again. Mr Porter, you're a sly one. But rest assured, I shall find you out. I shall get to the very bottom of you. . . . A cigar?'

We pierce then light our Havanas. You could rely on ffalke for a sound smoke. He smiles – all amiable relaxation. But I can read him. He's busy calculating.

'Do you happen to know, Mr Porter, by any chance, how that Mr Pinion on the unicycle gives such a convincing impression of owning two heads? I feel there are mirrors and papier mâché involved. Could you arrange for me to meet him?'

'It's a rum thing, Sir Frederick. But when Pascal isn't performing on stage, he's shy as a mouse's flea. Won't show his face. Or the other one. He claims people always stare at him.'

'Mr Porter!' The great man heaves with mirth. 'You're impossible.'

So I never told him. I wasn't going to have him steal my act, or swap it for a cigar. But I'll tell you.

My Act and Art

My secret's the very same as the Sphinx's. It is that I ain't got one. I only pretend. It's all a matter of retentive memory. Frankly, I ain't half so clever as some fellows suppose.

Take mathematics. When someone asks 'What's nine thousand, eight hundred and seventy-six times four hundred and thirty-eight?', don't suppose I multiply in my head to get the right answer. Indeed not. It's just that I've memorized the logarithm tables. So, by consulting the columns in my mind's eye, it's but a matter of adding or subtracting some decimals.

Or suppose a fellow asks me how many words there are in the Bible. It ain't that I know, care or have counted. No, I use a sleight of mind, and resort to approximation. I summon but a single page to mind, count the words to that, take it as a thoroughly reliable average, then calculate the grand total by supposing all the pages the same.

You just have to act brazen, be proximate to the answer, and suckers'll take you on trust.

Some wag in the audience always gets personal, trying to trip me up.

'How many sons I got,' he bawls, 'with wooden legs?'

Logic and reason confide in me. I take a third opinion from experience. They all agree – the answer's likely to be one or none. But the latter is the better retort; it gets you off the hook. For if the fellow shouts 'Wrong! My Frank has got a stump,' you can reply, 'Yes, I know. But gossip has it you ain't really his pa.'

The punters enjoy a snigger or two. And at least you got the jump on the sucker by promptly answering back.

Often you have to shuffle sideways so. To retain a proper authority. And show you've got the nous. If the exact and correct answer don't pop straight into your mind.

And there's simpletons too. 'If you're a know-all, what's my trade?' he shouts. He'll be in the fourth to tenth row – far enough away to be emboldened to challenge me, near enough to feel involved.

'Coster, ain't you, Bobby? You sell fish.'

He flushes and claps.

But there ain't no trick or gimmick to knowing. I once sat near him in the snug of the Mitre. And his name and scent wafted over, through the fug.

Then there's those who take a lewd swipe at you 'cos you're on the stage and their judy's laughing with you. They leer to those around them, then ask summat concerning nooky, regarding my habits or the size of their parts. There's a modest range of answers as suffices to silence the call. It ain't to my taste, but a fellow has to coarsen his tongue to survive on the stage. Specially in Islington or Covent Garden – where the common crowd hang out. With a bit of wit and wile you get by.

No. The worst is the earnest chappie: a tutor who wants to turn the proceedings wholesome, or a lepidopterist, up for the day from Sutton, to spread the gospel of moths.

'What's the wingspan of the common hawkmoth?' he enquires, with a strangled, quavery voice. As if the world might care.

'Male or female?' I demand to know.

'Male,' he concedes, severely.

'Northern or Southern?' say I. By which time the fellow's being properly hissed, for infringing upon an entertainment. Then I give an answer – haughty and authoritative – knowing any refutation shan't be heard. And, without pausing for breath, I answer the subsequent heckles.

'One and eleven eighteenths of an inch ... Blue Gown by three lengths ... Bruiser Yates in the twenty-sixth round ... Your wife Alice, sir ... Twenty-eight rats in a minute ... under the sofa with Flora Langtrey ... six and a half ounces, discounting the rind.'

For the crowd like racing, ratting, gossip and weights and measures. And there ain't never a mystery to those.

Then they clap and whistle, thinking I'm rare and wise. All because I know three wheezes and two wrinkles, and can remember what I've heard.

It's just a marriage of sense and reminiscence.

Every fine letter of Burke's *Etiquette* was inscribed on the rude tablet of my mind.

This served me well in duffing – telling me how I should defer to a cardinal to place him at ease. And when I found myself playing seven-card brag with an actor, an alderman and a Masonic Grand Master, I knew which ranked the higher, so could deal to them in the proper order of their precedence.

Though it's quare, I swear Burke stayed mute whenever I sought his frosty rulings in matters of my heart. There weren't nothing in the manual to guide me in wooing the Coleman Twins, though there were some tortured knots of protocol to be untangled. Does the fellow bow in turn to each, or but once to the both? Is it politesse to send separate or joint invitations? And supposing one accepts and the other declines? All Burke observes on the matter is that a man is no gentleman if he courts two ladies together. But I hazard, here, he was not making allowance for the loveliness and particularity of the ladies or the indecisiveness of the fellow as to which of the two he loved the more.

Faint heart never won fair sisters. I resolved to be bold. To declare myself frankly. So I invited them to lunch.

Pontius Porter Esquire requests the pleasures of the company of Miss Charity Coleman and Miss Chastity Coleman for luncheon at Davies' Dining Rooms, 117 the Strand, noon, Tuesday 4 October, to celebrate the recent entry of G. Garibaldi, Esquire, to Naples

RSVP

I used the camouflage of a pretext. And chose the discretion of private dining rooms so that the sisters should not fear to be stared at. Further, I supposed, if fortune favoured me, we might move promptly from pudding to intimacy without fear of interruption. I reckoned Davies to be a fine enticement. Flora Langton is known to have dined there once. It's famed for its exorbitant prices, excellent game and prodigious wine list.

'Who is coming?' asks Chastity. 'Will there be champagne and charades?'

'Is it a party?' asks Charity.

''A feast,' I brag, 'with the finest fare and choicest people. I've invited two of the loveliest ladies in London.'

'Then we might be free to join you,' Chastity concedes.

'We should be pleased, Pontius,' says Charity. 'How kind of you to think of us.'

There was a deal of preparation – ordering the floral displays, selecting the table settings, choosing from the range of cutlery, bribing the reluctant two-piece orchestra to play outside the door at the opportune time of 2.45.

The sisters rose to the occasion – wearing their black silk dresses with the fluffed sleeves, showing their collarbones to all the world – and were only forty-seven minutes late, by which combination of timing, clothing and co-ordination, they spoke their eminence, elegance, and mutuality as the sinister and dextrous halves of a pair.

'Where are the others?' asks Charity.

'Yes, where are all the gay people?' demands Chastity.

'All are here as are coming,' I explain. 'Mister Garibaldi and his party have been detained in Italy.'

'Are you trying to compromise us, Mr Porter?' Chastity demands, wrinkling her nose to an untidy shape. While Charity looks forlornly to her patent leather slippers.

'You might chaperone each other,' I suggest, 'and there's something dear to my heart I should like to say to you both, once we've toasted Italy.'

The *Terrine de Foie Ptarmigan aux Pruneaux à la Claude* nestled on a bed of truffles. It veered on the rich side. But they needn't have been so morose or grudging. It was a premier vintage St Lucienne.

We ate the skate with black butter in as much silence as the bones allowed.

Over the *Homard Flambé au Cognac à la Henri*, with *Crevettes et Langoustines frais sans Palourdes ou Praires Saint-Jacques à la Diable*, we spoke in desultory fashion of the sensitivity of crustaceans, the blueness of cognac flames, the incompatibility of crinolines and omnibus seats.

We'd reached a compromise and understanding by the time the waiter ushered in the *Cimetière d'Oiseaux Vulgaires à la Farceur Bulgaire en Boue Verte*. We spoke politely enough, with occasional shafts of friendliness.

'You'll find it's a quail inside the pheasant stuffed in the guinea fowl that's poked inside the goose,' I tell them, 'if you look closely beneath that green jelly. So keep a watch for bones.'

'Isn't that charming?' Charity says. 'What shall they invent next? Electric pianos?'

By the time we'd broached our fifth bottle – a Sauterne, as companion to the *Bombe Garibaldi Goute Revolté* – we'd moved a distance to amiability.

'It's a fine meal, Pon,' says Chastity, 'shall we take fruit and cheeses too?'

They did indeed – after the *Meringue Ivoire à la Creme* which we took with the Yquem.

No sooner had we broached the brandy than the party grew merry. Then both the orchestra struck up the tune behind the oak panelled door of our room.

'Our song!' gushes Charity.

'The soggy dog! It is!' yelps Chastity.

So they promptly commence to sing: 'Dadda, my doggie is dead, Dadda . . .'

It's a fine moving ballad if you're one of those with the taste, time and mood for it. But it does sound the better for a sober rendition with less vibrato or slur.

'I should like to speak to you,' I say.

' "Dadda, my darling, my precious, I've found/My puppy, floating. All sodden, quite drowned . . ." '

'I love you . . . Chastity . . . Charity,' say I. But they do not hear my declaration, so rapt are they in the song.

' " . . . Father wept. The daughter wailed and cried./Till both were quite moist as the doggie that died . . ." '

They were determined. I let them have their song, that I might then have my word.

' " . . . then the father spake. For wisdom moved him./He would buy her another. One that could swim . . ." '

Of course, I applauded them, clapping boisterously for the best part of twenty-three seconds. Which is an awesome long time in theatre. I beamed so broad, stretching my mouth so wide, that an onlooker might have thought it was the very first time I'd heard their song. And not the forty-eighth. My enthusiasm fell just short of demanding an encore. Which they surely would have provided. For artists are invariably vain.

'I love you both,' I said. For they were gazing expectantly to me, gluttonous for praise.

'It's true,' Chastity concedes. 'Our public do love us. We have a special place on the English stage.'

It is politic to look at a lover when you declare your affection. So I had to flit my gaze between their two flushed faces.

'You are very special artists,' I say. 'Truly, there are none others like you. . . . But, what I meant to tell you . . .' My brow furrows with sincerity. I lean forward and lay my palms upwards on the table, to show my lack of guile. '. . . Is that I adore you. That I love you as a lady. That you are the prettiest package in creation.'

Habit has me smiling first to Charity, then to Chastity. I nod to each in turn to stress my infatuation. 'I have never loved another as I love you. . . . Might I hold your hand?'

'The rascal!' Charity quivers with mirth.

'The scallywag!' Chastity titters, rolling her eyes in feigned wonder. 'Which of us is he talking to, Charity?'

'I believe it's me, Chastity. I swear the puppy is proposing to me.'

'Really, Charity. I could have sworn he was looking at me.'

'Forgive me, ladies, pray. I am unsure of the proper etiquette. I was speaking to you both – but individually, as is fitting.'

'Should you not choose between us?' Chastity snickers. I fear she isn't treating my ardour with her half of the solemnity it warrants.

'Yes,' Charity chides, 'won't you choose, Pon?'

'I can't, ladies.' I declare the very truth of it. 'For you are both too lovely. And quite strikingly similar to the eye – as others must have remarked to you. As for your temperaments . . . they are different. But both exquisite to my taste. And I cannot, for the life of me, prefer the sweeter to the sharper, the honey to the lemon. The clever to the kind. Each is the ideal complement to the other. It's the very truth, ladies – together you are flawless perfection.'

'Nonetheless, Pon,' Charity declares, 'we are two.'

'Indeed!' Chastity confirms, elbowing her sister, then whispering in her ear.

I have only myself to blame. They have drunk too much of too many wines. It has gone to their heads, and moved them to levity.

'I dare say it would be a lucky man indeed who won you both,' I declare hopefully.

'It would be irregular, Pon,' observes Charity. She clenches her little finger between her teeth as though pondering. But I suspect her seriousness covers mockery.

I take her at face value. 'I've thought it out. You are the best of chums. And sisters to boot. Naturally, you spend your time together. We have much in common and should get along famously. I should be scrupulously fair, and give no cause for envy to either.'

'It's true,' Chastity chuckles, 'I should not be jealous of you for winning Pon's love.'

'Nor I of you,' Charity chortles, winking at me. 'Ain't that strange?'

'But there are the ethics to consider,' says Chastity. 'God doesn't allow the arrangement. So one of us would be the wife, and the other the mistress. I'd be sorely shamed if my sister became a fallen woman. And I could never accept the career for myself.'

'My sister's a God-fearing woman,' says Charity.

'Mine too,' agrees Chastity. And both wobble and sway with merriment.

They had me flummoxed and no mistake. For I had not considered marriage.

'Nevertheless,' I suggest, 'we might get engaged. And worry for the future when that need arises. I'd buy you both a ring.'

The sisters shake their heads in unison, and we fall to a sorry silence. All consider the rum conundrum.

'I should not wish to come between sisters. . . . But I could love the one that prefers me – and be respectful friend to the other.' For I ventured that if I coaxed one into bed the other would surely follow.

'You can have him if you wish, Charity.'

'No. You take him, Chastity.'

'Sisters, sisters,' I protest, 'don't let me be the cause of bickering. Love is the stuff to resolve this.'

'If it's a matter of love,' says Chastity, 'I fear you'll be disappointed.'

'Yes, indeed,' Charity agrees. 'Yet it was a very fine lunch. And we both found you an unusual and witty companion.'

Then they rose tottering, as one, from the table, giggling with bonhomie, scattering cutlery, sending glasses atumble.

'It was a choice lunch,' declares Chastity, 'And will make a fine story.'

'An anecdote,' observes Charity. 'We could dine out on it.'

Then they peck me briskly on the cheek in turn, both yelping at the fun of it.

' 'Pon my word, I kissed Pon.'

'Me too. Ain't his cheeks hot?'

I've rarely known such humiliation, for it was in the manner of a double rejection.

I dare say I learned a lesson by it.

Being sneered at so.

By freaks.

They must have spread the story at the theatre. Compounding my shame. All that week I had winks fall on me, hard as hail. I weathered a deluge of knowing glances, and had my ribs bruised and battered by nudges.

Only Backstage–Nancy did not share the glee and mockery.

But, rather, reproached me through grand glares and niggling negligences.

She was contracted, for a shilling a week, to crease my trousers with a hot iron before I took to the stage, to leave a half-pint of ale in my dressing room before and after I performed, to wash and starch my shirts, keep alight the fire, and see that there was always a basin and water.

My trousers were indeed ironed – but scorched at the rump. My shirts were now so folded as to confirm Euclid's proofs of polygons. My fire was embers, my ale uncorked, the mug with yesterday's dregs.

It had been Nancy's way to leave a small posy of violets upon my dressing table. But these floral tributes ceased.

Naturally, the fellow was moved to remark to Nancy about the domestic irregularities. An artist requires discipline about him, and a regular regime, if his muse is not to wilt.

Nancy said she would as soon eat the bedding in a dysentery ward for tuppence a week as serve me for three times that sum. So I told her the way to St Bartholomew's.

She observed that I was heartless as a viper and had the manners of a toad.

I enquired whether some inadvertent word or act of mine had caused her any slight offence. She snorted in feigned amazement, raising her eyebrows till they were lost beneath her fringe.

On asking the precise nature of my offence, she observed that I was a loon and laughing-stock, that it was a treason against myself for a clever man to be so stupid. She would not say what I had done wrong, for I knew well enough, said she.

I observed that from a mere eighteen words she had built three contradictions.

She flung my hairbrush straight at my brow. I ducked. It splintered my dressing mirror. Then she hurled my beer mug, which caught me in the midriff, wetting my belly and lap.

She showed no remorse. But tartly spoke of my morals and appearance, likening me weasel, flounder, indiscreet bodily excretion, then Lord Derby's buttocks. I remarked that she should make up her mind. She proposed that I should, too.

Having sworn she would leave, she promptly sat in my lap. And wept! I stroked her crown to comfort her. She flung her arms around my waist and sunk her face in my sodden waistcoat.

Her feelings were volatile and jumbled, I suggested. No, she replied, she was dearly fond of me.

Did she not choose a rum way to show her affection, I enquired. I was thrice the fool she took me for, she said. But she would follow me to hell. I protested there'd be no need.

Whereupon we were intimate on the bare boards, till I was interrupted by the bell to give my second performance of the evening.

She was a poor, frail, bird of a thing. All ribs and elbows and knobbly backbone. So I was feared I should break her fragile pieces.

But she was eager to know me as none other before, fair bruising me with bony collisions and fearful clouts with her hips.

'Quick, Joey,' she jerks away at the clang of the bell, springing up, all smiles and twitters, as she rummages through the tangle of clothes, 'your breeches . . . we shan't be parted . . . there, your waistcoat . . . shall we eat at Porter's? . . . Here! The cravat . . . before we go back to your rooms? . . . Brush your hair, messy man. . . . Or should you prefer the Chop House? . . . All done. . . .' Then she pokes her quick, flickering tongue in my mouth before thrusting me through the dressing-room door.

By the time I'm off the stage, I'm betrothed and settled. There is collusion and conspiracy in the company.

Chastity and Charity beam in concert and give me gentle claps of approval. The mill-pond of Cecil Burney's face is stirred by the storm of a wink.

Ernest, doorman and sweeper, lays a large palm on my shoulder and tells me I'm lucky as Lucifer, and advises me that he'll thrash me to a pulp if I dare mistreat my sweetheart.

Nancy it is that is matter-of-fact. All knowing nonchalance as she leads me off by the hand.

Some matches are contracted in Heaven, I suppose, but

this one sparked its sulphur on the dressing-room floor.

And wasn't that a quare thing? How a fellow can set out to bed two ladies he loves, then find himself betrothed to another? Especially when he's a sharp fellow who's taken the trouble to make himself the master of his mind.

A Marriage, of Sorts

Frankly, I'd been duffed again – by common sense and sentiment.

It was quite a caution – how a fellow's slightest inadvertent gesture could be so misconstrued, by quite so many. For the chappie
had no declarations to make as he unbuttoned Nancy's blouse, and
meant no more than to remove the starchy obstruction. When she
wriggled free of her skirt, and unlaced her drawers, then splayed
her shaky legs, he thought to no contract beyond her immediate
promise.

As they bounced about on the boards, crashing their hips with
desperate, concussive jerks, he thought of nothing profound. But
worried lest he caught splinters in his sliding knees, and wondered
at the violent urgency of her frail frame, and watched her lids
flicker over closed eyes, and thought she needed proper feeding
to swell her hollowed belly. And he saw the sad, sunken gutters
between her ribs, and observed what a quare thing it was for two
parcels to be jerking so, and he cast an eye to check that the door
was closed, and looked about for his pocket watch, and felt her
tugging the hair to his neck, and it struck him that he barely
knew her, never having thought to watch her closely before.

Yet Nancy had seen it different, judging from the conclusions
she drew from the occurrence. It's often so. That two witnesses
to the same event observe quite different happenings. And when
one is a man and other a woman, you can rely on contradictions.

'Joey,' she remarks, pinching my wrist, 'I didn't know you
cared for me so.'

Well, a fellow does care for those about him. If he ain't
a brute. And won't cause another an offence, without good reason.

'We're lovers, ain't we Joey? And they shan't part us, shall they?' Only it's really an observation, spoken with such glowing assurance a fellow would feel a sour coot to disabuse her.

But, nonetheless, he ain't said so, ain't remarked upon his feelings, ain't presumed she cares a jot for him, ain't said anything to imply he'd like to take her out for dinner or home to his bed.

I dare say there was no connivance to her. It was just a meeting of different logics. And it was clear that others shared her readings of the implications. Seeing us as matched off.

And the fellow had achieved his ambition. Finding himself loved. Only the state weren't quite as he'd supposed it. For he'd hoped to choose his partner. And he hadn't accounted for the implied contract or its compendious clauses.

It's a rum riddle that a package that loves you so completely should want to change you so entirely. For, before one clear day had gone, she'd announced her plans to change my tailor, the cut of my hair, my ethics, sheets, the lie of the furniture, my stage performances.

Nancy further proposed I adopt pomade, cologne, ambitions, and adhere to certain fixed rituals in washing parts of my person – which she candidly named. She advised that I might buy myself a morning suit, purchase her a gold band, and acquire a piano for the both of us. Then she could play, I could sing, to occupy our leisure at home.

Naturally, I remarked that leisure posed no such problems for me. It was not a yawning gap to be plugged, but a pleasant pasture, over which I did not propose to push a piano. I further observed that home was a dull place, and offered but one of the many beds a man could find about town.

Nancy said she would take it amiss if I stayed out all night again. Then bullied me with her tears.

She had a rare skill for weeping. And brought her full vigour to the trade.

A fellow makes a harmless observation. Nancy's eyes moisten and sparkle. The rims of her ears go ruddy. Then her full face flushes and her nostrils flare. The waters well, sweeping over the bank of her lids, trickling down the slopes of her cheeks, the

110

droplets falling from her chin, or dribbling down her neck. She heaves, shudders and sniffs. Flinging her hands to her smeared face, kicking petulantly out with her feet.

When the fellow tries to comfort her, she flinches from him, as though he's a bruiser. And shrieks if he strokes her bosom, or his hand strays beneath her skirt to fidget beyond the frontiers of her drawers.

There's but one way to calm her. The fellow must perjure himself by promising – that he will not keep his appointment with Jenny, doesn't want to play poker at Langley's, will wear the polka-dot cravat she has bought him, wishes nothing more than to visit her mother in Chancery Lane, should prefer to leave corked that bottle of cognac.

He must say he loves her dearly, and none other. Then coax her grudgingly to bed. Till she recovers her warmth, beneath his playful fingers and avid tongue. Then, dewy damp, she twitches, moaning her flushed forgiveness.

So the fellow was properly saddened that he visited daily miseries upon the only woman that found him loveable. Nor could he free her from the suffering by leaving her.

He'd offered once, observing he was a poor, sorry burden for her back. She'd wept with raw ferocity. For the best part of an afternoon, wracked by shudders, wailing horribly, throwing herself against the wall, rattling her head on the plaster, scratching furrows on her arm, flinging china to the floor, toppling the table, tearing her skirt with her teeth.

He bought her a piano, resolving to reform himself. But for a fortnight she could not gaze on him without reproach. And would not trust him out alone on the streets. For fear he would abscond.

So love struck him as a sad patch of a riddle. A forlorn fabric; the criss-cross of the weave of passion and warp of pain, shrunken by tears, tattered by tussles, rent by strain.

There could be no disputing that she was fond of me. For she took me as her singular purpose.

She talked of me, behind my back, quite promiscuously, to all manner of folk. So in the morning on the landing, Ma Carey would accost me, enquiring of the progress of my cough and sniffing at my lapels.

'So Nancy rubbed your chest. Joey? With mutton grease and menthol?'

'She did that, Ma,' I say – though I'm sure my chest is my own concern.

'She said she would, Joey. After she'd got the broth down you. And are you regular today, Pon? Nancy was concerned.'

I think the privy well named, and always close the door. I don't expect the neighbours to follow my progress, or Nancy to report it.

'You ain't been gambling at cards again, laddie?' asks Cecil Burney.

'I?' I lie. 'No, Mr Burney. Why?'

'Nancy was concerned,' says he, turning on his heels after awarding me his distrustful scrutiny.

And when I ask for a bottle of brandy at the theatre bar, Fly Oscar – who ain't himself abstemious – slurs that Nancy has told him to give me no more than one a day. And 'tis clear they've exchanged views on my habits, and that his loyalty lies with her not me.

Then, when I slouch into the snug of the Firkin, to be amongst folk who give not a jot for my chest, regularity or gambling – and expect me to drink my share – Jessie Payne waves me over.

'Don't be late home,' she prods my belly with a warning finger, 'Nancy's braising some liver. There's dumplings and parsnips.'

Yet when the peevish fellow gets home to his chambers, he cannot bring himself to speak sourly to her. Though the parlour air is fouled by a stench of liver.

Nancy is bowed over the table pressing his socks; or has her eyes screwed tight in concentration as she darns a repair to his bootlace; else she's stitching his monogram on a handkerchief; if she's not polishing his tortoiseshell comb with beeswax; or mixing some potion of vinegar, laudanum and onions that she'll insist on poking in his ears, or rubbing between his toes.

'It's your Nancy's handsome gentleman,' says she, patting the swollen belly that holds my son. And though she shows a bold, beaming face, she watches me closely for warnings of a raw word. There's a nervous quiver to a corner of her lip, that says, 'Pray don't make me flinch or weep by speaking unkindly.' And her eyes are eloquent too. 'Tell me,' they plead, 'that you are frenzied for a slab of boiled liver.'

She's incorrigible – persisting in the pretence that I'm handsome. Saying as much in public, quite brazenly, so anyone can hear. Well, enough women have remarked upon my features. And I've taken the opinion of a mirror. And also wandered Billingsgate. So Nancy's perjury won't convince me.

'I ain't a pretty sight, Nancy,' I say wearily, 'and it don't help for you to jolly me with lies.'

'You're handsome to me, Pon. Truly. You're the prettiest man in England. To my sight.'

Well, it don't help either if I can't rely on either her savvy or sight. If it's her honest opinion I'm a good-looker, she'll be buying scarlet curtains, or having our son christened Augustus.

'I'm pretty, too. Ain't I, Pon?'

What's the fellow to tell her? Must it ever be a choice between lies and tears?

She has the wild, worried face of an urchin; hollowed cheeks; darting, burning eyes; lustreless black hair; tight thin lips.

The fellow had grown passionately partial, with practice, to her lean portions. Only, he wouldn't swear under oath she was Venus.

'You're the loveliest lady in England,' say I, 'and mother to my son. Shall we be married, Nancy?'

'Married?' she gulps. 'Like fancy folk?' Suspicion and wonder move her face in turns. Those flittering hazel eyes are frantic. She's blanched and all apucker, eyebrows dancing, mouth all twitchy. A vein to her neck pulses a violent spasm.

'Husband and wife, Pon? And Augustus born legitimate?'

For the fellow had resolved to order his life, grasp his obligations, act the proper father, honour his woman, and regain the lost kingdom of pleasure.

He would marry Pontius Porter off. Then waken Joey Blueglass from his slumber.

The young felon saw it clearly. He was vigorous. He was young. He had enough wit for two fellows to live their separate lives. Pontius Porter could bear the saddle of matrimony and fatherhood, acting the dullard family man. Then Joey Blueglass, who hadn't been seen for fourteen months, could reappear. And be as squalid and lively a chappie as he'd ever been.

It should cost him two rents, bind him to two careers, denying him kip, exercising his wits, straining his imagination, testing his powers. He'd be a proper duffer and no mistake.

Most folk stay cramped within a single life, stifled as a lone person, solo in their skin, owning but one temperament, knowing but one self, denying their other, the same tedious bod both morning and evening. It's a wonder they don't bore themselves.

Pontius could take duty, trudging the daylight hours. Leaving Joey joy, to fly by night.

All parties seemed the better for the arrangement. Nancy was radiant, the fuller each morning of child and contentment. And Pon was restful, resigned and dutiful, now he didn't have to reconcile the rogue within him. Who was Joey. Who was rarin' to live again, showing his face in his old haunts, and even being lewd, if the mood took him. He was back at cards and literature, for a fellow needs to earn a living. And he was quite taken by Jenny, who he guessed would prove an expensive item, and quite another story.

I first spied Jenny at Colquhoun's Novelty Theatre. She in the audience: I upon the stage, remembering.

After I'd spoken my piece on stage, I'd peered through the slit in the curtain. Seeing how taken she was by Renaldo Tescobaldi, Romantic Tenor. She rocked, wide-eyed and white-faced, mouth agape, to his rendition of 'A Mother's Tears at Sunset'. And when Renaldo had wept his finale, her hands were the blurred flurry of starlings' wings, her face a chatter of delights. She bit her lip in rapture. Whilst her man companion sat dour, sour and still, his right hand resting upon her shoulder. As if holding her captive. As though he owned the lovely.

I saw her next in Regent Street. She had a scuttling walk between the stores. Then fell to awed pause before each window

display. She was avid for the ladies' gowns. I recognized a familiar, sorry story. She had the passion, but not the wherewithal to
purchase.

So I determined to play the Honest Stranger – in its most
innocent guise.

'Excuse me, Ma'am.' She turned, eyes widening in impassive
surprise, unsmiling. 'I believe you dropped this piece of paper,'
say I. 'If I'm not mistaken, it's a banknote.' Then I laid a five
pound note in the palm of her puce-gloved hand. She looked up
at my face and arched her brows. She looked down at the folded
money, protruding the tip of her coral tongue. Then gazed back
to me.

She gulps, like the fish as it snaffles the bait.

'Ah, my money,' she giggles, breathy with delight. 'Ain't
I the careless one?' Her fingers snap down, like the bar of
a mousetrap, to imprison the note.

I smell her perfume – patchouli and jasmine. I sniff her
beneath those layers – creamy, then the tang from deeper. I see
the flutter of fair lashes above those eyes of duckshell blue. Her
wet china teeth glisten between amber lips. A fellow can see faint
the purple routes of veins beneath the pearly sheen of her neck.
And he wishes himself inside her too.

The chappie fair throbbed with his ache for her. She was
one of those hundred-odd women he desired most in London.
One of those orchid beauties he kept a daily watch for. Amongst
those few he ever followed. And one of only twelve with golden
hair.

'Will you walk my way?' I ask.

'Why young sir, what a notion! Does your mother know
you're out?'

'It ain't far,' I explain, 'and p'r'aps if you drop some more,
I shall be there to hand you the money.'

They were striking places she had hidden about her, undercover.
Smooth as silks, lush as Epsom downs, striking as a clout to
the brow, confidential as a rosebud, dewy as dawn, aromatic
as Floriss and Lacey's, delicate as a finch, rich as clotted cream,

mysterious as Assumption, candid as snow, eager as a puppy's tail, imperious as General Frobisher, liberal as Mr Gladstone, lavish as Dionysus, intoxicating as six pipes of opium, exotic as Tientsin, shy as unicorns, bold as thunder, frisky as a squirrel, gripping as thighs, compelling as a sneeze, luscious as plums, sublime as sun, subtle as infinity, fresh as bluebells, profound as the moon, sly as an itch, grasping as a monkey, wracking as fever, urgent as a siren, jerky as a stammer, sticky as honey. Ah. Now. Jenny.

I dare say Joey was as soft for her as Pon was for his Nancy.

On Friday he gave her twelve pounds which she needed for some gowns. Saturday he loaned her the fifteen guineas she must find to pay off her milliner. On Monday she required another twenty.

He could find the money. From his career of letters. Only he worried if she cared for him.

'Calling me a tart?' demands Jenny. 'Money don't come into it. Why ...' She has narrowed those lax blue eyes to gimlets, piercing my brow with shafts of loathing. 'I'm a decent married woman. If my husband Oscar were here ... he'd crush every bone in your body. Calling his wife a whore, indeed.'

'I thought you were fond, Jenny. Like you'd taken a fancy to me.'

'I'm a lovely woman, Joey,' says she. And there's no disputing her contention. 'I shouldn't go around picking up the likes of you, now, should I? Not for nothing. ... All I ask is you help me with expenses. So I ain't the loser by it.'

'The likes of me?'

'You know, Joey ... you're just a boy.' She softens now and fluffs the pillow. Leans back, so her breasts lie coaxing. 'You're a kind man, ain't you? You'll make a girl laugh. And tell a rum story. But look to yourself, Joey. You ain't God's gift. Are you now?'

'I ain't God's gift.'

'I mean you ain't the maiden's dream. You ain't going to steal Ninette from the Duke of Devonshire. Are you? I don't suppose Flora Langton would pay you to give her your body, Joey.'

'Not Flora,' say I.

'I mean,' Jenny sucks pensively, struggling to explain this, 'if Lady Caroline Lamb had had the choice of you or Lord Byron . . .'

'Lord Byron,' I concede.

'Yes,' says Jenny. 'Or supposing a girl had let you dance with her. And young Albert Edward, Prince of Wales, came up and said "Excuse me".'

'I understand, Jenny.'

'Or Blanche Ariston had a vacancy for another beau . . .'

'I understand, Jenny.'

'Or, if I wanted some excitement. . . .' She shrugs and shakes her yellow tresses. 'But I thought we had an understanding, Joey.'

'An understanding?'

'Expenses,' says Jenny firmly. 'Such as a girl incurs.'

He had the love of one good woman. Nancy. Who was more than he deserved. And he loved his Jenny and would grasp her terms, as readily as her loins. For it would break his sorry heart to be parted of her chest, exiled from her thighs, cast from the garden of her lap.

Only it struck him as a forlorn world where Nancy loves Joey, Joey loves Jenny, Jenny loves Oscar, and Oscar spends his time in Brussels, but Brussels cares not a jot for Oscar.

What a pretty life it should be, and tidy, a fellow thought, if each person loved their proper partner. Yet it seemed more than ingenuity or human hands could contrive. But then, he supposed, if it weren't for the glamour of other men's wives, and the allure of other wives' husbands, everyone might stay at home, and society might halt. Certainly fashion would be drabber, and there'd be less music and fewer restaurants if we were each content to park our feet on the hearth and sup on boiled liver. So it struck a fellow that adultery might be part and parcel of the divine design, and a fitting portion to marriage.

I left Nancy howling for me, like a bitch for her last, lost, pup.

As I strode along, whistling to declare my regained freedom, I pondered the curse she had screamed upon me. And I recalled how ugly she looked, her face bloated crimson by weeping.

It was then, at the corner of William IV Street and the Strand, that I was visited by feeling.

'What's that, Joey?' I asked myself. 'In your mind, there? That irritation. That itch. Like a fly on the rump of an ox. Squatting on the back of my pleasure?'

' 'Tis guilt, as I recall,' say I.

'Well, now!' I tell myself. 'He's a sour and vindictive runt. As always pipes up, to taint any jolly occasion. Don't you suppose we'd be better without him? If I let him have his say, he'll ruin my recreation. Can't we do our best to forget him?'

'Yes, Joey,' I resolved, 'and let's take some snifters first. For here's the door of the Mitre.'

But I did not realize, slouching along, that this was to be the pivot of my life. The very day I met my Florrie; when we first crossed our paths and purposes.

Florrie at the Crossroads

Sprawled upon my prison mattress, the straws pricking me through the calico cover, I recall a choicer berth, reclining upon Florrie, upon Florrie's couch. It is a broad chaise longue, upholstered in hide, on which are laid pillows and quilts filled with duck down.

Being narrower than a bed, it was required for me to lie on Florrie, or Florrie on me, or for us to tie ourselves in a tangle, or snuggle, skin upon skin. So there was always some stretch of her close, as a treat to mine eyes. And I made it my business to know her minutely, from all vantages and perspectives, visiting her every stretch and curve, hair, freckle and wrinkle. That I might hold her entirely, to her finest details, in my mind's eye, and rotate her through my vision, on the spit of my desire.

Why, to my mind, it's a longer journey, and infinitely more exotic, from her thumb to her wrist than from Rue Saint Clement to Drury Lane. And I could write a lyrical guide book for the tourists, saying where to stay, and what to see in what order.

Six feet from the end of Florrie's couch is Florrie's reflection. A cheval mirror, taller than she, and tilted, so that Florrie can watch herself supine and standing, and never be without her fair image, nor forgetful of herself. Which pleases us both. For she and I are tied, equal in our love of her form. Which is the knot that binds us.

Reaching up both her hands, she swivels the mirror to study her length – and questions me on her breadths.

'Would you say my hips were wide or narrow?'

'I could not say either, Flo. It is a matter of proportions, and your proportions are exact and correct. Yours is the perfection of a violin.'

'A violin?' she protests, scathing. 'Like fiddlers scratch on?'

For Florrie is contemptuous of poor metaphors for her form. Always finding a hidden hurt, or slur of palest praise. You should have heard the kerfuffle when I carelessly compared her to a rose.

So, on the haphazard routes of conversation, we pass by her hair, to her ears, along her thighs, thither leaping up to her nose. Unlike me, she's loathe to favour any part of her person above another. So every nook and cranny is called into question. And she will have me peer into her ears, quarry her throat, or pass judgements on the tints of her fluids. Which I take as both trusting and choice.

'Come see my pee, Joey. Do you suppose I'm sickening?'

When our opinions part, she invokes the wit and learning of her brother Clarry, who can be wise ás Solomon but plainer spoken.

You would no more say she was vain than observe that water is wet. For folk would think you a dull 'un. In conversation – Burke's *Etiquette* reports – it is the first feature that we should mention least and last. Society would be dull, you can be sure, if we passed our time reporting the grossness of elephants or opacity of fog. And poetry would be the poorer too.

You would never catch me talking so much of myself, for vanity don't visit me. But each of us is cast different.

I cannot help but think back to how I met her, at the crossroads of my life.

Ain't she a quare thing, life? Ain't she whimsical, bountiful and brutal? Jerking a fellow, like a puppet, to the dismal, joyful dance of his life, with her casual plucks of the gossamer threads. And the filaments so fine you can't see 'em.

Suppose you make so bold as to chomp one of Manzini's mutton pies. There ain't no knowing what lies within it, loitering beneath the crust – gristle, indigestion or epiphany.

If you meet an Airedale terrier, there's no predicting what'll happen, as I know from my own experience. She may beckon you to join her profession. But a passing collie may do no more nor less than pee on your boot.

So it's a sheer miracle of whimsy that ever I met my Florrie. If the waiter at Whistler's had been quicker or more tardy in totting the bill, if I'd sipped another brandy and hadn't paused in Drury Lane to buy the *Chronicle*, if I hadn't complimented Jessie Forbes on her floral bonnet . . . I should never have met my Florrie. For she'd have accosted another man.

'Excuse me, boy. I fear I'm lost.'

On the contrary, miss. I've found you.

Well, I never. Not in my seventeen years. Ever saw. The like. Of that lovely. Ain't she just. Perfection.

Flame hair. Red and gold. Ivory skin, freckle-speckled, dainty as a duck egg. Wispy, golden, fluttering lashes. Flittering, searching, mocking eyes. Lapis lazuli. Forget-me-not; as if I might. And what a fragile delicacy of nose. Flared, to provoke a fellow to adoration. And gorged lips, pert and pursed.

'Am I correct, young sir?' She stabs a hole through the yellow fog with a white gloved hand, pointing to the steps of Macey's Dining Rooms. 'In supposing this is Lime Street railway terminus?'

I gulp. 'They serve a good rack of lamb,' say I, 'but you must look elsewhere for a locomotive.'

'Then I am truly lost,' says this maiden, her eyelids dancing a pleading flutter. She slaps her palms together and stamps a foot in exasperation.

'I dare say you ain't from London, miss.'

'Much Hadham,' she declares.

'Pardon, miss?'

'I'm from Much Hadham,' says she. 'My father has a butcher's shop there – William McTaggart. You've heard of him, I'll wager.'

'Indeed not, miss.'

'Really, sir?' Her brow creases. 'He has won numerous prizes for his sausages and faggots. And he is a church warden.'

'I've never been to Much Hadham, miss. I've never known the need. You'll think me a foolish bumpkin.'

'It is a smaller town than London,' she explains, 'but sweeter smelling and a great deal prettier. And the harder to get lost in.'

Oh, but her voice. Herr Schubert never wrote a prettier melody. She makes a nightingale seem graceless and shrill. They say Fanny Larkspur, on song, sounds lovely. But compared to Florrie, she's a croaking toad. And, with the breathy pauses, a fellow can see the flush purse of mouth, and a wet, rosy slither of tongue.

'Ah,' she squeals, clutching at my sleeve, 'look there!' But I see nothing except Elsie Owens about her natural business.

She has touched me. The lovely has gripped me. Has clutched at me for comfort. I have felt the urgent press of her fingers on my forearm. She is lost and she needs me.

'What,' say I, 'has disturbed you, miss?'

'There! What's that old woman doing, crouching in the gutter?'

'Answering a call of nature, I believe, miss.'

The lovely one flushed. She made it clear she was bemused by the ways of London, and disapproving of our customs. Then she was promptly distressed again by a weeping urchin, tugging at her hem.

'Look!' commands the lovely. 'This poor infant is naked. And pulling at my skirts.'

'Why yes, bless him!' say I. 'It's a stripped child, ain't it?' So I give the child a threepence piece − as deposit for a pair of breeches − and advise him to crawl away.

'Stripped child?' she gulps. 'What can you mean, sir?'

We watch the bare-arsed nipper teeter down the pavement.

'Someone's stolen the clothes from his back,' I explain. 'Don't folk do the same in Much Hadham?'

'No!' she protests. 'Who could be so wicked?'

'A thief, felon or scallywag,' I explain, 'for there are many in London. But it ain't all for the bad. I dare say the lad has learned a lesson by it, concerning trust and suchlike. . . .'

She shakes her head and puckers her nose. 'I must leave this wicked town,' says she, 'so I would thank you to direct me to Liverpool Street.'

She's properly perplexed by the directions and distances,

declaring that a girl should find it easier to go from Upwick Green to Paddlemore Heath, though it's a good seven miles down the Midgley road.

I offer to accompany her in a cab. She shows a distrustful hesitancy.

'Are you a Christian, sir?'

'I am so.'

'And you respect women?'

'Above any other class of person,' I tell her.

'And you are a respectable man?'

'Gracious, miss!' I declare, 'I'm a writer.' Which answer, oddly, seems to satisfy.

Then we are together in the gloom of the swaying cab, alongside on the plump, cushioned, hide seat.

It's a quare thing, but I can never look on that buttoned upholstery without being reminded of the sunken vortex of a lady's navel. And the plump padding prompts me to think of plush curves of buttocks and bosoms. But I do not mention these compelling comparisons. Lest I cause offence.

As the cab fills with her fragrance – a confection of musk, citrus and sandalwood, the name of which I know – and I cast discreet glances at her exquisite profile, and note her tight, wasp waist, and see the wriggle of her thighs on the seat, and glimpse the tap of her dainty bootees on the floor, and see the fragile delicacy of her folded fingers, I think how I shall steal her, and hold her to me through life.

I ache, throb, pulse, squirm, yearn, for her. Never have I known such a loveliness, or sniffed such an essence of innocence.

She, for her part, sorts the contents of her wicker hamper with neat, nimble fingers. Then she jerks her head to regard me, her face a radiant white in the gloom of the cab. Her mouth gapes, mute and stupid, before she can speak her mind.

'My purse! . . . My purse is gone!'

I ain't surprised, this body could lose herself in a bath, or mislay her leg in her stocking.

'Lost?' I ask, helpfully.

'Stolen!' she declares. Then she shrinks back from me, pressing her back to the side of the carriage, holding out a palm to fend me from her. 'It's you,' she gasps. 'Thief. Ruffian. . . . Be warned, I shall scream for a Constable.'

'Miss,' say I, 'I should never steal a lady's purse.' Which is the very truth. For I dip in men's hearts with my literature, not into pockets with my paw. I'm an artist not a felon. 'So scream,' I advise, 'it gives relief when misfortune strikes.'

She gazes reproachfully at me, then resentful. Then she releases a warbling scream, 'Thee-eef.' With fine projection for such a fragile frame, and a deal of theatrical conviction.

The carriage jerks to a halt. And, announced by a deal of coughing and cussing, the driver peers in at the window.

'Well, Master Joey?' says Fly Frank. 'Is it a fire, flood or last judgement?'

'This is a lady, Frank. She's been flimped by some felon in the fog. And now she declares it's I that's dipped her purse.'

The lady weeps, her cheeks puffy, all adribble.

'It wouldn't be Joey,' Frank tells her. 'He may palm your confidence, but he wouldn't pocket your purse.'

'Thanks, Frank,' say I. Though I could have wished for a better reference.

'If the lady's lost her purse,' says Frank, with slow concern, 'I dare say you'll be paying the fare.'

'Drive around, Frank, till I say different. The lady and I will discuss her misfortune.'

Miss McTaggart leaks muffled moans, declaring herself friendless, lost, forlorn. So I swear that I am her protector and friend – which, in truth, I hope to be – saying I shall provide her with lodgings for the night and reimburse her loss when my bank opens on the morrow.

She pauses by the door as I light the lamp on my desk. The orange flickers show her calmly assaying my parlour. Her gaze flits quickly from the desk drawers, to the silver figurines on the marble mantelpiece, to the oil painting of Maccabeus, Mare and Foal between the windows, from there to the stuffed Springbok, on to the travelling case beneath the chaise. Then the lovely image cast back at her from the cheval mirror captures and entrances her.

When the flame burns full, she steps boldly into the room, skipping a circle, sending her skirts aswirl.

'You live alone, Mr Blueglass?'

'I am a shy man, Miss McTaggart,' say I, 'I keep an accordion for company.'

'Then stay shy,' says she, lifting my silver paper knife from the desk, weighing it in her palm, then holding it to the light to catch the hallmark. 'For if you think to get frisky, I shall stab you with this.'

But she needn't mind. I'd never storm her by force.

I send out for shrimps, a game pie, fruit and claret. We take our polite repast. But both have other concerns. I must feed my addiction. She must think to her trade.

'Shall you be comfortable on the chaise longue, miss? I must retire to my bed. Take care to lock the parlour door.'

I shall leave Nature to steer her course. Much Hadham, indeed! Do I look a glock?

I smoke four pipes.

All is hush till three in the morning, when I see from the flickers beneath the door that she has re-lit the parlour lamp. I hear my desk drawer yield, splintering to a lever.

Ain't she destructive? It is Queen Anne, and, anyway, I left the key for her in the ink-well.

Now, if I were robbing myself, I should take the figurines, ivory statuette, gold medallions, icons, and the cash from the riding boot as small change. I could fit them all in a Gladstone bag and scarper unobtrusively, thinking myself lucky to travel so rich and light. Discretion is the better part of thieving.

But we each have our own estimates of beauty and value. Miss McTaggart was determined she must have the stuffed antelope. Which made for a droll sight, and weighed her down in her flight.

With the sabre belted around her waist, my greatcoat on her shoulders, a deer carcass beneath one arm, riding boots clutched in the other, and a travelling case in each hand, she might have just returned from cavalry service in the colonies. It made her an easier quarry to stalk. For she'd handicapped herself mercilessly, in heavy going, against a quickish colt.

In raglan and glengarry, I sloped behind, on the opposite pavement. Twice she dumped her heavy load, pink-faced and panting. And, though she saw me clearly, as unlikely as the corpse dancing at the wake, no flicker of recognition played upon her face. If I'd walked up to her, I dare say she'd have propositioned me with a smile, to help her bear the load.

No, miss! Not a pawnshop. They'll give you a bare fifth of the value. And if you must hock it, don't you know no better than to plead your case at Fleck's. He'd have you pledge your mother for thruppence, then demand you deposit your teeth, or leave your ears, as insurance on the loan. And when you called to redeem poor Mamma, you'd find that Fleck had traded her for a ukelele, sold her as a coat rack, or put her to work as a chimney brush. Yet, still, he'll insist, you owe him seven shillings interest.

Miss McTaggart leaves the shop lighter of burden. But with a sorry, perplexed expression. Still, she perseveres with the antelope. I dare say it means much to her.

Now she has only the beast and a single case. I can't bear the forlorn sight any longer.

'Excuse me, miss,' say I, pointing to Drury Lane, 'is this the road for Paddlemore Heath? And ain't you Princess Casamassima?'

At least she had the wherewithal to blush. I so surprised her that she quite dropped her antelope.

'Come,' say I, 'let's take some breakfast. We'll both feel the better for it. You must be famished and parched after all that portering.'

Gustav, the head waiter, fingered his whiskers and rolled his eyes in protest. For he was as loath to stable our antelope as I was to keep its company in the paddock of the Grant's Dining Rooms. He's a proper stickler about who you bring with you to his tables.

Miss McTaggart sipped tea and nibbled feebly at some dainty triangles of toast. Before she took to harvesting the table settings.

For my part, I followed the kedgeree with Cumberland sausage, kidneys, gammon with pickles, duck eggs, muffins with clover honey and Devon butter.

It weren't till the second pot of coffee that I thought to mention her conduct.

'What made you suppose I'm a glock, miss? Do you think my head's vacant premises?'

She don't answer, but looks forlornly to the table-cloth, where her nonchalant fingers stalk the silver-plated cutlery, poaching the smaller pieces.

'Unpocket the salt cellar, please miss. I'm known here. And they trust me not to steal the condiments.'

She fidgets in her lap and retracts the lost item, but her darting eyes cast dainty daggers at me.

'Thieving is more a mannerism than a profession with you, miss,' I observe.

'I'm sorry, Mr Blueglass,' she concedes, 'that I inadvertently took some small sundries from your room.'

'It ain't the loss,' say I, exasperated, 'it's the how and what of it. To be frank, Miss McTaggart, I should far prefer to have been robbed by someone qualified in the craft. For you've insulted me, playing me for a fool.'

No, miss. Don't flirt. I ain't finished yet.

Don't cry neither. Tears won't float the navy. Ain't you got no pride? Nor self-control?

Pass me your bag. I mean to go through it.

Lordy, miss. Ain't you fond of cutlery! And handkerchiefs! And gentlemen's watches! Do you suppose it betrays you? That you rattle when you walk?

What shall I do with you, Flo?

I have an inkling, close wrapped in my desire.

Flo's Toes

The chaplain called on me in my cell this morning. He advised me I was a sinner.

'Joseph Blueglass, you shall find relief from your misery if only you confess. Then Jesus may clutch you to his breast, for he loves the repentant sinner.'

I dare say.

We creak and sway in the rickety chairs, either side of the warped pine table. I run a finger along the splintered edge. My warder breathes heavily bronchial behind me. A caution this – lest I think to assault an agent of God.

The Reverend George Gully means to have me, to hear me divulge, then repent. That I may be released with his blessing. I thought it a shame, to disappoint a decent man.

I told him I had sinned with women.

'Good, Joseph, good,' says he, nodding soberly. But I suppose he approves not so much of my fornications as of this first teeter down the path of confession. Perhaps he thinks I shall progress to concede to worse.

'Was it often, Joseph, that you sinned with women?' And I was surprised that he was taken with the mathematics of the matter.

'As often as I could, sir.'

Her toes. Florrie's toes. That first day I knew them.

Are a secret association, snuggled coy in conclave, pink and plump together, furtive in her doeskin boots, beneath a silken sheeny skin of stocking.

The littlemost members are perfections of precision and proportion. Diminutive. Exact. They fair make you giddy with yearning. For a fellow thinks, if nature has taken such care of the peripheral parts, how consummate she must be at her core.

It is a paradox of her person that to travel hopefully, commencing at her distant territories, you must start out brazen, nearer the crux, unrolling that imprisoning stocking, snapping back the ruthless garter that bites into the plump bounty of her thigh.

I tug against the tyranny of her doeskin boot.

'Careful, Joey! Those boots cost a guinea.'

I mean to have it off. Oops, there! She is exposed. Her foot is out of hiding, free of the coy sheath of shoe.

She gazes down with detached sadness, as I kneel at her feet, unwrapping her leg, tossing the flimsy gossamer web aside. Now I hold a raw, naked portion.

'Sir! It tickles. When you lick my toes.'

They are moist and salty, sweet and sour. There are secret wrinkles between, hidden away from civilization. I dare say few adventurers' tongues have travelled there before me, drinking these unnamed flavours, speechless, drunk on the scents of her, his dawdling lips in her private places.

She does not know what she has; how much she gives me. Vain as she is, she is inured to the beauty and wonder of her body. She knows it only as a pretty place; not as a palace of mystery.

'Oh! So you're one of those fellows who's fond of feet?'

I shall have her slowly. Piece by piece. I shall eat her.

It straightens from its languid droop, this itsy bitsy toe, and flushes candid, pulsing hot to the wet flicker of my tongue.

Oh. My. The arching curve of her foot, jerking to escape my predatory desire. And the pale, soft, hidden underside, writhing at the play of my fingers.

Then I meet those twin mounds of her ankles, and the satin sheen of her shin. I can see the very pores of her. I gaze at her smallest, most private openings. The intimate entrances. And I am too gross to venture in.

'What's to do, Joey. What's that you're staring at? Have you found a blemish?'

No, ma'am. All is as fine as a fellow could wish.

She swells here as I meander upwards. There is the soft, slack, gravid hang of her calf. Kiss it. It yields to the print of my lips.

'Oh, sir! Do you mean to kiss me everywhere?'

Your thigh, madam, we touch upon it now. Lip, lap, lick. Glancing, skittering, dancing tongue. Ah, if that's the inclination of your flesh, this is the deviation of my desire. My winding indulgence.

'No, Joey! You'll make me all soggy!'

Ain't it a sleek, slithery, skidding path, supple and pliant, beneath my snail's trail. I shall pause and graze here.

So far. So downy. A hair's breadth.

Ah. There's the rub.

A fellow could skulk here the day long. So swell. So plush.

A dimple on the tender, pliant, underneath. Unbend, madam. Will you yield?

The ascent of Florrie, by the sinuous, tortuous, swerving path. The laying on of hands. The merging, meeting, brushing, stirring, glancing of skin on skin. The coincidence of me on she. No scant regard. No skimpy kiss.

'What are you doing? What do you mean by that, sir?'

Don't look so coyly bemused, miss. We shall come to the naked truths of it.

By and by, we shall lie in the lap of it.

Oh, your eyes miss – open. Oh, your eyes flickered closed. The rent. The tear. The split of them. The blue depths. The moist opening. The closing and the holding in. Ah, the lashes.

Your lips, too, miss. That groove. That niche. Those swollen banks. The snug coral snatch of mouth. The quivering flick of the frothing tongue.

Yes. I shall undo you. Unlace you. Have you properly defrocked.

'There's buttons, Joey. Don't tug!'

What slender, lissom arms, miss. Flimsy willows, bending to gusts of my passion.

Jesus. Good God. Sweet Virgin. Your collar-bones and shoulders. Oh, my glad eye. Ain't you supple. How shall I finger you. Clasp, smother and cherish.

Oh, and the rosy flush. We come to the heart of it, beneath, behind, this high, defensive, armoured breastplate.

What accoutrements. What a garrison. Now. This man shall scale the ramparts. Come. Let us have it off your chest. Make a clean breast of it, ma'am.

Gracious. Glory. Mother of God. 'Tis no wonder you guard them closely. A fellow is faint at the sight of them. Ain't you favoured? Ain't I blessed?

An illumination. The word made flesh. Where women keep their chest, Florrie holds Revelations. What, pray, are the names for these. Fonts. Of the milk of human kindness.

Yes. Twitch and shudder. So do I. We're fingered by a miracle. In the dazzle and glare of a Manifestation.

That iridescent sheen. Of those bountiful mounds. How gravely they sway and judder.

Palely. Reverential, I kneel. I press my lips to the Grail.

I take Communion.

These are truths eternal here, miss. You are blessed to bear them before you; as I am to revere them. Pray let me worship here, ma'am.

'Gently, Joey. They're my bosoms. I need them to last. They're the only pair I've got.'

Ain't they beneficent. Blind and mute. All they know is giving. Don't they show a lesson to us all. For they don't ask nothing in return.

See, miss. We ain't never met. But up she rises, to give to me, stretching firm, swelling between my lips. Indulging this needy fellow.

'May I, wondrous stranger?' enquires my teasing tongue.

'Take me,' says the gorging nipple. 'And have my sister too.'

Oh, but your freckled belly, Florrie. Ain't she a sight. How she quivers and shivers to my sneaking finger.

'Your hands, Joey. Ooh, they're chill.'

This is the frontier. The no-man's-land. Beyond is the Golden Fleece. But it is in the dark, under wraps. One crossing, one transgression, lies between us. A boundary of lace and satin. This is the separation. Of you and I, Florrie. Shall we meet what lies ahead of us by shedding what comes between?

May I, ma'am, visit your places? Might I part you from this modesty? And ease you from this reticent garment, thin pretext, loose cover, flimsy concealment?

'Ain't you got no manners, Joey? . . . That's my privates.'

Would you think me rude? Or impolite? I shall not snatch. I will knock before I enter. I'm anxious to please. I keep a civil tongue in my head – that wishes no more than to devour you.

'Boy! Ain't a lady permitted any secrets?'

There, yours. Oh, my.

What a joyful surprise, and wondrous disclosure.

This is the country of my dreams, Florrie. I visited here last night. You are too kind, miss, to show it to my blinking eyes. 'Tis a fair land, that fairly makes me giddy. Wait, till I catch my breath.

There's a shaded glade beyond the golden thicket. And, lo, the secret grove.

'Tickles! Oh, tickles!'

I swear I smell the salty sea. I must hurry forth to sink. On the slithery slopes of the swollen banks, I taste bliss and scent eternity. Back to the ocean whence I came.

Oh, to drown myself here.

The perisher must plunge in, to die his several deaths in her depths.

'There, Joey, boy . . .' her azure eyes dazzle. Her face shows cunning and pity. 'I said you'd find me a comfort. . . . Now, shall this room be our parlour, or my dressing-room?'

What were we, she and I? The haddock and gazelle. The cold and cautious, slithery package of scales and fins: the sleek, svelte, nervous, prancing parcel. The submerged and the aerial. Calculation and reflex. Depth and surface. Mind and body.

I didn't presume her mine. But took her as some divine loan, heavenly body, fallen to my orbit.

She was beauty bent on burning – like some gaudy moth that wants no more than to incinerate itself in the flames of a candle.

What did she find in me? A pleasant perch, I dare say

– four fine rooms in William IV Street, with a south-facing dressing-room. She supposed me a wealthy fellow, who could afford those tastes she wished to acquire. For she took to the pipe as to a sacred calling.

Perhaps her unthinking wit, her wise folly, had found her a fellow who cared.

And I moved her, to laughter or tears, when I spoke my vexations. For she weren't without those faults which clung to her foibles, alongside those whims in which she hid her vices, which any fair-minded accountant would offset against her cheer, bloom and beauty.

Her carelessness pains me.

'Flo, my duckling,' say I, 'where's those letters I left by the chair?'

'Oh, Joey! Was that paper papers? I used it to light you a fire.'

'Flo!' I say. For I'm stern in the flush of the moment.

I judge her light-fingered. For she's loath to part any place – restaurant, shop, park, street, theatre, church – without claiming a secret souvenir of it.

'Where'd you find this briefcase, Florrie?'

'Charing Cross, I think, Joey – if I remember right. Does it matter?'

'And do you know what's inside?'

'Documents,' she says, regretfully. As if she'd expected oyster wrapped around pearls.

'Government documents,' I tell her. 'The Cobden-Chevalier Treaty of Free Trade between France and Britain. A proposal to repeal Paper Duties. Some Fiscal Plans. And a report on the blockade of Confederate ports.'

'Is it valuable, then, Joey? Are we in the money?' She beams at her coup.

'Were you seen, Florrie?'

'I'm a handsome woman, Joey. Men can't help themselves eyeing me. I'm pretty. They're weak. They stop and smile and pass the time of day.'

'And the man who owned this case?'

'We spoke,' concedes Florrie, 'of this and that . . . before I had to scarper. . . . I believe I know his face from somewhere.'

'Stupid . . .' say I, 'bitch.'

Then I say more and worse. For I'm sometimes roused to anger, and quite forget my manners, not to mention the polite strictures of Burke.

Then I move her to tears.

When she's cheery, she's a glorious palette of colours. It's her hues, in part, that make her so special – amber, copper, cream, coral, bronze, caramel, roan, sorrel, russet, foxy. And it's a flawless scansion. And the assonances so delicate.

So the fellow's properly grieved. That his rude words have smashed the prosody, rent the couplets. Turning her to reds.

The tips of her ears are crimson; burning coals by the flames of her hair. Her scarlet cheeks have swallowed the field of freckles. The creamy sheen of her brow has puckered ruby raw. That delicate, rust-speckled nose has flared to a gaping wedge of a thing.

The chappie's disfigured the face he loves best. Pummelling it with his blunt, brutal words.

Tears are atrickle down livid, pulsing cheeks, swollen fat as a cavy's.

'What've I done wrong now?' She spits milky flecks, which glow opalescent in the air. Her nostrils are spread to the size of almonds. The face is stripped raw. The mouth twists, slewed by loathing.

'Sorry, Florrie. . . . Only you mustn't do it again – steal the case from a minister. Not when there ain't no profit to it. It only attracts attention.'

'Minister? He weren't wearing a dog-collar.'

'Minister of government,' say I. 'You've flimped a Secretary of State.'

'So. . . .' observes Florrie, considering this. 'No one's perfect. Is it cause to shout at a girl?'

Another vexation – her vagueness as to her history and antecedents. She creases her face, rolling her eyes, in the strain of recollection. But she can't produce a convincing account for her place in this world, nor tell a tale that don't contradict the one before.

On Tuesday her pappa was dead. By Wednesday he's progressing to recovery. He lives in Bristol, Exeter, Hackney or Glasgow, quite as her fancy moves him. You've never heard tell of such a diligent, versatile fellow. For he's been baker, butcher, corpse, debtor, farmer, all within three days.

Florrie's mamma is a prodigiously resourceful and good-natured woman – as she'd have to be, given the travel and adjustments her spouse requires of her. Not to mention the range of disabilities and ailments her daughter loans her.

Florrie has a brother Clarrie. When she is not an only child.

She doesn't seem a mite disconcerted by the contradictory and volatile family, or the impression they give to outsiders. She simply squeals and giggles when I protest them fanciful fictions.

I felt I had reason to ask her of men. But of these she proves least reminiscent. She's heard of them, but is fair flummoxed to remember any she knows outside the magic circle of her kin.

I know I must send her packing. This woman is danger and disorder, while I need caution and control to keep me from the jug. So I stare her bold in her azure eyes, bear witness to her freckled face, and tell her truly – that she is precious to me, that I love her and am resolved to make her happy.

'What do you want of life, Florrie?'

And when she told me, it struck me that she'd be easy enough to please. If she really knew what she wanted, and wanted what she said —

A kind man, husband even, who didn't wish her to work, and sent her shopping every day: accounts at Ffolkes and Morrisey's, Florix and Stoogeley's: a vacation in France: a five-bedroomed house in Brockley or Peckham (respectable places) with a large garden; a tiara; five strings of pearls; with time, a daughter called Elvira, and a blond-haired boy called Oscar; never to rise before twelve; a maid or two; rum truffles, whenever she fancied; supper at Sloane's; a night (I believe she meant an evening) with the Prince of Wales in his box at the opera; a meeting with Dr Livingstone; to bathe once in asses' milk, just to try it . . . Oh, yes – and never to grow old, and always to be happy.

'The things that can be bought just ain't a problem,' I assure her. 'I'll use my influence with time to tell him not to finger you. . . . We'll have a sign on the wall – "Bless this house" – warning misery to stay away. . . . Dr Livingstone is in Africa. But when he gets back, I know a man as knows his niece. Then I'll have to work on an introduction to Princey. Which opera, Florrie, would you most like to see with him?'

'Joey,' she giggles, 'you's a dreamer.'

'Florrie!' I grasp her shoulders, and lose my focus in her forget-me-not pools. 'I'll do my best for you. Be mine. I'll get you what you want.'

'Jasus, Joey. You're a quare 'un.'

I lift a floorboard behind the chaise, reaching down to lay my fingers on the familiar grain of the leather satchel.

'Here's a hundred pounds, Florrie. Why not buy yourself some thingummies – and some whatsits if you fancy.'

'Joey!' she's all agog. 'How much money do you have there?'

'Enough for jellied eels and mutton pies. Here and hidden. I've been saving for a day like this. And I'll get more promptly. . . . But money ain't never the problem is it, Florrie?'

'It ain't?'

'No. It's finding the proper use for it.'

And the strangest part of it? It was the only day we spent together that we didn't lie together. Yet it was one of our happiest times, planning our future and all.

Had I tried before, I would have known. There's no choicer labour than striving for the happiness of another. And you shouldn't believe the serene silence, when you bid your own desires to hush their clamour.

I had made a brief calculation how much it would cost, without skimping, to procure for Florrie her happiness. To the list of desiderata she'd spoken, I added some items she might have forgotten – pony and trap, wedding licence, maternity dresses, children's toys – and added a hefty premium to pay for her foibles.

It was a wonder of economy. For, in the first year, it could all be bought for two thousand, three hundred and seventy five pounds. And, I dare say, the initial outlay on house and home would make the first year the most expensive. So a couple could live on less thereafter, and still not be strangers to comfort.

And of the first year's costs I already had a full eighteen and six-seventh percentage. Which, though it could not transport Florrie the full distance to enchantment, could make her cheery at least.

Thus resolved, I devised some new opinions for my head.

Time was when I was never satisfied. I'd eat an apple and lament the core, or gorge on salmon but regret the bones. Till I realized the fault was mine. Pleasure is a matter of attitude and will. Our tastes are our very own doing. So I told myself that pips and bones were the very best bits, and sewed the prescription in mind. And, bar two choking attacks, the opinion's done me no harm.

After all, I ain't going to be advised by a stilton rind, or fish head, whether he's tasty or not. He's got a vested interest. It'll be I, not the object, that determines my desire. For the object ain't objective.

So it was I perfected Florrie, quite wiping the few blemishes that nature and culture had awarded her.

'Contrary to appearances,' I informed myself, 'buck teeth do suit a lady. As do a sprinkling of pimples.'

'And it's a charming lilt,' say I, 'not a lisp.'

So what if she were a bare-faced liar? A mythomaniac is just a poet, taking a short cut to work.

She says she could expire in your arms, Joey. She always says so, after nooky. It pleases the fellow to believe it.

French Leave

However conscientiously a man strives to forget his past mistakes, or the evils of the world, still they sidle up to surprise him.

Ladies address me in the streets. They know my name. Their faces flicker with familiarity. Some call me Scarlet. One claimed she had lain with me.

'Oh, madam,' say I. 'Pray don't remind me. If I do forget a face it's for some good reason.'

Whereupon she swings a frisky hand upon my face. Smacking my cheek, fair rattling my faculties.

And I do damage easy. Without my noticing. For some mornings I witness in my shaving mirror fresh man-made blemishes. There is a purple mound on my brow, perhaps, or razor cut upon my neck, or knuckle marks embossed in bruise upon my chin. For the life of me, I can't recall how I incurred these costs.

Or, I'm seated in Langley's, engaged with a plate of chops, when a fellow casts his shadow over my plate and the best part of the linen table-cloth. I look up to find a chappie as corpulent as a bull, swaying barrel-chested, jerking a neck as fat as a tree trunk.

'Blueglass,' says he, blowing heavy through his spread nose, 'you're a pimple on my futtocks.'

'I am, matey?' say I. For I hadn't known.

I dare say he's a bruiser or a scallywag. When a nose has spent more time broke than entire, it acquires a telling character and won't sit quiet and straight on a face, but slumps and spreads its crimson bark. If a pair of ears have been twisted and torn, they'll not sit tidy and discreet. Eyes that have been gouged and busted open watch out for themselves, more peevish and suspicious than most. A brow that's been butted and pummelled carries more splits and creases than maturity awards.

'A hundred and fifty pounds,' he snorts, Delphic as the Oracle.

'Is a deal of money,' I opine.

'That it is, boy. It's what you owes me.'

'I, sir? You, sir? Are you sure that we're acquainted?'

'Pay up, boy. Then I needn't bounce your head on the pavings again, or slit open your nose.'

The ammoniacal scent of his sweat hangs heavy over my luncheon.

'What's your name, sir?'

'Don't be tricksy, boy,' says he.

'Remind me, sir. My memory ain't what it was.'

He leans over. 'Jack Gumm!' He gobs it in my face.

Let me see, now. I must consult my reminiscence.

Guinea-fowl, vomit up
Gullet, biffed on
Gumboil, fork in
Gumm, John, pugilist, thumped by

His bulk sways over me. His black pig eyes swivel his menace. There's spittle dribbling from his mouth. 'Oh!' I say, 'I'd clean forgot you.'

My heart's knocking to come out. For another portion of memory confides that a Jack Gumm once felled Bruiser Yates (fourth minute, twenty-second round).

'Come outside,' he coaxes, whispering, gentle. Then lays a hand close-aside my plate and near as large.

Being frail, I'm averse to a brawl. My heart ain't in it. Each to their own trade, say I. He's a bruiser. I'm a duffer.

Seeing no other means of safe conduct, I affixed his hand to the table top with a sharp downward stab of my steak knife, taking aim to split some bones and part some tendons ... I tossed coins to the table and strode hastily from the chop shop. Leaving him squealing and spurting like a stuck pig.

139

Word spread. Folk called me foolhardy.

'You should have paid up or let him hurt you,' says Frank Logan. 'He ain't one to forget a slight.'

Whereas I am. That's my way. Call it forgiving and tender, but if folk do me a wrong, I try to fling it from my mind.

But I thought it time to fulfil my promise to Florrie; to take her across the water, and account it our honeymoon.

Florrie and France. A surfeit for the senses. Two vistas, a duplicity of tongues, a double-dealing of manners, a brace of beauties, a deuce of journeys, a befuddling couple. When my nose wasn't gorged on the scents of it all, my palate clogged by the clotted richness, my eyes blinking from the scorching beauty, ravishing loveliness, my ears were thrilled by the warbling, giggling suites of it – a double concerto for Florrie and France.

I dare say I was too choked and stuffed by the combination to give a fair, measured, reverence to each. The sensualities are tangled in my memory, entwined like the legs of lovers.

Normandy in Spring. Florrie ripe and gushing, in the flush of her beauty. The budding, blooming bursting of the hedgerows; the lush roll of greens beyond. And the harvest hues of Florrie – yellow, gold, russet, red, amber. The meandering rivers charged to their banks, threatening to flow over. Florrie, swollen as ripest fruit, throbbing to the pulse of this vernal season, fair bursting her chemise. The vast flats of the golden sands, lapped by the languid grey-blue sea. Hillocks and swells, clothed in tufted grasses. Hidden, stranded pools. The smooth, creamy stretches of her thighs. The ebb and flow. Low tide and high time. The wondrous expanses exposed. Where the fellow loiters, lazes and lounges in the pulsing warmth. The lick of waves, and answering murmur, the caress. Alone with the golden beauty.

Scallops with coral roes, whiskered oysters, fat mussels, crayfish, crab and lobster. Salty, tangy, wicked tastes. Plump, moist, mysterious shapes. Naughty food. Creamy, red-veined, pink and whites, furtive and coy, behind nature's chill, stiff corsetry. Prise them out and prize them. Luscious, crude, primordial bodies, raised from their secret depths. Startlingly, shockingly naked to the exposure of man's eyes.

Fat beef, creams and butters. Flesh flourishes, is favoured here – spilling and squirting its juices.

Chaste cheese, powder white. It yields to the touch and exudes its molten centre.

Crisp white wines. Calvados. Golden cognac. Laid, matured, for this moment of its taking. Biting your lips, sending your throat athrob, basting you at the core. Till you are quite befuddled and legless. Then you decide you must drink more. And you sink helpless into that black velvet tunnel of night.

Le Mont St Michel. Oh, choicest sight to pilgrim's eyes. A shrine on a holy mound, commissioned by an archangel. Quicksands surround. You must cross the fortified bridge, then climb the giddying heights. Lucky traveller that finds those peaks. Many have sunk in treacherous sands beneath.

St Malo, hiding its cleft, chasmic paths behind those towering ramparts. A fellow counts himself fortunate amongst men, to have entered in through the narrow gate.

Clécy, where the Orne sweeps through its secluded valley, then tumbles down the slopes to the spuming rapids.

Bricquebec. Good Queen Vicky passed the night here after visiting Cherbourg.

Les Cuisses d'Or, Les Monts Stupéfiants, Entre Deux Jambes, La Forêt Châtaine Rousse, Relais du Désir, Le Ravin Sacré, all in the magical regions of Joey sur Flo, where the fellow passed his mornings and nights, between the urgency of ecstasy and tossing, fitful sleep.

And I gained some proficiency in two further codes of speech – French and Florrid. Both pretty, fanciful tongues, more concerned with mood than truth, preferring pretty effect to vulgar meaning, much taken by possession, sensitive to the smallest nuances of gender, preferring the soft satin curves of vowels to the stone and steel of consonants, relishing small differences of inflexion, stressing self, plurality and sensuality. The feminine is an addition upon the masculine, and may take unlikely forms. Both French and Florrie enrich themselves by borrowing. For which they do not require permission. Both Florrie and French pay special attention to their lips. There is a deal of pursing, pouting, blowing and bluster. There are a deal of irregularities to be mastered. Certain surprising acts are described with casual familiarity – though a Cockney lacks the verbs to do these things himself, at least with a tranquil conscience. French and Florrie constantly remind the fellow of the familiarity and intimacy allowed him, by the names used to address him. French makes much use of tu and vous. Florrie deploys Joey, you, fish-eyes, Mr Blueglass, glock, arse and dearest Joey. By these distinctions, the fellow knows how close he may stand, where he may lay his hand, or how much it shall cost him.

Both languages, I should hazard, rank above English in sensitivity and power for pleading, passion, possession, or poking superlatives at perfume and petticoats. And are prettier to the ear than my own guttural grunts. Only if I wanted to peel some potatoes or sharpen a pencil, I should use the sharper edge of English.

The fellow should be a fool to presume that the same words mean or sound the same on all three tongues. Take Florrie herself. Who means blossom in French, dearest angel to me, but something different again to herself. Or that commonplace word which means yes, piddle, or me, depending on who voices it.

So we had our confusions, and diplomatic incidents. For when I said 'perhaps' I meant precisely, 'never – if I have my way, as I mean to'. I believe this is the common usage in our native kingdom, but she always mistook it for an affirmation, and spoke her later disappointment with tantrum and tears.

Or take 'I love you', which I misunderstood as a phrase of endearment, promptly thanking her. But, here, I was amiss. For when she spoke it to me, it was a form of demand. It said 'Tell me you adore me. Pray mention the beauty of several of my parts. And remark upon the sweetness of my nature.' Or 'Shouldn't you like to purchase something pretty for me?'

We had our love of yarns in common.

Her stories were pretty narratives. She was determined to write the world anew. In her own fair image. And make it well again, nursing it in the clinic of her imagination. There was none better than she, at doctoring the truth. For her mind was a kind, forgiving, forgetful place.

So all she said had the unspoken preface 'Once upon a time, in a magic land . . .', and was never a description of the sorry tarnished truth, but an observation on how life could be the finer, if she were the Creator.

For which high-minded yearning I could always forgive her much. She knew there was poverty, malice, diphtheria, lice and squalor; that milk turned sour; that love withered; that a face grew creases; that teeth and monuments crumble. Only she chose not to mention it, preferring to weave a prettier web, reforming our very being.

Truth was a state we knew of, from dark and dismal rumour. We didn't think to mention it, but made a richer, freer, warmer, larger place – the size of a double bed – governed by desire, not gravity. And if the rude world ever knocked upon our door, I'd try to leave her at rest, nestling under the quilt.

And the world did keep poking some of its impudent snouts round our door, startling us from blissful reverie to rude awakenings.

In Deauville, a sour wizened hotelier blocked our path as we sought to leave his musty establishment at dawn. He quite accused Florrie of stealing a parasol from the salon, a Limoges sauce-boat from the supper table, the lace curtains from our chamber.

'That cannot be so, Monsieur,' say I, 'for my wife is the niece of a bishop. I've heard her tell kindly untruths. But it is not within her compass to steal.'

The exchange being spat in French, Florrie knew no more than the sourness. She sought to stem the acrimonious flow, so foreign to her amiable spirit, with the balm of her innocent bosom. With pouts, and beguiling heaving of her *décolletage*, she winked at the man.

'Stow your bust, Flo. This is one unpleasantness that your chest can't cure. The buzzard swears you've flimped him.'

'He dares accuse me? This evil prune, this raisin-face says I've stolen from his hotel? A watch did he say? And a parasol? And he says it's me?'

143

'He didn't mention a watch, Flo.'

'The knave shall not blame me, Joey. Tell him I am the daughter of the Queen's Physician. Tell him he is a slanderous nark. Say we shall sue him.'

'Monsieur. . . .' I commence, swelling my chest.

'Monsieur,' his wrinkled face splits to a gaping sneer, 'this prune speaks English. This raisin understands much more besides. This buzzard will have your luggage and persons rummaged. If I find the evidences, I shall place them before proper, officious persons.'

'Monsieur,' I protest, 'noble patron,' I coax, 'our persons are intimate. Our possessions are private. We traverse your fine establishment without guile to ourselves or our baggage. We can disclose nothing but ingenious innocence.'

'No, Monsieur. You are pillagers, purloiners, peculators, filchers and fiddlers. Your woman is a whore. And you a pimp.'

'Patron,' I remark, 'your English does you credit. You speak with felicity and grace. It is a pleasure to talk with a scholar. Have you perchance read the works of Mr Dickens?'

'Spoliators,' he continued, in his malicious whine, 'malversationists. Huggers-mugger. Immoralists.'

'It's a compendious lexicon you entertain in your gross faculties.' I observe, 'Truly, sir, you have the wisdom of a thesaurus.'

'Misfeants . . . Anarchists. . . .'

I observed we were making progress. At least we were wearing him down, by exhausting his epithets.

'It is very misunderstanding,' say I. 'Shall we eat the apple of discord, rather than gnaw the bone of contention? P'r'aps we can confute the wrangle with amity, like friends.'

'No, Monsieur. Like merchants.'

'Merchants?'

'You may bid for my discretion. Also tender to reimburse my sanguine humours.'

'Very well, Monsieur.'

'Eighty livres,' he observes pithily.

'Eighty!' I exclaim. 'It's a deal of money.'

'Eighty,' he confirms, 'or I shall call on authority.'

I near empty my pockets and purse in his palm.

'Now, please leave with vital immediacy. And Monsieur . . .'

'Yes?'

'If you please – as you go – don't allow your woman to purloin my escalations.'

'Really, Joey,' says Florrie, pink and peevish, 'I never thought you'd let Frenchy better you so.'

'Keep the watch as a present, Flo. I hope you like it. It cost me a hefty sum.' I dare say I'm sour.

'There's pearls besides, Joey,' she protests. 'Three strings with an emerald clasp. Like those the Comtesse wore last evening. Like you promised you'd buy me.'

We spent our happiest day at Boulogne, watching the races. It's a fine, lush, flat course. And a smart gathering. Florrie looks the swell lady she is, in her azure damask frock patterned with a motif of iris blooms. Above her wide straw bonnet, trailing dust-blue ribbons, she twirls a choice parasol – silver-handled, ebony-stemmed, with a lacy canopy.

I dare say we were both excited – to be back amongst fine folk, away from the dusty provincials who knew only donkey dullness or peacock gaudiness.

'They're discerning, refined folk here,' says Florrie.

'Yes, Flo. They're haut bourgeois. We're with our own kind at last.'

We perch our folding canvas seats on the turf, open the wicker picnic hamper and spread the fare upon snow-white linen. Florrie selects the finest silver cutlery from the selection in her case.

We have two bottles of champagne, a smoked duck, two dressed lobsters, velvet-skinned nectarines, brandy-soaked walnuts, coarse pork paté, crayfish mousse, a pungent goat cheese, crisp fresh loaves, truffles and a bottle of pickled mushrooms.

As we meandered through the elegant company, Florrie admired the ladies, their dress, jewels and escorts, while I kept an attentive ear to the play of the odds.

I don't know French pedigrees or form. So I rely upon the flow of bets to guide my own wagers.

I've never been a friend of the favourite. Its odds overestimate its chances, being dictated by popular feeling which confuses the likely and the probable. And the more money goes on it, the more money it then attracts. So a chancer becomes a winner, before the race is run. And it ain't the task of a racehorse to lecture the public on the fallacy of hope. It's got its work cut out just galloping round the track with a mean dwarf perched on its back.

And why bet a pound on the favourite, to win another pound? You might as well labour for a living. And raise your cap to a master.

But I'm a wishful thinker, not a thoughtful wisher. I cherish the outsider. I look for the unlikely nag, the flier. Whose odds suddenly sprint. For, then, you can be sure, some sage punter knows what others don't. And there's the sniff of a coup or a scam.

Which was how I came to wager a thousand francs on Anonyme, a dappled, winking, frisky nag, who tumbled from odds of twenty to tens within a blink of his liquid chestnut eye.

He romped home, by twenty lengths, over fifteen hundred metres. All without the jockey stroking his flanks with his whip, and without any sheen of sweat.

I'd won ten thousand francs. I'd seen a marvel. For he was fluid motion. He just stroked the turf with blurred hooves. All chilling grace and scorching pace. So I set my mind to calculate the strength of it.

A furlong is 220 yards . . . is 201 metres. A metre per second is 2.23694 miles per hour. . . . As for the weight carried, there are .4536 kilos to the pound. . . .

So, adding five per cent to his speed, if the jockey pushed him . . . adding three per cent for a lighter, surer mount . . . subtracting nine and a half per cent for heavier going, subtracting five per cent for the effects of a channel crossing, followed by unfamiliar stable and hay . . . and even assuming my timing was a full second awry. . . .

'Jasus, Florrie. You've seen a miracle. That little hoss there could have beaten Clarion at Epsom over eight furlongs by a clear four and a quarter seconds.'

'That so, Joey? And ain't he a pretty creature? And don't his rider look fine in his blue silk blouse? See how those breeches hug his thighs.'

But we couldn't procure what was needed in Boulogne. So we took ourselves back to England. For laudanum just don't satisfy. A fellow needs his smoke.

I Forget

What I miss most in my cell is not my pipe, nor fine food and wines, nor the freedom to go where I choose – for I have the free run of my memory – but the company of Florrie.

I thought myself the luckiest rascal in Christendom. To have her.

'I'm ugly, Florrie.'

'I shouldn't say ugly, exactly. You're every bit as handsome as your features will allow.'

'Look at me!' I clout the side of my head with my knuckles. 'Tell me I ain't the spit of a haddock.'

'I shouldn't say a haddock, exactly,' she screws tight her eyes in scrutiny. The sight of me ploughs furrows in her brow. 'There is something fishy about you, though. But fish aren't half as unsightly as some folk pretend.'

'You're the loveliest piece in creation, Florrie. And I'm ugly. It's a riddle that you're mine.'

'I shouldn't say I was yours exactly, Joey. I'd say I was my own. For I can leave whenever I choose.'

I hug Florrie's back and gaze over her freckled shoulder at my own reflection. Looking all sniffy and hurt. There's no disputing. I look like a cod that's taken umbrage. There's something to the sculpting of the brow. And my dark, still eyes make it seem I'm peering perplexed from the depths.

It ain't just her beauty. It's her character too. For she's every jot as deceitful as I. So she ain't one of those tyrannical women – like Nancy -- who oppress a fellow with the yoke of her virtue. No. She was a duffer like me. We held our profession in common.

Only the trouble with our trade is that it makes a habit of distrust, and finds delight in deceit.

And though this had brought us together, it threatened to tug us apart. For there are times when a couple can benefit from truth and fidelity, if they're to stay securely tied.

I should have been more contented if I hadn't felt the need to check, after we'd had nooky, that she'd used the distraction to empty my wallet.

And I felt properly peeved every time she pawned my watch. Nor could I take it with equanimity when she stayed away all night. For her whoppers stretched the corset of my belief. I couldn't credit her bald explanation that she'd merely got lost on the streets. For I'd heard that story once before.

Naturally, then, I took to following her. So, every day to forgive her, I'd strain myself to forget.

'Would you say my waist was plump?' Florrie swivels her hips before the mirror, patting her belly, smiling all winsome at her own reflection.

You are my hourglass. I will be your sand. Spilling my drops through the waist of you.

'You are choice, Florrie.'

She turns to face me, breasts abounce, and, frowning, examines my face for a sign of mockery. There is none to be found. For I gaze upon her with reverence.

'Pout,' say I, 'I love it so.'

'Are you jealous, Joey, when other men look at me?'

'I am so, Florrie.'

I am jealous of your corset – who can clutch your breasts so close, so long, without you bidding it desist. Envious of camiknickers, that enwrap enchantments, clinging so intimate, brushing those satin slopes with their silken touches, kissing those lips. I should be your pillow. Come lie on me, and hollow me to your shapes. Turn and brush your cheeks against me. I am cold and forlorn without.

I would be your buckskin gloves. Clasping your hands tightly wherever you go. Never releasing my grasp of you.

Resting my chin upon her shoulder, I take in the bouquet of her body, warm and milky, together with the scent of cologne, and the lingering musk of our sport.

I raise a languid hand to goose the golden down of her throat. 'Now, Flo, duckling, I'll have those sovereigns. If you please. They've fallen into your boot.'

Oh, those days of enchantment!

A chilling spring morning in the Strand. All is yellow fog. The air is sulphur, overlaid with coffee and ordure. I hear a station master, across the river, command a locomotive with his shrill pea-whistle. There's a clattering of hooves and grinding of steel wheels, but I cannot see the dray as it passes. Across the road, Elsie is chanting the price of lavender. We are home again, bleary-eyed from a night of pleasures.

Our rooms in William IV Street are in ripe disorder. Books, ornaments and clothes are spilled across the floors. For a moment I struggle to understand this measure of mess. How is it that we keep such a disorderly house?

We've been ransacked.

There's few more dispiriting sights for a fellow than to see that some sneak thief has come to snaffle his hard-won earnings, laid clammy hands into the recesses of his privacy, trod hobnailed over his homely places, tearing through the domestic web.

But, no. It weren't a common burglar. Valuables are left. My porcelains stand untouched, yet Florrie's gold ear-rings are crushed where a brutal heel has trod.

Florrie's Springbok has been disembowelled through a gaping belly wound, spilling its innards of horsehair. Its head has been wrenched clean off, and watches us, through incensed red eyes, from its new perch on the mantelpiece.

The bedroom showed worse attentions. A violent knifesman had torn twelve diagonal gashes through the quilt – but found no more than duck feathers.

Florrie squats moist-eyed and silent amidst the tatters of her wardrobe. Every item has been rent or slashed. The floor is spread

150

with split-seamed dresses, footloose boots, armless coats, knotted stockings, brimless bonnets. Strings of lace had been torn from hems. A pair of knickers had gained another vent, lay desecrated at the base of a candlestick. Two corsets had been quartered.

The air is stale with cologne and musk. For all the perfume bottles have been crushed or emptied amid the rags. I stamp my foot and raise a dust-cloud of face powder.

But the quarest thing! Every one of Florrie's silver teaspoons, mementoes of the occasions we've dined out, is twisted, bent or broke. Quare, that.

I turn on my heels and climb the stairs to the loft. The rope is where it was, hanging limp and damp down the side of the water tank. I pull upon the chill strands to raise the box. It is sealed, locked, unmarked. They haven't found what I prize – my secrets and valuables.

Ma Lovesey, my landlady, knew nothing.

'Nothing, Joey.' Her gaze wilts from my chest to her feet, never having risen so high as my eyes. She holds the door between us, so she can keep me out on the landing if I turn quarrelsome or piqued.

'So you ain't let anyone in my rooms?'

'No, Joey. You said I mustn't, ever.'

'And you didn't hear anything, ma?'

'Only the rats, Joey. And the wind rattling the panes.'

Florrie rocks doleful amidst the rent rags of her fashion. She shakes her lovely auburn head.

'It's only ownings, Flo. They don't matter half so much as our necks.'

Shopping cheered us. We purchased a spanking fresh start. Florrie replaced her wardrobe and procured a spinet. Neither of us could play the beast. But it were a pretty piece for the parlour; with its ivory keys and rosewood cover. Then, to ice the cake, Florrie bought a selection of mirrors which, she promised, do really furnish a home.

Abed, I nuzzle her ear and stroke her tresses, and think to broach the several issues.

'Flo, duckling. The world's a wicked, deceitful place. And people can be properly spiteful. . . . We're making more 'n our share of enemies. Barely a day goes by but someone says you flimped him or I've duffed him. . . . And it's a rare thing to find a faithful friend, unless you buy a puppy and train him. . . .

'So it strikes me, Flo, we've got the same problem and might reach out for the same solution. . . . We both need a package to love, and a parcel to love us in return. Else we're nothing but skin bags, Flo, porkers waiting their turn for the butcher's knife, flies on rotting meat, fleas meeting and mating on a patch of cat, trash in the gutter of life.'

'Is that so, Joey?' She snuffles, rolling over to watch my sentimental eyes.

'So I thought, Flo . . .' I kiss the tip of her nose '. . . that seeing we share lodging, and a bed, and are fond and the like, and enjoy similar pastimes, and both work in the same profession . . .'

'Yes, Joey?' She raises her brows, teasing with her smile.

'That, if you took a fancy to the notion . . .'

'Yes, Joey. Tell!'

'That we could do worse . . .'

'Yes?'

'Than choose to love each other.' I blurt it out and blush. 'And be redeemed by it.'

She traces a languid finger down my nose to the split of my lips: 'What would be different, then, Joey?'

'We'd speak the truth to each, Flo. You'd trust me. I'd trust you. We'd spill our secrets. We'd be proper partners.'

'Love,' she sighs. 'Truth and trust.' She savours the words on her palate. 'Proper partners.' Then she smiles.

'A bargain?'

'A bargain, Joey?' she giggles. 'Between duffers?'

We shook hands on it there and then.

'Truth to tell, whoever ransacked our rooms, Flo, was trying to teach you a lesson.'

'How do you reckon that?' She raises herself against the headboard and pulls the quilt to her chin.

'They searched me, but they savaged you.'

'Savaged?'

'Tore, ripped, slashed, bent, gashed – in effigy, through your clothes and spoons. Disfigured you.'

'Who'd want to hurt me so?'

'Tell me, Flo. What have you done that I don't know of?'

She'd flimped some men, she said.

A surgeon who lived in Gower Street; a scribbler in Eaton Place; a cleric who had rooms in Dean's Yard.

'Think, Florrie. Are there others?'

A parliamentarian who took her to Vauxhall Gardens; a man with a bulbous nose on a Brighton train; a lawyer from Gray's Inn whose name began with M or W; a captain of the Welsh Guards; a painter without a sot worth taking . . . and divers men from several professions.

'The earl, Florrie?'

'Earl?'

'The flash Clarence at Boulogne Races.'

'Were he an earl? The cheeky fellow. He told me he traded horses.'

'What did you take from him?'

'Just a wallet, and a pocket-book that came away with it. He got frisky, so I left him smartish. There was forty pounds odd in the wallet . . . and a letter. Scented – Nuits de Luxur.'

'What did the letter say, Flo?'

'Jasus, Joey! I didn't look. I don't read a gentleman's letters.'

'Well, Flo. There's someone as means you some harm.'

'There's a Jack Gumm . . .' she observes.

'Tell me, Flo. I know his name.'

'I know things about him that I shouldn't.'

'What, Flo?'

'He fixes races.'

'The world knows that, Flo.'

'He's got plans for the Epsom Derby.'

'Flo! Tell!' Ain't she a fount of wisdom. Knowing in advance is a different matter.

'He's got two horses that look the spit of each other, on account of them having the same mamma and pappa. One's a dud and one's a flier. And he's sold the flier saying it was the dud.'

'Why, Flo?'

'He made the new owner promise to run him in the Derby. Does that make sense?'

'It does, Flo. He can bet on a likely winner at the odds they'd give on a milk-horse. He'll be planting the money now.'

'Then we can bet on him too, Joey! If I can remember the name.'

'His best horse is Clarion. Clapperclaw has the same dam and sire?'

'Clapperclaw!' shrieks Florrie. 'That's the nag he spoke of. Ain't we clever? Shan't we be rich!'

A fellow shouldn't pry. Every package deserves its secrets. Only we've become partners. And tonight is a time of revelations.

I should like to be told of the locket. For in the flux of Florrie, in the kaleidoscope of clothes and ornaments, there's one fixed nugget as never leaves her. A gold heart-shaped locket on a fine belcher chain. When she slumbers it rocks and quivers to her breath, snug in that niche above her breastbone, shaded by a tendon of her neck.

The chappie has opened the enigma while she slept and pondered the twin conundrums within. In the right ventricle there's coarse, lustrous curly hairs locked behind blue glass. On the left there's an italic inscription—

F.F. and P.K.F. 4th July 1856. And eternity.

'This, Flo?' I prod her secret casket, which shudders about her lowered neck.

'A keepsake.'

'It could have been a present. From husband to wife say, from a P to his Florence.'

'Curiosity'll kill you, Joey.'

'Are you married, Flo? Are you another man's wife?'

'Not so as you'd notice, Joey.'

But I had noticed. She was married, I knew, to a moist-eyed, moon-faced, pot-bellied grocer on Whitechapel Road. By the name of Percy Fox. First I knew, she'd take herself to the shop on Thursday afternoons, to see to the welfare of her daughter

Polly. Now, she's started calling in on other days. She smiles at the grocer. I've seen her do it.

I dog her there, and follow her back. She ain't never seen me, skulking thereabouts. I don't mention our excursions.

Man and woman must trade with tact.

Grace and Fortune

It's hard to credit the fog of deceits and clouds of dupery that veil the inner workings of a horse-race from the credulous eyes of the punter. Why, Derby day makes a Commons debate or a rat match seem a fair and innocent contest.

There's switching and nobbling, bribing and doping, conning and conniving. Men of all classes assemble for sociability's sake, and for the pleasures of cheating each other over the motions of nags.

And if Dobbin could talk, what tales he might tell. Only I suppose he'd swish his tail, regard you with his moist, candid eyes and, swearing through his eye-teeth, say 'neigh, it were an honest race, squire.' For he'd have been promised a twist of barley-sugar, romp with a dappled filly or sackful of oats. Besides, he wouldn't want them to geld him.

The master had a system for ranking deceits, according to their honour and art. He didn't flatter the chicaneries of the turf. It's an honest duffer, he observed, who'll cheat a man to his face, rather than lurk behind the flanks of a horse.

The lowest form of deceit, said the master, was the bare-arsed lie. All a fellow need do is twist his lips and issue a small gust of breath. It's as artful as breaking wind. A man should be as proud of lying in society as of farting at the opera; so the master said.

Above the lie – but just – comes the collusion. Two men lie in concert and orchestrate their burps.

Next comes fishing, in its several forms. You don't need to be a sage to dangle a worm to land a flounder, but there's a pleasing morality to it. A greedy fellow eyes a helpless, wriggling chappie

156

and resolves to eat him for luncheon. But no sooner is the bait in his mouth than he finds himself caught; that he himself is another's supper.

Beyond this, there's juggling, legerdemain, magic, business and preaching. At least there's a morsel of art to it. For it ain't every man that can palm an ace, quote the Book of Proverbs, sell firewood in August, or discover a goose egg from a lady's nose which her senses hadn't told her was there.

Then – proposed the master – comes science, spoofing, leg-pulling, cricket, wit and hoaxing. There's an honour of motive to these deceits. The duffer's doing it for sheer passion or pleasure, not for mere monetary gain.

Above all these lesser connivances lie the grander forms of deceit. There's fraud, hocus-pocus, sophistry, jiggery-pokery, politics, hanky-panky, perfidy and honest duffing. There's a deal more to these than meets the eyes or greets the ears. Most of the labour must be concealed. To succeed, you must combine art, psychology and scholarship; and gain a moral ascendancy over your mark.

Suppose a duffer stands as Liberal candidate for Eton and Windsor, or markets an embrocation to smooth the wrinkles from ladies' faces, or a paste to regenerate hair on gentlemen's scalps, or tries to sell the shooting rights in Hyde Park to a Moscovite Count . . . then there's a deal of work to be done, afore you can hope to succeed. You must descend the deep mines of morality, to quarry your clients' voices. For the scam will depend on a full ethical audit and diagnosis: and its completion must preach the virtues. Then, the fellow must artfully contrive appearances – his own façade, and those of the world. All must be based on rigorous research and scholarly method.

When you play your hand, and lay the trap, you offer the sucker a sporting chance. For if the mark knows more of the matter than you, can see beyond the glare in the window of appearance, and ain't preoccupied with his own reflection, knows his vices, subdues his greed or vanity, doesn't seek to purchase what cannot be bought, then he won't be suckered. He won't vote for you, smear your patent potion on his skin, applaud your chorus, or open his heart or wallet to you.

*

So Clarion was running under Clapperclaw's name. Would I bet on him? I wager I would. For I'd trust him to beat the field eight romps in ten. And his odds were twenty-eight to one. So he were the nearest to a certainty you'd hope to find – and at the price of a rank outsider.

It pleased me that I should make money from Jack Gumm's labour. I reckoned he owed us – Florrie and I.

Placing fly bets is a deft, delicate gesture – like lifting the fob watch from a sleeping bully. If you move too jerkily, or lay too heavy a touch, you'll wake the bruiser from his slumber.

I needed to place a sizeable sum without raising alarm. If I slapped a thousand pounds on the counter, there'd be suspicions. The bookies would sniff a scam. At the least, the odds would shorten.

Anyways, I'd need to lay the money in small packets – so each could afford to pay me my winnings. It's a paradox that to fleece the bookie, you must protect his purse. If he owes you all his money, he'll only scarper, or have you fitted for an eternal waistcoat.

I pondered the dilemma awhile, then resolved that the wisest procedure was to act the glock.

I chose those houses I haven't traded in before.

'Excuse me, sir, is this one of those emporia in which an honest man can win a fortune by staking small money on a race?'

'You can lay a bet, at least,' says the surly clerk.

'On horses?'

'Especially on horses,' says he.

'Then I am resolved to bet on Clawhammer to win the Derby.'

'Ain't no such runner.'

'There must be, sir. My wife dreamed last night that a horse of that name would win the race.'

'Still ain't a Clawhammer.'

'Then a horse of similar name. Is there a Sledgehammer, perhaps, sir? A Mallet? Or a Gavel?'

He shakes his disdainful head.

'Not even a Maul, sir? Or a Peen? Hammerhead or Cudgel? Or Clapper?'

'There's a Clapperclaw.'

'Clapperclaw!' I exclaim ecstatically. 'That's surely the winner. Wouldn't you say so, sir? And its name begins with a "C", too. Mary Ann is never mistaken. Not when she's asleep.'

'Then bet on him, boy. There's handsome odds.'

'What's odd about him?' I demand to be told.

The clerk explains with terse ill-humour.

'Then, sir, if I bet a penny on him and he wins, you'll pay me two shillings and fourpence? And give me back my original penny? Surely that ain't fair on you, sir?'

'I'll take the chance,' says he.

'Then I shall stake him here and now. How is the contract transacted? Do we need a notary? Is there stamp duty to pay?'

'No, boy. You put your hand in your pocket. I give you a card as receipt. How much should you like to stake?'

'One hundred and six pounds,' I declare proudly.

'A hundred and six! On Clapperclaw!'

'Sir!' I protest stiffly. 'My wife is a very perspicacious dreamer. She dreamed I should become a double-entry book-keeper, and that she should become pregnant of a baby. And each time before it happened. . . . So I'm resolved to stake my inheritance. When Mary Ann dreams it, it comes to pass.'

The clerk retires to consult his master. I hear mutters and scoffs. The bookie leaves his desk to come out and stare at me. I dare say my wide-eyed smile reassures him.

'It's a lot of money,' says the clerk, 'but we can oblige you.'

So I heave the fat wadge of notes from my pocket, lick my fingers, then count the sum and lay it on the oak counter.

With a sorry shake of his head the bookie checks the money before passing me my stake-card.

I played a variant of the scene in seven different shops in London and three in Brighton. I swear each bookie took me for a glock. A few were kind enough to glance on me with pity. One cautioned me to lodge the money in a bank instead.

So it was done and the money laid. Florrie and I need not

159

worry for our future. I dare say nothing is certain in life. But Clarion carried my confidence.

We're stowed abed early, that night before the race – snug as two pigs in their wallow, or rabbits in their burrow. Life can be a fine thing.

Two bottles of champagne lie empty, forlorn, tinsel torn, on the rug, alongside a carcass of a duck. Some grease from this bird lies as a golden sheeny smear on Florrie's lips, lit by the flickering glow from the dying fire.

'All gone,' observes Florrie, rustling the wrappers in a tin of *petits fours*. 'Ain't marzipan a charming stuff?'

'Another brandy?' say I.

'Sir, you'll make a lady tiddly,' but she jiggles her fluted glass before me.

I lick the spillage of cognac from her chest. It tastes better and different there – warmed by her flesh, mixed with the salts of her skin.

Bless her, she's dribbled. So I snaffle up the trickle down her chin with a languid sweep of my tongue.

'Home is a fine place,' say I, 'God bless this house.'

'There ain't much worth doing that you can't do in bed,' observes Florrie. 'Shall you pass me an orange?'

I feel the acid spits of juice on my neck as she struggles to undress the fruit, wrestling the rind, pinching and tearing her way through. The citrus scent lies pretty as perfume over the tang of our hot moist bodies.

'When we're rich . . .' I stroke her satin flank.

'How rich, Joey?'

'Thirty thousand, seven hundred and fifty-four pounds.'

'That's a deal of pigeon pies and roast chestnuts,' says she.

'To Clarion,' I propose. We clink our glasses.

'To Clapperclaw, bless him,' Florrie squeals.

'Another brandy, Flo?'

'As it's a celebration, Joey, I'll concede to take another. And shall you pass me the almonds and the nutcrackers?'

'When we're in the money, Flo, we could take life easier.

I shouldn't have to write any more. And you needn't flimp gentlemen's watches.'

'Or suppose I carried on flimping,' says Flo. 'It'd just be for the sport of it.'

'You could have a new gown each day, Flo. When our horse comes home.'

'I've got a new dress, for the races tomorrow, Joey boy.' She slithers up against the headboard, pulling the quilt from our chests, scattering almond shells. 'Shall I show you?'

She shall. For she slides from the sheet and topples to the boards. Rising, swaying, she walks an unsteady arc to the wardrobe, tugging open the doors which shudder on their hinges.

Her plush thighs and rump catch the dancing light from the hearth. There's a tearing of wrappings, then a rustle of crêpe paper.

'There!' She turns, clutching a marigold taffeta dress to her, then staggers some circles, her tresses aswirl. So I see her buff and covered, naked and clothed.

'It's grand, Flo. If you've got to wear clothes, you couldn't have found finer. Only you're choicer raw.'

Which is the very truth of it. To this fellow's taste and sight. For there ain't no fabric to compare to her sleek, satin skin. And I worship her like this – as midnight knows her.

The dark embraces her; moonlight languishes upon her chest; the night stirs her unlit places, hugs the taper of her waist, snuggles between her thighs, shades her curves, shadows her swells, caresses the slopes of breast, clings in her crevices.

When she turns her back I see the sign of the cross, joyous to this sinner's eyes, drawn upon her in ebony. Across in the crease between her buttocks and thighs: its length in the sinuous curves along her spine through the cleft of her rump down the fine, wedge split of her legs.

Florrie, joy of Joey's desiring. The Lord lays his gifts where man shall find them.

'Come abed, Florrie. I'm feeling reverent.'

So she drops the bodice of her dress to expose her chest, and shrugs her shoulders, causing wicked judders to her breasts.

'Come, Flo. I wish to pray upon you.'

And she topples, giggling upon me.

I dare say all men know this time. Theology is made flesh. Arcane truths are inscribed between thighs; the purse of wisdom is opened to him; he finds axioms of logic manifest in hips; each thrust presents a new postulate of stupefying beauty; and the giddying calculus claims his mind. He is as old as liturgy. Clever as Newton. Profound as Proverbs. Witty as Disraeli. Inventive as Mozart. Urgent as a maelstrom. Vehement as Vesuvius. For he has a timeless truth to tell. There is something he must express. A matter he must spill.

And he wakes to find himself at nooky. Panting, trickling sweat. Thrusting like a mad 'un. His belly makes a ripping sound as it tears itself up from the lady's. And he ain't as noble as his reverie bragged. And the spirit that moved him was cognac.

'Gently, Joey. What's your hurry?'

'Epi . . .' I gasp, '. . . phany, Florrie.'

'What's that?'

'Divine, Flo. I've had an experience.'

'That's nice for you, Joey.' There's a puzzlement on her brow. 'I ain't. Not yet, I haven't. Not a spasm.'

She shouldn't come to the races, I know. There'll be fellows there that'll want to harm her – Jack Gumm, the earl, others maybe.

I thought to dose her brandy with laudanum, so she'd sleep through to tea-time. But it wouldn't be proper to treat a partner so. And it'd break her heart to stay away: to show her dress down City Road, instead of on Epsom Downs.

I dare say there'd be concealment for us in the throng. Last year – some reckoned – there were four hundred thousand legs at the Derby, and that weren't counting the horses.

She lies candid in her slumber. There's a pout to her lips, twitch to her nose. Her auburn mane coils and curls across the pillow towards me – dark chestnut in the gloom, save for those tresses glimmering in the moonglow. For a strip of light falls between the curtains, slicing our bed.

162

'Er . . . aar . . . eee.'

She whimpers softly as though in a stifled protest. Then, she catches her breath.

'Percy!' she sighs.

I stroke her tresses. The filaments crackle and rise to my touch – charged and charmed. There are gurgles from her belly. Her chest heaves to an uneven rhythm. My lips graze her brow and send her closed lids aflutter. Every part of her is alert: and none of her is conscious.

Florrie, duckling, I was a base and squalid man. Before I was redeemed by the love of you. The master would be proud of me. If he could see me now.

Ah! Her freckles. Amber constellations scattered through the creamy firmament. Down her cheeks, cheeky on the ridge of her nose, perky on the curves of her nostrils, brazen on her brow, basking in celebrity. There's a gregarious swarm, favoured in the flat of her chest. Some luminaries straggle the swells of her breasts. There's a fat braggart sprawled on her belly. Vigilantes stand secret watch on the inner slopes of her thighs. There ain't a place I've visited on her that a freckle didn't find first. And all of them belong, and take their place in the divine design. I'm nifty with figures, but I'm flummoxed to count 'em all. I tried once. But I'd got no further than her neck when I was forced to concede to infinity.

Her nipples have flattened, retiring for the night into their crimson bedding.

Her belly quivers and tightens as I whisper to the golden downy hairs – teasing them with my breath.

Florrie parts her legs. I reach down to lay my hand in the splay. So my fingers flatten the springy tufts and part the warm, wet gape.

'Scuse me, Flo! For she rolls away with a snuffle. Wriggling her rump, she turns her back upon me. It's a poignant vista. Lovely as her front, yet more mysterious. There's a gullet-grasping, breathtaking, melancholy-making, aching sadness to naked backs. The long groove, nobbled with spine. The wistful rumour of her breath. A tormented, submitting, twitch to her shoulder-blades. Those ridges of rib – showing the naked frailty of the fleshy fullness of her. Twin shaded hollows before the proud salience of rump. The chasmic cleft of buttocks. The still, solemn monument of hip: a profound and mighty arch, fashioned from those long, smooth curves of her.

Oh, Flo! The scents of your liquescence. I should be bee to your bloom; sucking the secret saps and juices, my darting tongue clandestine between your pink petals.

The heady blend! Piquant sauce; gamy relish; tangy twang; fruity ripeness; honeyed musk; spicy syrup; foxy balm. Acrid and ambrosial.

When I have my fortune I shall commission Monsieur Corot to try to paint your likeness, then have Monsieur Florix bottle your intimate scent.

So I lie some uncounted hours, snuggled to her, my lips on the small of her back. I am giddied and drunk on her, lost in grace.

At dawn, I secrete a pellet of paper in her locket – telling her where I have hidden the betting slips. Lest we become parted.

It'll be the knell for us, I know, if her grocer husband comes between us. But she won't leave me – now we have our fortune.

She could part the world like this, she's said, lost in my arms to take the big sleep.

'Florrie,' I whisper to her sleeping head, 'I'd give up my very life for you.' And I stroke her lovely speckled nape. 'I'd swing for you.' Say I.

Derby Day

I am rendering the final deceits to my face, regarding myself in the chest-top mirror, when I see the body beneath the quilt wriggle awake. She stretches and, languorous as a tabby, yawns a smile at my back.

'Good morning, duckling,' say I.

'Jasus!' She spies the reflection of my earnest face, refashioned for this Derby Day.

'Me, Flo. Ain't you never seen me in beard and spectacles before?'

'Joey! I ain't used to waking with strange men.'

'I look older, Flo. Don't I just? And different I dare say.'

'Like a demented fishmonger, Joey. Or a rogue preacher. Take that hair from your chin. I ain't escorting no Esau.'

'It's flesh of my flesh now, Flo. Glued to me with Hattersley's Patent Fixative, as never comes unstuck. And I've figured it for a disguise. . . . And you, Flo – you'd better wear a veil.'

'A veil!' she spits, cheeks wrinkled and nose hunched. So she looks sour and contemptuous as that camel in Regent's Park Gardens. The one that curls his upper lip and tries to gob in your face when you proffer him a candied tea-cake. 'If I wear a veil, the folks shan't see my pretty face.'

There ain't no agreeing. She won't conceal herself. I surely shan't shed my beaver. So, muttering, we both don our fancy dress.

I look dowdy, dingy and drab as a mouse in my dusty bowler and faded grey serge frock-coat. Florrie's a florid ostentation. It's clear she aims to be noticed. I dare say she'll frighten the horses.

For she's the spit of a titanic ambulant daffodil blossom – in her cadmium yellow flounced dress, flame hair capped by a gold straw titfer sporting crocus-coloured ostrich feathers.

We wave down a carriage at the peak of Whitehall. Fig the expense, I'm a wealthy man. I'm damned if I'm going to hang my head through the window of the Derby Special, have my shoulders used as a luggage rack for some matron's hamper, entertain five elbows on my chest, or have some sixpence-a-day clerk exhale the smoke of his ha'penny cheroot in my ear. I ain't a snobbish chappie, but a fellow must think to his position and comforts.

'Got no manners, man?' slurs the cabbie. 'Got no eyes? This lady hailed me first.'

'We're together,' say I.

'Together, indeed!' He tips back his cap and considers the rum conundrum. His red rheumy eyes mock us in turn. 'Not Epsom, I don't suppose. I shouldn't think you'd trouble me to carry you to Epsom.'

'The Derby,' I agree.

He rubs his blue jowls with his fat brown knuckles. He adopts the regretful unfocussed gaze of a professional mourner. 'If I was to take you, I shouldn't be back afore evening. Not with the crowds, the roads and all.'

'Come, man!' say I. 'You'll be going anyway. I'll be paying you to take yourself.'

'Eighteen miles,' he observes. He looks forlornly to his nags who gaze dolefully back at him. There's resignation writ in three limpid eyes. One poor Dobbin is one-eyed.

'Four pounds,' I offer, 'and I'll pay the toll onto the Downs. And tell you the name of the winner.'

'Sulphur,' the cabbie observes, 'he'll stroll it with Titch on board.'

'A fair horse. A fine jockey. But Clapperclaw has the beating of 'im.' I wink.

'Clapperclaw,' he spits some brown stuff to my feet, 'or my nag Nelson here.'

'A deal?'

'If I was to take you,' he drawls, 'we'd need to stop in Kennington to collect my lunch and brother.'

*

The world and granny are off to the race. Parliament's adjourned for the day. Factory gates are bolted. The striped blinds are pulled down in barbers' windows. In Berwick Ground Market the stalls stand empty and abandoned, sodden and weeping from their dawn drenching. The costers will be trading at Epsom. Alongside our carriage, matching our pace and eyeing us amiably, two stray dogs pad purposefully. The hounds are coming too.

At Nine Elms and at Waterloo there'll be mêlées of artisans, battling for a sight of the station gates, then brawling for positions on the platforms. The apprentices will walk. Gentlefolk and professionals – the likes of Flo and I – are packed in traps and carriages. A continuous snaking chain, muzzle to box-seat, round the Elephant, through Clapham, Merton, Morden, all the way to Epsom.

Two hundred thousand people. With an average height of five feet three inches.

'If you laid us all end to end, scalp to toe, Flo, all of us as are going to the Derby, we'd reach one hundred and ninety-eight miles, one thousand five hundred and nineteen yards, two feet, nine and a half inches.'

'Is that so, Joey? And how'd you get them to lie down in the wet, then? And where'd you find the ruler long enough to measure 'em?'

She's got a practical mind has Florrie. It provides ballast for my flights of fancy.

We rest at the Swan in Clapham. Our nags sink their heads in bags of oats. Their master takes three pints of porter. Florrie and I have breakfast. Pigeon pie washed down with a burgundy.

This sustains us so far as the Cock at Sutton. The horses have no more than water; their groom cheers himself with stout. Florrie and I take an early lunch of veal, tongue, beef, salad, dressed crab, smoked eel and some hocks.

On the road again, I set myself to work on Dorling's Derby Race Card. Thirty-four runners. Sulphur and Gladiator are joint favourites. There are two horses – Brown Gown and Imperial Sherbet – I don't know of. Brown Gown is ridden by Harry Dye,

167

who's too good a mount for a trash nag when he's sober, and too risky when he's lushed. Rumour is he's reformed and don't mix his whisky with riding no more.

Then we're at the Spread Eagle in Epsom Town. The fraternity gathers here – bookmakers, owners, trainers, jockeys and bruisers.

There ain't no trouble knowing who is what. The flash top-hatted gents are the owners, swaddled from the rabble by their retinues. Those jerky dwarves, with haggard faces and wasted frames, are the jockeys. There's fear etched in their faces.

Bookies pace the yard, chanting numbers, speaking tongues, declaiming to the heavens, like mad mystics.

Most money's riding on Sulphur. Gladiator has slipped. Guinea Piece is gaining ground. Black Bonny is out of the shadows. Clapperclaw has shortened to twenties – which causes some wry remarks and puzzlement.

Some horses are passing by in their boxes. A cheer goes up for Sulphur. He snorts through a window in the planking. You can hear the eager clatter of his hooves on the timber. There's a cordon of minders slouching alongside, lest anyone thinks to toss him a poisoned carrot or scare him with a thunderflash. He shan't be nobbled in public.

Yet I'm taken by the box behind. For there's something to the strip of speckled flank as commands a fellow's attentive admiration. I am touched by the sight. I know awe, respect, then fear. Promptly I feel cheated. For I see a pricked ear through the strips of boarding. And, as the box draws level, a bold, mischievous brown eye regards me. Then winks.

Anonyme. Anonyme, the flier at Boulogne races. I won on this nag. Now he's set to cheat me.

Two ringers. Not one. A scam on the scam. Ain't folk dishonest? Plain deceitful. The Earl. His owner. And him with a silver spoon and Fanny Larkspur.

'Who's that?' I shout at the driver, 'who are you carting, matey?'

'Brown Gown,' says he, disdainful. 'Tis clear he feels demeaned by his passenger. 'Last year I had Musjid.'

'I'll back him then. Maybe you bring 'em luck.'

I've got a thousand riding on Clarion. And I'd rate Anonyme to beat him by four or five seconds. Which don't augur well for my fortune.

First cover yourself, Joey boy! That's my injunction to myself.

But I don't have the serious money to back him. I've no more than a hundred pounds about me. His odds are forty to one. I'll win no more than four thousand. And a quarter of that'll be loss on Clarion. And Flo and I had set our hearts on a fortune. To bring us comfort and leisure.

First cover yourself, Joey.

'Who'll give me Brown Gown?' My voice cracks and trembles.

'Hundred to thirty,' shouts Sly.

Quick, Joey. He's shortening.

'For a hundred?'

'Done.'

We shake on it. Sly Hobbes and I.

'Got some fancy for him, have you?'

'Sentiment,' say I. But he looks hurt and reproachful. He suspects but he don't know. And it ain't his way to decline a hundred pounds. Not on a no-hoper. Not fresh banknotes.

Now, Joey? What shall you do? Sell my watch and Florrie's jewels, to raise more stake? No. I shan't raise enough to make a difference.

You've covered the nag. Now try to stop him.

How?

Tell!

The Earl? The Jockey Club? Sly Hobbes? Leviathan Brown?

No. Jack Gumm. We've interest in common.

'Boy! Here's a shilling. Find the fattest man in the lounge and give him this. Tell him where to find me.'

I scribble a word and fold the paper. 'Ringer,' it says.

When the boy's inside, I take myself to the other side of the yard, and retire behind a pillar. In case Jack Gumm don't know a kindness when it's poked beneath his nose.

And in complicity with shadows, I realize how the business might be done. Don't nobble the pretty horse. Douse his lush of a jockey.

My supposition was right. There wasn't a stouter party than Jack Gumm. Not in the lounge. He's coming alone. Nimble and awesome fast, considering his bulk. Purple-faced, cutting a clean swathe through the small tumbling people. The boy runs panting in his wake.

I saunter out, compelling myself to boldness, trusting to the concealment of beard and unfancy dress.

'S'im,' declares the boy, 'as called you fatty.'

'Ringer,' whispers Jack Gumm, clutching the tip of my nose in the vice of thumb and finger. 'Ain't no ringer. And I'll crumple a man as says different.' He presses his chest into my face. It ain't just his solid mass that impresses, for he whiffs as sour sweet and strong as a stable when it's first opened in the morning.

'Brown Gown,' I splutter, into his steamy shirt front, 'is a Frenchy horse called Anonyme. He's got the beating of Clarion.'

He shuffles back to glare on me. The veins on his brow are thick as pipe stems. 'What's Clarion to do with it?'

'You own him,' I observe him. 'He's the fastest I know in England. But this nag's quicker. Four, five seconds, over the Derby distance.'

'Suppose . . . what's it to me?'

'Same as to me, I dare say. Our stakes are on another runner. My money's on Clapperclaw.'

'Why tell me?'

'You've got the wherewithal to better the cheat. Scupper the scam, sir.'

'How would I do that?'

'The jockey's a lush, sir. If a fellow was to lead him to his first few tipples, I suppose he'd find several more hisself. It's just a matter of re-acquainting him with the bottle. For, currently, he's lapsed from the booze. But I've seen him ride drunk, sir. He don't think as cute nor steer so straight. Sometimes he rides a different course to the other jockeys.'

'Suppose . . .' says Jack Gumm, 'there'd be a fellow in the know, to tell the tale.'

'Who?' I ask.

'You, man,' says he.

'Not me, sir. I'd be vanished with my winnings.' And I step back a pace, then saunter away, leaving him watching me with a scowl on his raw face. I dare say he's forgotten how to smile.

I've done the business as best I can. But ain't I forgotten something?

Florrie!

Find the lady, Joey!

'Gone off with a gent,' says the cabbie. 'Told me to tell you she'd meet you at the Grand Stand.'

'What gent?'

'Topper and tails. Finer manners than some I know.'

I pay him off.

On a clear day on the Downs, there shouldn't be any difficulty in spotting a yellow woman against the lush greens. But on Derby Day you can't see further than the next fellow's bowler or his lady's bonnet.

Thread your way through the throng and you meet a crowd – cheering at the bare-chested lady boxers, heckling the minstrels, jostling at the canvas booths for luncheon of baked meats, pummelling a prostrate pickpocket, jeering the puppeteers, grappling a coy constable free of his navy breeches, wrestling for entry to a beer tent, ogling the portraits of celebrated murderers.

Florrie! Flo! Ain't you a reckless one. This ain't no place for a solitary lady.

And suppose she stoops to dip a pocket! If the crowd nabs you, they ain't forgiving as a court. And if a constable has you, you're up before the magistrate in the Grand Stand, and off to Coldbath Fields afore you've passed the post.

You wouldn't believe the vulgarity of the mass. There's bright yellow judies in every gathering. Turn a circle, I spy seven. Ain't none of them my lovely.

I pay my five shillings to enter the Grand Stand. It's most parts gentry here. Should be fewer women dressed as daffodils.

I swear I glimpsed her above in the first balcony, swaying a tipsy path down the aisle of seats. Yet when I reach there, she's gone. And she ain't in any of the booths in the refreshment room, nor in the Grand Salon.

I work with method, from left to right, circling the rooms, peering at any woman in yellow. On the stairs to the second floor I'm made delirious by the sight of auburn hair pinned high above an ivory neck and yellow frilled collar.

'Flo, duckling,' I sigh, blowing on the nape of her neck, reaching for her elbow.

The lady squealed. Her escort shook me by the lapels. Some bystanders mutter about my manners.

'Don't you remember me, lady?' say I, to cover my confusion. 'I'm a chum of your brother's. What's the scallywag doing these days? Still grappling?'

'Sir ...' says she, her face shot scarlet, 'Alfred is still Viceroy. Thomas is still deceased.'

Furk the fancy folk! If they want to keep themselves to themselves, they shouldn't parade in public. We all make mistakes. And there ain't no shame in having a wrestler for a brother.

I'll have to find you later, Flo. There's roars and whistles from the ring. The nags are being led out.

Sulphur's a handsome fellow, the glossy prancer, calm and proud. Guinea Piece is skittery behind his blinkers.

Brown Gown's a choice, lean, glistening nag. And a part of his class is horse sense. For he keeps pricking then dropping his ears, turning his rippling neck to blink at his rider. He shivers and bucks.

Jack Gumm's done it, bless him!

Henry Dye sits ramrod straight, eyes tight focussed on the distance. You can see him twitch his lips to blaspheme at his horse. He's a practised drunk, versed in the deceit of acting sober. But the saddle of a shying horse is a precarious perch – when you're fair piddled – and he's stiff and tight to stay in the upright. I dare say he'll be harder pushed when Brown Gown speeds from his trot to a gallop.

Clapperclaw looks fair enough. Appearances are fearful fibbers. You'd be flushed with pride to ride him hunting. Only he don't look the Derby winner. Still there's enough faith in him in stake money for him to have dropped to fifteen to one.

He swishes his tetchy tail as he follows the others, cantering from view, round Tattenham Corner towards the start.

You don't know more than the distant roar of the crowds, which rises to crescendo then falls, then swells shriller in the shrieks and whistles of derision.

Four false starts.

Then you know they're away to a level start. The roar holds then grows, building towards us at the speed of the nags.

A horse rounds Tattenham clear. He's half a furlong down the straight before the following group have turned. And there ain't no mistaking his grace and ease, the stretched neck above the pounding pull of his forelegs. It's Anonyme. And he'll stroll it. Only he ain't got a rider.

Looking straight down the course, you see the effort but not the speed. The legs are stretching, throwing turf to the air, the necks rise and fall to the rhythm of the gallop. It seems there are six in a line. Half a minute and they seem barely nearer. Frozen in their frenzy. As though they'll never reach us, sentenced to an eternal race.

Clapperclaw by half a length, whipped hard, wet black and frothing. Guinea Piece two lengths before Sulphur.

It ain't a popular result. Too many have lost.

Now, Flo, let's be having you. Let's commence our ecstasy. Come, lady. Show yourself. We'll take a brace of bottles of fizz. Then we'll think to our pleasures.

I've done him a favour and won him a pretty packet, but Jack Gumm ain't smiling as he crosses the ring towards me. He beckons me with an arm. I look around me. He points me out to his two companions. Bruisers. I drop down below the rails. Through the slats I see them break into a run. They ain't slouches. I'm no athlete.

Calm yourself, Joey! I hear my master's words – when you're being followed, it's better to walk than run.

I rip the jacket from my back. Tread my glasses into the turf. The beard comes away with some skin. I stand up and straddle the fencing. Then stride-walk calmly towards them. The thugs jostle past me, searching for a different-looking chappie . . .

Jack Gumm eyes me different, now I'm bare-faced Joey Blueglass. And though he's grunting purposefully, in earnest pursuit of another, he can't resist a passing comment.

'Can't stop,' says he, 'but I ain't forgot. I'll take a knife to you when I've got the leisure.'

I pause, watching the ripples to his retreating bullock back.

Thirty thousand pounds in winnings. And I ain't a penny in my pocket – threw it away with my jacket.

I need to be scarce. I don't know the measure of Jack Gumm's malice or leisure. If I ain't a rogue preacher no more, I'm Joey Blueglass with blood upon his chin, spilling down his shirt. I don't need no sharks to sniff my gore. There ain't nothing like a wounded chappie to entice the carnivores.

And where, I ponder, is Florrie?

She's at hazard. Else she's left me. She ain't home. Our rooms ain't been visited. She ain't dunked herself in the Font, nor moistened herself in the Wheatsheaf.

Where'd she go? My daffodil. Where'd she bolt, my duckling? Where'd she find seclusion?

Supposing a fellow had snatched her pretty person? Or she'd set up shop with a grocer? Or left me for some other?

Does she love another?

Don't even whisper it. Stifle the mouth that says so. Strike it out of mind. Throttle the thought. Take a stranglehold on that cold shoulder. Perish the thought. Twist it from your deceiver's head. Nip the faithless flower in the bud. Consign it to oblivion.

The truth, Joey, lies in the secret locket of her heart.

Yes, be calm. Stay quiet and still.

Now, walk awhile, Joey.

Two in the morning, slouching home by boot. Feel sickened of a sudden, skewered by a shaft of fear. Concerning Florrie.

I run a distance, stumble panting, trudge, imagine, vomit, run.

Yes, there's a flicker of flame playing upon our curtains. She's home, my duckling, where she belongs.

The Cut Flower

When a fellow's in the salt-box, waiting his turn to dangle, to be hung out like the washing, he's accorded certain privileges by way of compensation. They allow me pen and paper. And I have benefit of clergy. Chaplain Gully calls daily, enquiring discreetly of my soul. He only lapses from stern but sorry sympathy if I ever plead my innocence. The turnkey calls me by name, not number.

'You're a poor, wicked bastard, Blueglass,' observes my guardian, in his booming whisper, rolling the tips of his moustache to needle points, narrowing his eyes, furrowing his brow, as if I were a more curious sight than he. 'They're going to stretch your neck.' He tells it as a confidential reminder, lest I've forgotten.

And, because of this final, grand correction, I am spared the lesser corrections, meted out to lesser rascals. I need not strip my shins treading the mill, nor stoop in line to ferry cannon balls – which are fearful labours making strong men howl and whimper.

No. If I wish it, I can curl on my pallet like a child, suck my thumb, and sleep the day away.

The morning of my arrest, I trudged the streets alone, pondering, burdened by foreboding. My betting slips are gone and with them Flo. Which I count a colossal compound loss.

I didn't recognize my front door till it struck me in the face.

Some burly fellow quite bars my way on my doorstep. So I

scamper beneath his outstretched arm, and up the flight. I hear him pounding the stairs behind me.

'Joey!' Ma Lovesey shrieks, as I pass her on the landing.

Our door is open. Florrie lies on the chaise, staring at me, wide-eyed.

'Do you know this woman?' asks a fellow sprung to my side. But I don't look to him.

Ain't a woman. Ain't Florrie. It's a limp, dead, cold thing. Ain't my rose. It's a cut flower.

Blood has leaked from an ear. Dried to a flaky rust on her neck. Lip's split, swollen, gaping – mouth within a mouth.

This is a mocking mask. Wide-eyed. Frozen in a bewildered stare. A puppet made in Flo's likeness. The arms don't rest right. The neck's twisted to an unlikely angle, such as a backbone don't allow. Like a toy upon a shelf, taught a lesson, by a peevish child. Then abandoned.

Her legs lie straight, stiff and splayed, like a doll's, along the length of the chaise.

Florrie's a dancing, prancing, squealing package. Lithe as an eel. Ain't this chill porcelain doll.

'Are you Joseph Blueglass?'

I see it's her. I know it ain't.

'I must ask you not to handle her, sir. She counts as material evidence, see.'

She's quite cold and stiff. It's not her flesh, skin of my dreams. It gives to my touch like a boiled ham. The mouth don't twitch, giggle or gurgle. Her cheek retains as a dent the touch of my finger.

Nor her eyes. Neither. Her blue, to be sure, to a tee. But these are still, glassy beads, frozen to a marbled scare.

Florrie don't frighten easy, nor hold an expression. Moods bore her mind and flitter from her face.

That locket's gone from her neck. Strange, what a body notices. There's the links of her chain, bitten purple on the soapy white of her. Someone's torn it from her.

'Is this the woman known as Florence Alice McTaggart?'

'Was,' say I. 'Now her neck's broke.'

Quare, what a skin-bag finds himself saying to another.

'She was a lovely one, living. Makes you weep to see her so.

'Man . . .' says the stranger, looking to me with sympathy, 'you've been in a tussle ain't you? There's skin off your face. Blood down your front.'

'Flo, Flo . . .' say I, 'you ain't safe without me.'

The stranger takes out his pocket-book to jot a note. Licks the end of his stub of pencil, then looks warmly back to me.

'I'd have taken proper care of her. Only she would wander off. I warned her there'd be trouble. But she never heeded a caution. . . . And now she's broken.'

'You were angry,' the man advises.

'She should have stayed with me.'

'You loved her,' he prompts, 'like a mad 'un.'

'She was my duckling. We were proper partners. Promised, we did. Shook hands upon it.'

'. . . hands upon it,' the man observes to his book. 'And now you're sorry,' he suggests.

'Sorry, sorry. Cold and shrunken. Sorry, sorry. Sorry thing. Ain't a use to life without her. . . . And it were in my hands to stop it.'

'. . . my hands,' he writes, compliant to my every word. 'Now is there more you'd wish to tell me, before we go?'

'Go?' say I. 'I must stay with her.'

'There's a place I know,' he offers, 'where there's plenty room for you. And when you're ready, you can speak some more about it. Details and such. . . .'

'Weren't she a lovely one?' say I. 'You can see, can't you? Even now?'

Next morning, I recover some tenure on my being. I wake in a cell upon a straw pallet. 'Tis a relief to find myself here, in a kinder place than my dreams. Only, I find a stout man with a small mind and stubby pencil has mistook me for a murderer. He tells me I've confessed to him.

Vengeance is mine, saith Joey Blueglass. I shall wreak it. Yet a

178

court of law is not the place to gain it. I shall have my justice when I find her killer.

Court number seven, The Old Bailey. Regina versus Blueglass. The murder of Florence Fox. Mr Basil Spurling for the prosecution. His colleague Joseph Blueglass, new to the law but eager, represents himself. Lord Justice Manning presiding. All be upstanding. Silence in court.

There's a deal of sleights, scams and quirks to the law, as I've discovered – from my perusal of Matthews' Criminal Jurisprudence, vols one and three.

'The accused is acting in his own defence?' The judge slumps forward at his bench, spreading his elbows, displaying his ermine cuffs, to peer down to me, with the condescension a gaudy muscovy duck might award a sombre slug – before snaffling it. He's here for some days. I'm here for my life.

'If you please, your lordship . . . Regina versus Capstick, Rex versus Cannington. . . .' So say I. For we talk in code in the legal profession, citing precedents.

'Very well. How do you plead?'

'My client – myself – is innocent of this murder.'

'We shall record the plea as Not Guilty. The law, in its reason and wisdom, does not allow you to call yourself Innocent.'

'Rex versus Conningsbury?' I ask.

'Regina versus Blueglass,' says he, ignoring this. 'I decide the law in my court. Now . . . Mr Spurling . . .'

. . . is a horse of a man. A stallion of a cart-puller; heavy framed with fat fetlocks bulging neath his spats; the tails of his coat lie tight over his sturdy hocks. His sad brown eyes roll in his broad Dobbin face. He retracts his top lip to display long yellow teeth. The tight wig rides his scalp like the knotted mane of a nag prettied for a show. I dare say he's slow; but he's sure and he's practised. Aside him I'm but a novice, despite my shrewder wit.

The deceased is a Mrs Florence Fox, née McTaggart, of Whitechapel, aged thirty-one years, separated of her husband and six-year-old daughter. She was a woman of good character, not being previously known to the police.

She had suffered blows to the cranium and mouth. Her

head had been twisted through one hundred and ten degrees, parting it from its mounting on her vertebral column, rupturing her spinal chord. This proved fatal.

The forensic doctor spoke numbers describing the inches of her height, pounds of her weight, some vertebrae of her spine, contusions, degrees fahrenheit of her corpse, hours of her demise, rigors of her mortis, years of his experience, date of her death.

I asked him what he made of the chain mark upon her neck.

There was no such mark, he observed, consulting his papers, for his records would have noted it.

'Was it a powerful man that killed her?'

Strong or violent, he observed coldly, with evident distaste for me.

'Was the deceased moved to the chaise after her death?'

'My record does not show this. She might have been. It could have been so.'

'Do you not suppose from her posture . . . ?'

'Are you a doctor, too?' he enquires.

'I have read Brady's *Forensic Pathology*.'

'Then you have been poorly informed by an unreliable source,' he says, gazing lax-eyed towards me. 'Mine is the accepted text.' And, I realize, from the reprimand of his opaque eyes, the expert is near blind. . . .

'Did the deceased have freckles?' I ask.

'My record does not report so.'

'Can you see me, doctor? And do you see how many fingers I have raised to you?'

His eyes wrinkle in scrutiny. There are titters from the public gallery. Lord Justice Manning cautions me on contempt.

Sergeant George Todd of Rochester Row reports the discovery of the corpse. Flicking the pages of his notebook, he reads with jerky passion.

'. . . the accused said he was sorry . . . that it was done by his own hands . . . he had threatened the deceased . . . but she still left him . . . there were bloodstains on his shirt . . . cuts upon his chin . . . "I am a wicked man, Sergeant," said he. "I broke her neck." '

'Had we met before that night, Sergeant?'

'No.'

'So how would I know to address you as "Sergeant"?'

'Ah . . .' he nods and smiles, 'because I would have spoken my name and rank, then cautioned you, as is Proper Police Procedure.'

'But your evidence did not report this.'

He flicks back through his pages: 'No.'

'So how do you know?'

'I remember it clearly. And it's Procedure.'

'Did I attempt to escape?'

'You did not. You came like a tame one,' says he, 'on account of your remorse.'

'It is a difficult profession, catching villains, I suppose?'

'It is.'

'You have to go in pursuit of them, I dare say, rather than wait for them to come to you?'

'That's the way of it,' he agrees with sober regret. 'They don't want to be caught. On account of the consequences,' he explains.

'So it is rare in your experience, Sergeant, that a criminal returns to the scene of the crime to confess to an Officer of Law.'

'Yes,' he agrees. 'Not every felon shows a decent remorse like you and presents himself for arrest.'

'You may be an honest fool,' say I, 'and more a dupe than a perjurer.'

The judge declares starchily that he shall have me removed, unless I mend my ways.

'Regina versus Baker,' say I, 'the Court of Appeal.'

'Silence,' he rages.

'But it's my life,' I protest.

'That's for the court to decide,' says he.

I suppose Ma Lovesey told it as she saw it. Once, she said, I went into a heedless rage. I tore all Florrie's clothes and wrecked the rooms.

'Tell them, Ma. Have you seen me angry?'

'No,' she squeaks. But she's winced, turning to avoid my eyes, as though my gaze might bite her.

'Did you hear us argue?' But she won't reply. 'Tell me,' I demand.

'Yes, Joey . . . I heard you shouting and she weeping. You called her certain names.'

'What was it about, did you hear? Were your ears tight enough to the wall?'

She shrugs.

'And what did you hear on the night of the crime?'

'Feet on the stairs. Hers first. A minute later there were a man's. I hear this scuffle on the boards. Then, she screamed and shrieked. Then it went quiet. Then I heard the man running out down the stairs.'

'What were the man's footsteps like?'

'Like yours, Joey. Like yours.'

'Are you certain they were mine?'

'No . . . only they sounded so. Familiar, like yours.'

Thank you, Ma.

'What is your occupation, Mr Blueglass?' Mr Spurling enquires with polite concern.

'Gentleman, sir?'

'Good,' he observes amiably. 'It is a respected and dignified profession. May I ask what manner of gentleman you are?'

'Self-made,' I concede. 'You shan't find my name in Burke, but folk often remark upon my manners.'

'We'll come to your manners by and by,' says he pleasantly. 'But how did you spend your time as a gentleman?'

'I attended to my correspondence, took an interest in races, visited theatres, dined out.'

'Yes. Correspondence. I mean to ask you of that. In your rooms there were papers pertaining to a Pontius Porter. Can you identify him to the court, please?'

'That's me.' I declare a proper pride. 'It was my stage name in music hall.'

'There were also letters addressed to a Thomas Trevelyan.'

'Me again,' say I. 'A *nom de plume* – to avoid confusing my public.'

'John Gillymore?'

'A pseudonym, sir.'

'James Birch?'

'A *soi-disant*, sir.'

'Joshua Cave.'

'An allonym.'

'Richard Roe?'

'A *nom de guerre*, sir.'

'You wrote begging letters under these names?'

'That's a view on it, sir. Seen through the spectacles of disapprobation, and spoken through the megaphone of rebuke. But in truth I never asked for money,' say I, haughty. I shan't have him paint me a scoundrel. 'It was a perpetual surprise, sir, that gentlefolk would send me money as a cure-all. Whatever plight I described, they answered me with tin.'

'So you would describe yourself as an honest man, Mister Blueglass?'

'I am that. An honest man and a Christian.'

'You are an honest man with seven names?'

'Exactly so, sir.'

There are titters and guffaws from the public gallery. It is often the way in theatre that the audience seek some comic relief within the dramatic flow.

It's a full house. The gallery is choked. I flatter myself that many gentlefolk and journalists have pledged an interest in the justice of my case. Many bring their luncheon with them, so they do not lose their seats over recess. Some ladies have their opera glasses ever trained upon my face.

'And you smoke opium, do you not?'

'It's something to put in my pipe,' say I, 'as makes a change from tobacco.'

Mr Spurling is playing to the gallery. I see his intention. He's trying to cast me as a rogue, so folk won't believe my testimony.

'Besides being a . . . writer, you are a collector. Is that right?'

'Yes, sir. Paintings and porcelains. I do enjoy pretty things.'

183

'Bent spoons, too? There were hundreds in your chambers. Also watches, handkerchiefs, hymnals, pepperpots, fish knives.'

'Those too, sir. I have wide interests and broad enthusiasms.'

'Also purses and wallets?'

'Those too.' In for a pepperpot, in for a purse. And I ain't about to shift the blame to malign the dead. It wasn't legal, but it was an innocent foible – a distinction the law can't comprehend.

'How did you acquire this museum, this extensive collection?'

'The items came to hand, sir.'

He nods. Enough said.

'Are you a violent man, Mr Blueglass?'

'Certainly not, sir. Like I say, I'm a Christian.'

'Then you're confusing me. ... On the occasion of your arrest, you had a revolver on your person.'

'Yes, sir. To frighten thugs.'

'Let me understand this – you are a peaceful man, who carries a revolver to frighten folk, in case they themselves turn violent? Is that so?'

'Exactly so,' say I, only the way he phrases it, it sounds sinister. If I were Jack Gumm I should never need a firearm; for I'd caution folk with a blink, or flicker of my eyebrows.

'Mr Blueglass, what was your relationship with the deceased? What was she to you?'

'My love, sir, my duckling. An epiphany. Light of my darkness. I worshipped her.'

'You loved another man's wife?'

'Yes, sir. It's a common enough occurrence – in society – I believe.'

'Forgive me, Mr Blueglass, if I suggest you were an adulterer. But I put it to you that you had knowledge of this woman.'

'Oh, yes. A deal of knowledge, sir. And all of it dear to my heart.'

'You formed a licentious, squalid union?'

'Venial, yes, sir. But never squalid.'

'And one day she said she would leave you. So you broke her neck.'

'No, sir.'

'You bludgeoned her with your fists. You twisted her neck from her shoulders.'

'No. No.' I dare say Mr Spurling has fine manners. Yet he's mighty presumptuous – loaning me some incriminating words and vicious actions. Which he can't justify. It's all innuendo.

'In the course of the struggle she scratched at your face. And blood was shed on your shirt front.'

'No, sir. A man did that.'

'I see,' he says, raising his brows in polite surprise, 'who was that?'

'I forget, sir,' say I. 'I always forget an unpleasantness, so as not to bear a grudge.'

'That's convenient,' says he.

'I find it so,' say I.

'And do you expect us to believe you, Mr Blueglass?'

'A fellow can believe whatever he likes,' I observe, 'and whoever he chooses. If he has a mind to. It's but a simple matter of tinkering with your head.'

He surveys me with some confusion. Then, puffing out his chest, he accuses me again.

'You returned to the scene of the murder. You told the officer in attendance that you were sorry. You told him her neck was broken. You confessed it was your doing.'

'No.'

I sensed the tug of the tide, turning against me. Those jurors that will meet and return my gaze are chill in their regard.

Then a thought came into my mind, of some notions I'd forgotten—

Grimace, her face when
Gristle, Manzini's pies and
Grit, intransigently lodged in nostril
Groan, as I twist it
Grocer's wife, bend spoons of
                     , teach lessons to

It gave me quite a startle, you can well imagine. Till a reassuring note appeared in my mind's eye, written in my own shaky hand, on prison paper in fresh ink.

Joey, boy, it's a quare coincidence. No more. There's thousands of grocers in London Town. Most are married. Spoons bend easy, being flimsy items. You ain't never had an ounce of violence in you. And you ain't a vengeful man. And Florrie was your duckling. Best forget what can't be remembered. For it's no more than the hearsay of gossip, rumoured in reminiscence. Take care. Don't tug at what can't be opened. Your own self. August 17 1863.

So I'd examined my case thoroughly. Barely a week before. And, though I'm a harsh judge, I'd properly acquitted myself. For there just weren't any evidence to convict.

I ain't a man to distrust my own judgement. Only it quite distracted me from the proceedings. For I'd begun sifting through splinters of broken mirror, in my mind's eye – thinking how they might all fit together.

Though the jury were out three hours, I could assemble no more than a corner piece, no larger than a playing card. And I could see no sharp reflection in it. For its surface was a spider's web of distorting fissures.

'Guilty,' say they. 'Of murder.'

No, say I. Not so. There ain't the evidence to prove it.

No. I've been condemned by a blind expert, perjuring police-man, insinuating lawyer.

The Lord Justice has raced to hasty judgement. He reckons to intimidate me, donning a black cloth upon his wig. As though his scalp is mourning its natural hair.

But they shan't get the better of me. I've a fair mind. To forget them.

My Release

God Almighty! Ain't there no end to your wit? I knew you were comic, sir, but am I to be no more than your brief quip?

That conceit with men and women, sir, is the drollest of puns. Such a slight difference in design, between He and She – but to such comic effects. A simple matter of joinery. The hasp and clasp. The latch and the catch. Such a weight hanging on so slight a union. And don't we creak and screech at the join?

And money, matey, weren't that a waggish invention! The business of the rich and poor. Ain't that a tease to us all?

Lordy! The purse, the loins and the lavatory. Ain't you been dipping your playful paw in our pants!

Jesus Christ! I do believe you meant to show us. That at our centre we're a jest.

Only you made us free, didn't you just? To wriggle like tadpoles in our puddle, or maggots in the rot. So I jiggled my very own dance, sir. Being sovereign of my squirm.

I may only be a wiggling worm in a turd, thought I, but sometime I may grow, frolicsome as a flea, or buzzy as a bluebottle, or flighty as a gadfly. And gladden your eye, as a flicker. Or catch your ear as a throb in the pulse of it all.

So the grub of me grew, from larva to pupa, from boy to lad, apprentice to man. Only it seems I'm no sooner out of the chrysalis, than a hand has swat me down.

Yet I did my utmost, sir. To be the best of fleas.

Fashioned myself, I did. Furnished my mind. Scribed fine

principles in my head. Forgot all ugliness as best I could. Loved as often as I might, especially women. Forgave those men I could not like – by casting them from mind.

I struggled, sir, to reconcile my conscience and conduct, by adjusting the one or the other. And I lived by my beliefs, and changed them quite as often as the need arose.

I took life by the scruff, sir, quite as you intended. And strained the talents of my carcass. I communed with women, snatching at every sacrament. I chuckled like a cherubim and sniggered like a saint, chanting your liturgy of jest.

God Almighty! Have I missed the point? What have I forgot? Why do I suffer so?

'I ain't a normal man, sir,' I tell the Reverend Gully. He nods, ponderous with regret. 'I've lived faster than most. Now I'm an old man.'

'How old, Joseph?'

'Seventeen, sir, and nine months.'

'It's true you do look older.'

'Now, I'm rotting,' say I. 'My memory is going. There's white to my hair. I ain't quite the Adonis I was. I'm shedding my teeth. I feel wearied now and old as a prophet.'

'You do believe in God Almighty?'

'Surely, sir. For I've proved him, see. Three ways – by mirrors, numbers, and from his doings – in church, courtroom, parliament, abattoir and brothel. In the blossom and the pustule. He's a stern chap, ain't he just?'

'He forgives sinners.'

'He do?'

'If they confess and repent. So confess to me, Joseph.'

'I would, sir.'

'Well?' He folds his arms, waits on my yarn.

'Only it's hard to remember causing much offence. I dare say I'm innocent as the next fellow. I've lived a good life, sir, else some sins have slipped my mind – but I do recall, sir, how I once snaffled a duckling from a grocer.'

*

A concatenation of signs, each an ambiguous whisper, combine to a welling chorus, to keep a condemned man alert to the imminence of a certain public ceremony.

Now, the spluttering light burns night and day in my cell, and will not be extinguished till I am.

A warder, or another, is ever with me to watch me in this light, lest I pre-empt the just-throttling by devising for myself some ingenious device to slice my soul apart from my body. This feeble candle must flicker on till the law snuffs it.

A man who lives by killing others – and who is no craftsman – will call upon me this day to assess his work for the morrow.

When I stand at the cell window I can see a hole being dug in the earth by the northern wall of the yard. Over the nervous surprise of sparrows I hear a distant, dismal hammering.

I am told that the chaplain will call on me at five. After him, it's said, there's sausage for supper. It ain't often these days the fellow has meat.

'Boiled or fried?'

'Don't know boy. But after you can have a smoke of my pipe.'

'Thanks,' say I, 'I'd enjoy a puff, and be grateful for the kindness. I ain't got no friends to treat me, now that Florrie's gone.'

'There's a deal of interest in you, boy. Here in the stir.'

'Interest?'

'Money,' he explains. 'Wagers on how you'll take it.'

'Only one way to take it, ain't there?'

'Some blab, boy, an' fight, an' kick their legs so you have to carry 'em. Some go quiet and dignified. Odds on you are evens.'

It's quare what folks will gamble on – nags racing to a post, bull-terriers ripping each other's faces, rat matches, fellows dangling, the price of coffee, the charm of a fiancée's nose: justice, stocks, religion, marriage, beasts and gravity.

'What's your bet?' I ask him.

'Five shillings. It says you'll go quiet and carry your composure with you.'

'That's how I'd bet,' say I, 'if I could stay to collect my winnings.'

He nods solemnly: 'Try to ignore the mob,' says he, 'they

189

can put a fellow off his stroke. Like as not they'll jeer and howl. . . . Best to be prepared, so you know what's coming. You're a popular villain, so you'll draw a handsome crowd.'

'I'm used to performing in public,' say I. 'Used to be in music hall. You can't get a nastier crowd than at the Lyceum on a Saturday night.'

'Just do your best, boy,' he's gone gruff and shuffles his boots. 'Can't ask more 'n that of you . . . got a lad your age.'

'Good boy?' ask I.

'Good . . .' he confirms. 'Honest, respects the Lord. Strong lad.'

'Good,' say I, 'good.' Then we lapse to silence, sunk in our different concerns.

Brady's *Forensic Pathology* observes that a good hanging dislocates the spine – at the juncture of the second and third, or fourth and fifth vertebrae. To achieve this, the knot must be placed asymmetrically to one side of the jaw. The drop must be judged in proportion to the weight of the fellow. Too much slack and you rip off the fellow's head. Too little and he strangles slowly. So you have to climb on his back – lend him your weight to finish the job – else tug on his legs. The pressure of the rope cuts off the blood to the brain. There can't be much consciousness to speak of, after a while. Though the heart beats, with waning vigour, for ten or twelve minutes more.

The eyes pop, the tongue swells, on account of the increased pressure of fluids, within the chappie's cranium. The legs draw up and part – as though he were riding a horse.

I dreamed my death last night. Foresight, I call it. Always think ahead – that was the master's edict.

There's the snap of the wooden panel, drawn back from the outside, in the observation window of my cell door. I raise my head slowly to greet the bright, passionless stare. I dare say that's him – Joseph Ruxton, hangman – peering in on me, his face pressed to the bars. He has brilliant, sunken, button eyes above a sharp hooked nose. All else to his face is wiry black hair.

'I shouldn't mind him visiting me,' say I to the warder. Whereupon the panel promptly clatters shut.

There's the squeal of a key turning in the top lock, then the easy, oiled clunk of the other. The door is swung open. He fills the frame – a hunched bear of a man, sober in black as befits his desolate, solitary trade.

You couldn't have a hangman sporting a mustard waistcoat and paisley cravat. Society and his employers would reckon him facetious.

Is he a wag in the public house? The life and soul of the gin palace? Or do fellows and neighbours leave him alone? Does he talk of work to his wife, and brag to his son – that he's hung a man well that day?

He ain't famed for his efficiency. I suppose he'd have to work smarter in an abattoir. What with the number of beasts to be dealt with and all. They say he took three tries, and twenty minutes, to dispose of poor Edward Coxmoore.

'Eleven stone, three pounds, sir,' say I, deducting half a stone to be on the safe side. 'Five feet, eleven inches. Size sixteen collar.'

But he don't speak nor move his eyes from their fixed stare.

'I mention it, sir, because I reckon the science to your trade lies in calculating the differential equations of downward forces, when bodies of various weights are dropped through variable distances. Ain't that so? You're a physicist when all's said and done, sir?'

He doesn't reply but paces a circle around me at a radius of three and a half feet. At least he's sober and treads crisply. I ain't seen a pair of bigger boots – which is saying sommat in the stir.

'I dare say you've calculated the drop at around four feet seven inches, sir. That's the slack I'd give it, if I were in your shoes, sir. Over five and half and you'll tug my head off. . . . But I suppose you've worked it out yourself, sir – with your algorithms and those tablets of logarithms as can be purchased from Brady's in the Strand for no more than sixpence.'

191

His tread stops behind me. I feel his eyes on my back and neck; which is disconcerting.

'It's in both our interests, ain't it, sir, that the job's done clean and quick.' I chose not to mention Coxmoore. I shouldn't want to antagonize the man. Not when my life's in his hands. And I suppose I've said enough to convey my drift.

Then he strides from the cell without a backward glance, and the door clanks shut behind him.

'Don't mind him. He ain't a chatty chap,' observes the warder, 'not to the prisoners nor to the turn-keys.'

'In his profession,' say I, 'he must find that fellows avoid him. And no sooner has he worked with a man than he's lost a colleague.'

'You're chipper today, Joey. Considering . . .'

I smile at him. For I'm touched. It's the first instance my warder has called me by my Christian name. You can rely on a fellow's sympathy when you're in a jam.

My eyes go moist, for I think again of Florrie.

A sausage is a sausage. A spud is a spud. Only I'd have sent them back if they'd been served me at Langley's. On account of one being rancid and both being cold. Only the taste and tenor of food depends on the season and context.

This was a sausage served with sympathy and mustard. It was a sad, shrivelled body, as made a chappie think of the wrinkled cheeks of widows, the brief careers of pigs, the separation of soul and body, our insides and outsides, and that each of us is no more than a skinful of offal served up on the platter of society, that however unsightly a dish we are there's sommat precious, divine, within us.

'Don't weep, boy. It's only a sausage.'

'But ain't it pretty and wise?' I splutter, spitting a nobble of gristle to the floor.

'Take a swig of tea.' He biffs me in the small of the back. 'Shouldn't rightly do that,' says he. 'Regulations. Mustn't touch a prisoner, unless he fights.'

The tea is strong and stewed. It has some body, warmth

and sweetness to it. I find myself swilling the leaves along the sides of the tin mug. The way Mamma taught me to read my future.

'I dare say this is breakfast, too. I've an early start tomorrow.'

'Feel all right, boy?' He's caught my open eyes as I turn in my sprawl on the straw pallet.

'I ain't been to a hanging before,' say I.

How do you feel, Joey?

I feel humbled by your grace, Lord, that you should've taken such time and trouble to fashion me so particular and peculiar. For I've never met another like me.

And perplexed, Lord. As to your intentions. Is it right that I should hang?

I'm vexed as a bear in a broom-cupboard. Twitchy – as the pig feeling the butcher slash a gash in his throat. Puzzled – as the chicken that's lost its head or head that's lost its chicken. Doomed – as the oyster slithering down a diner's gullet. Adrift – as a shrimp in a storm. Abandoned as a drowning puppy. Randy – as the boar on the sow's back. Unwanted as the flea in the lady's bush. Chased as the fox, when the hounds snap at his brush. Odd – as Joey Blueglass.

Also anxious and melancholy. Fearing for my future. Much concerned. Troubled.

But I had Florrie, and Florrie's love. I drank the finest wines and ate the choicest dishes. Heard Jenny Lind sing Cherubino. Saw Spangle win the National. Lay in the laps of warm women. Returned my face and mind to the world in a daughter. Practised my craft. Gave joy to Mamma. Bettered myself. Dedicated myself to Art. Improved my mind. Forgave by forgetting. Lived. Loved. Learned. Spoke jokes. Wrote myself. Scribed my own conscience. Obeyed its dictates. Had nooky. Gambled. Smoked. Drank. Lived better than a grocer.

Spent my last day in the company of a good, kind man. Better fellow than I'd supposed. Most are better than we suppose.

Ate a poignant sausage. Saved the last piece in my pocket for this morning. Hear the chorus of sparrows. Drink the fresh dawn air, gusting in over the stench of piss-pots.

The bell says I've fifteen minutes more, here on God's earth. It'll toll again, for another quarter hour, to announce that I have gone.

I sit up and tug on my laceless boots. Scrape cold, clumsy fingers over my scalp. Arrange my hair for my public.

He has risen from his chair, red-eyed from the vigil, and beats his chest with his arms for warmth.

'I'll come quiet and calm,' I promise, buttoning my shirt, 'only don't let them rush me. Or have me by surprise. . . . They'll put a hood on me?'

He nods. Flicks some lint from his sleeves. Straightens his belt, so he'll look smart for the Governor.

'Thanks,' say I. 'You're a kinder man than I supposed. Goodbye – I shan't look at you no more.'

I stand up, walk to the centre of the cell, facing the door – so as I'll see them come in.

Breathing heavy through the canvas hood, both my wrists held firm by fellows. Feel two points of finger pressed to my back propelling me on. Head's hot from my captive breath. But my body shivers to the chill morning air. Doors must be opened, which affords the fellow further time.

Hand rests upon my shoulder. Door shrieks. Wind gusts on my naked ankles. Crowd howls, my ears throb, legs splay limp, spine melts, as though I'm poleaxed. Fellows grasp me by the elbows, carry me on. Yet I won't kick or scream.

'Yer gonna swing, boy, swing.' So the crowd chant.

Feel it pulled over my ears to rest heavy as a chain on my shoulders. Jerked tight up around my neck.

Hush. Clatter. Cheer.

I'm gone.

I drop through chasm and part from time. Falling, hurtling,

194

tumbling. Feel my blood spurt upwards to crowd my head. I'm coming, Flo, to you. We shall have broke necks in common. We shall look askance on the world for eternity. We shall ever watch over our shoulders.

Quare what a fellow thinks, as he's hurled on downwards. Quare how long he has to consider his fall.

Till the grocer severs his neck with cheese wire. And an infernal device detonates within his head, squirting the mucus of his mind through the surprised, parting sphincters of his ears, nose and mouth. So he's extruded from his body in a long explosive sneeze.

So he's a cloudy, slimy, bogey suspended in the air. Quite separated from his rude body.

Praise the Lord, I shan't suffer the like again. Ain't known such discomfort since I was born. Don't we suffer, though? With our comings and our goings.

That's your husk there, Joey, the shell you used – twitching and jerking on the wire. And ain't it a pathetic, unsightly parcel of rag and bones. Quare, how you were so attached to it. Found so much joy in its sordid doings. Its solids and fluids, its ins and outs. When you weren't entranced by squeezing things in, you were besotted with squirting stuffs out. And all of it weren't no more than a sack of offal, hunks of squirming organs joined by pulsing, slithery tubes.

See, there! It ain't done even now. There's dark stains to the lap of your canvas breeches. You've wet yourself – twice, boy. First in a final violent spasm. Trust you, Joey, to be lewd to the last. Then a second stream in the warm gush of your water down your thighs. And all the folks can see. Only it don't matter. Not now. There's worse crimes than piddling yourself in public. And it ain't your body no more. They claimed it, they can take it. Bury it in lime.

Jesus, you felt a smile on your face, wrestling with the boggle-eyed grimace.

And ain't I won a large and various public, pressed to a heaving, screaming swarm in the square; leaning out from the windows; swaying on the roofs of the carriages; entwined around the lamp posts. They'll have paid a hefty price – those parties in the upstairs lounge of the Swan Revived – for their privileged view of my last performance.

There's all emotions to be seen, dancing over those faces. Passions play with them, like breezes from all points of the compass, rippling the heads in a field of wheat.

Many are creased with smiles and leers. Chanting – 'Swing, boy, swing . . . See the man swing.' Yet others are solemn and quiet. There are blanched faces, staring wide-eyed. A blond-haired judy at the doors of the Feathers is retching on the paving: heaving at the sight of me, else moved by the persuasions of a duff meat pie.

I swear that's Bent Frank beside her, climbing onto the barrel to catch a fuller view. Sentimental chappie! I ain't spoke to him for three full years. Yet still he's come to say farewell.

There's hawkers, doing a brisk trade in sheets of my image. Folk like a memento of an occasion. And, if they look to my picture, they can imagine my face beneath the hood.

Festive folk. But so am I – frolicsome and free. And this ain't just a hanging, but a triumph of life besides. In the midst of a dangling death, there's hungry living. They laugh at what they can't comprehend. They're chuckling at the leering face of horror. They're still governed by the plumbing of their tubes. Don't know there's life beyond the piping. So they buy a muffin, chestnuts, mug of ale, to complete the celebration. Flush their systems. Say 'boo' to death. Call her a goose.

And, I dare say, it ain't all folk that'd enjoy a hanging. Those that come have more robust palates, tougher spirits, than those that favour the church or opera. But each to their own, say I.

Ah, good. The fellow's going up.

A Quare Place

It'd be a quare soul who didn't think back to the day of his death.

I rise above them, light as thistledown, fluff on the breeze. There's a grace and charm to weightlessness. I'm gliding a spiral on the rising airs.

Looking down, I spy my kernel far below – no more than a small stick man, hanging by a thread of cotton.

The crowd's a dotted mosaic; specks of hats and heads. Their hubbub is hushed to a murmur. Can't smell their revel, sweat or breath no more. Nor any juices of their life.

The air thickens and darkens, heavy with the fragrance of pine resin, clouded by the acrid fumes of burning sealing wax. There's the insistent squeaks of scurrying mice. A bell tolls far away.

I'm at the gaping mouth of a golden tunnel and reach out to stroke the chill stone walls. Hear voices calling, coaxing, round the bends of the winding burrow. I stumble in, and lurch down the darkening path.

So that's where I am. No wonder the place feels so familiar. I ain't vain, but it occurs to me that I couldn't have been sent to a more fitting place. I'm lodged in my very own mind.

Now ain't that a quare thing. Paradise being fashioned in my own image.

It's a maze of dark passageways. Underfoot there's a deal of debris – shards of broken mirror, playing cards, lobster shells, numbers cut from sheets of brass, empty bottles, cigar butts, betting slips, gnawed bones, crumpled papers, crusts from

197

mutton pies. Scribbled everywhere on the dank stone walls are observations I've made, travelling through life.

Every story is enigma. For more is withheld than told.

If the world offend thee, pluck it from your mind.

prob nooky (Charity or Chastity) = prob (Charity) + prob (Chastity).

XXXXXXX XXXXXXXXXXXX don't frighten me.

Florrie says she could die in your arms.

Quare. Every corridor mingles different scents – camphor, beeswax, Folie de Florix, stale beer, opium fumes, menthol, human juices, havana smoke, mustard, blood, mutton fat, smog, sulphur, musk, fish.

At the forking branches of the dingy tunnels, there are signs daubed large in chalk, in my own precise hand, directing the lost traveller.

Sixteen ruses: for avoiding creditors.

Duffing: moral philosophy of.

Self-improvement: four principles for avoiding hubris.

There's the echo of voices, murmurs of midnight streets, lapping of waters, the glug of bottles pouring, rumble of horse's hooves on turf.

I can hear the master declaiming in the distance. 'Correct breathing,' he observes, 'is essential to the maintenance of a man's composure.'

'Mr Rivers!' I call through the megaphone of my hands. 'Where do I find you?'

'There are fifty-two positions,' comes his echoing call, 'excluding two jokers. We'll meet recurrently at odds of eighteen to one. I'm the king of diamonds. You're the knave of clubs.'

Then I hear Mamma, singing, distant down a tightening path. I'm forced to stoop, then crawl, till I am thwarted by the narrowness of the passage.

'Sometimes a light surprises . . . the Christian while he sings.'

How I melt to her voice: 'Mamma!' cry I.

'That you Joey? Back so soon? Shall I fry you a herring in oatmeal?'

'Empty the hat,' slurs Clarence, 'we'll treat ourselves to a tipple or two.'

'Can't get through,' I howl. 'The path's too tight.'

'Yes, Joey,' observes Mamma, 'you've grown so big and grand.'

I slither backwards, till there is room to rise and turn around. 'Florrie, my duckling? Where are you?'

I tramp the labyrinth. But she don't answer to my call.

So that's the strength of it. I'll have to retrace my steps, down the dark paths of the maze of memory. To reach back to where I lost her. I must look out for likely signs.

I clutch my watch to my face, to regard its augury in the gloom. Usually it's seventeen minutes past nine. Sometimes the hands are a blur of backward motion, sometimes they move with forward languor. Most times they are stilled. At nine seventeen.

Time is different here in mind. From the way it is in the Strand. It don't proceed, but ebbs and flows, back and forth, like the line of water on a beach. There are pits and holes to its surface. I dare say a fly might feel the same, wandering the craters of a crumpet. A fellow heaves himself back up, till he topples down the next chasm. But it's disconcerting when you're in a hole – as though the world has stopped and all stands still and frozen.

I ain't been here more than sixteen minutes, I reckon. Only it seems like a fair portion from the pie of life. On account of the forward and backward motions, and frozen stretches.

'Ouch,' say I, 'hell. Damnation.' For I've promptly trod on some splinters of mirror.

Ecstasy ain't all a bed of roses. Even in paradise you need to mind your step.

Some passages are bricked or barred.

Nancy's curse – deleted.

George Mulltravers lives down here – best retrace your

steps, Joey boy. Hereabouts ain't safe. Turn left into the Epsom Derby.

Frankly, I feared I shouldn't find her. It seems an endless snaking maze – my mind – interminable as my cleverness.

Then my nose commences to twitch. It's the scent I seek.

'Florence, duckling. Where are you?'

I know she's nearby, stirring in the bedroom gloom. I have her in my quivering nostrils. I hear the rustle of her thighs wriggling on sheets.

'Florrie, Flo,' I chant my joy.

'Joey, boy?'

Quare. She sounds fair puzzled to hear from me.

I sense a divide between us.

'I'm dead, Flo,' I call out to her.

'No one's perfect,' she giggles. 'I'm dead too. Don't it chill your bosom?'

Oh, my freckled lovely. My ivory treasure. My satin-skinned, sleek beauty. Plump-breasted duckling. Honey pot. My pink-petalled rose. My prize. Golden fleece. Moist mystery.

'Where are you, Flo?'

'Here!' she chortles. 'In bed eating oysters. Snug as a bug.'

Quare, that. Her voice seems to rise from a crevice by my feet. As though she's locked away. In some catacomb below.

'Where, duckling?'

'Hidden away, in the folds of your kind mind.' Florrie's breath catches on a strangled sound.

'But I can't see you, Flo?'

'It's your mind, Joey. . . .' she gurgles. 'You find the way if you've the mind to. . . . Don't say that you've forgotten.'

I see some parts of her, scattered over shards of fractured mirror. . . . Her blue vacant eyes, wild copper hair. Limp, lean body. Twitching lips.

And that's you, Joey boy! I recognize a part, shuddering on the slivery skin, pivoting on her pelvis, between her jerky splayed legs. And your hand reaching up to her neck.

We're closer, Flo. I feel the burn of it.

I scrape at the floor with my fingers, but the rock won't yield to my clawing hands.

I got fair flustered; every degree as impassioned as a dead man can be.

Then my eyes beheld a scrumpled letter. On the ground to the sinister side of my left knee. Just where a fellow scraping the ground is most likely to look. On account of the rick and the twist to his neck. It was a most helpful and calming memorandum, addressed to myself, from myself, advising the soundest course.

Joey, boy
You've been here before. It's the wrong place to start.
To find her, you must retrace your steps. And start near the beginning.
Don't worry about time. You shan't lose any. However long it takes you. It'll still only be nine seventeen.
Go back to the start. Then you can't miss her.
Affectionately,
Ever yours,
Your very own self, Joey.

Florence. Oh, Florrie. Flo. My auburn-tressed beauty. My freckle-nosed, twinkle-eyed, rose-cheeked, satin-flanked, plump-breasted love. My chortler, squealer, giggler. Guardian of secret dimples. Moist rapture. Liar. Thief of teaspoons.

I know how I must seek you.

Now I know the passage I mean myself to find.

What's the time? Ah, yes, nine seventeen.

Now, where was I? Oh, here.

And it's a pleasant enough place to lounge. Despite the monotony and confinement. And if a fellow gets bored, why then he can count his toes, or make some rhythmic noise. By plucking away at his umbilical.